FORGIVE ME MY SINS

AN ARRANGED MARRIAGE MAFIA ROMANCE

THE AUGUSTINE BROTHERS
BOOK 1

NATASHA KNIGHT

Copyright © 2023 by Natasha Knight

All rights reserved.

No part of this book may be reproduced in any form or by any electronic or mechanical means, including information storage and retrieval systems, without written permission from the author, except for the use of brief quotations in a book review.

This is a work of fiction. Names, characters, places and incidents are either the product of the author's imagination or are used fictitiously, and any resemblance to actual persons, living or dead, business establishments, events, or locales is purely coincidental.

Cover by Coverluv

Photo by Wander Aguiar

Model Andrew Biernat

PROLOGUE
MADELENA

Present Day

"*Forgive me.*"

They were the first words he spoke to me. I can still hear them, still see the look in his eyes as he took my hand and said them. I couldn't turn away from him.

Not until I saw the flash of the blade he produced out of nowhere.

I blink, and the room comes into focus. I open my hand to trace the thin scar across my palm, the raised flesh bumpy. Does his match mine?

The surprise of it had shocked me at first, then the pain. The latter should have been familiar, but strangely, it wasn't. It depends on who's holding the knife, I guess.

A key turning in the lock on my door disrupts my thoughts and draws me into the present. I catch a glimpse of my reflection in the mirror, dark hair around a too-pale face and eyes lined heavily with black. Little Kitty, he calls me. It sounds almost tender, but it's not. It's his mockery of me.

I don't have time to think about it as Sister Catherine opens the door, the key dangling from a chain at her belt. She never has bothered to knock. I brush my hair and watch her in the mirror as she surveys the room. My bags are packed, and I'm sure she can't wait to be rid of me.

Behind her, Mr. Abbot, the groundskeeper, stands in the doorway.

"Take it all down," she tells him sharply. "Load it into the car."

My heart thuds against my chest because it's time. This is it.

"Not that one," I say, pointing to the oversized, still-unzipped tote on the bed. It's the one with the things I actually care about.

Mr. Abbot looks to Sister Catherine, who shrugs and approaches me. She takes the brush from my hand and stands directly behind me at the vanity. I watch Mr. Abbot sling my duffel bag over his shoulder and lift the two suitcases. They have wheels, but he carries them anyway.

"Goodbye, Mr. Abbot," I call out. He pauses at the

door and glances at Sister Catherine, who tugs too hard on my hair. He gives me a small but warm smile.

He was always kind to me.

The door closes, and I look up at Sister Catherine's pursed face. It's not quite resting bitch face—more of a forever-constipated face. I mentioned once they have things you can buy over the counter for that. She did not appreciate it. Remembering the moment makes me smile.

"We should have had this cut," she says, tugging the brush through.

"Too late," I say with a smirk. She's made sure I knew exactly what a burden I was from day one. Exactly what she thought of my kind, as she put it, and I always reminded her how easily she took money from *my kind*.

My kind being my fiancé, the heir to a crime family. This was where the Augustine protection had come in handy. She had limited power over me. I could say what I wanted to say, and all she could do was lock me in my room and deprive me of dinner as punishment. Yes, she'd made the last two years of my life as hellish as she could, but she couldn't really touch me. I've survived worse than her.

I wince as she tugs and pulls, but I bear it. My eyes fill up, but I don't let a single tear fall.

"You'll do well to remember to keep your mouth shut with your husband."

"He's not my husband yet," I say, earning another tug. I turn the diamond ring on my finger, trying to keep my face neutral, trying not to show how anxious I feel—how much I dread what's to come. Because it's only a matter of time until he is my husband, and there's no way out of it.

She puts the brush down and sets her hands at her back. "Stand up."

I glimpse the thin leather strap that hangs from her belt, which is another thing I was protected from. I've seen what she's capable of doing with that strap.

I stand, turning to face her. I'm taller than her, and she doesn't much like it.

She looks me over, and I want to ask her why she hates me. Why she hasn't helped me once or offered even the smallest comfort. It's not like I chose this, or like I can stop it.

No one can.

Because five years ago, I was promised to Santos Augustine. We signed the contract in blood, mine and his, while our families watched.

I touch my thumb to the scar as Sister Catherine's hard gaze meets mine. I press my fingernail into it, the pain grounding me.

She looks me over, likely making sure I'm wearing the dress I've been told to wear. I am. She nods and turns to walk out. "Come."

I put my brush into the bag on the bed and zip it, slinging it over my shoulder then following her out of the room that's been my prison and my sanctuary for the last two years. I don't look back. I can't.

Because today is the day that contract we signed is

fulfilled. No one—not my father, not my brother, not even fucking God can stop what is about to happen. Because Santos Augustine is God, and he made clear five years ago and at every opportunity leading to this day, that I belong to him.

1

SANTOS

5 Years Earlier

Marnix De Léon is a fucking coward, and it turns my stomach to have to look at him. In contrast, my father stands tall and proud. To anyone not present in this room, you'd expect the opposite—De Léon with his head held high, with my father's bowed low, face in shadows. I'm not sure you'd expect the Augustines and the De Léons in the same room at all, actually. Not as equals anyway, but here we are.

The Augustines have returned from exile, patriarchs of each family present and accompanied by attorneys, as if the transaction we're carrying out is in any way legal.

The next generation is here too. My brother, Caius. Me. De León's son, Odin. No women, though. They're not necessary for this part. Not yet.

Even then, we only need the one—although she's not quite a woman yet. That's the part that bothers me. It makes me lose sleep at night, but I know what I have to do, what role I'm meant to play.

And she will be a woman soon enough.

"Santos." My father calls my name.

I shift my gaze past Caius to him. Should Caius be the one named on that contract? He would be if it hadn't been for me. My father adopted Caius when he married our mother. I am not first born, but I am blood-born. Caius stands like a statue, hands folded in front of him and face as unreadable as ever as I proceed toward the older men. I wonder what my brother is thinking. Would he want this if it was his to take? If she was his to take? Spoils of war.

"Father," I say.

De León's irritated gaze follows me as I step up to the desk. You'd never know looking at him that he buried his brother-in-law today.

I don't bother acknowledging him. He fucked up. Overreached. This is the consequence of thinking too highly of oneself, believing oneself untouchable. No one is untouchable.

De León turns the fountain pen over to me. I see where the ink of his signature is drying, smeared where the crease of his fist had rubbed against it. He signed with a flair I'm not surprised to see. He's arrogant. We've always known that about Marnix De Léon. That arrogance has led to his downfall.

I meet De Léon's flat eyes, which are colorless and washed out. I glance to my father, who gives me a victorious smile. I don't take the pen. "Where is your daughter?" I ask De Léon.

"She is unnecessary. I decide for her."

Is he trying to protect her, I wonder? Fatherly love? No, that's not it. I know enough about the family to be certain of that fact.

The corners of my mouth lift into what I don't think anyone would call a smile. "You don't decide anything," I remind him. He used to, but times have changed.

He gestures to one of his men standing by the door, but De Léon's son, Odin, steps out of his corner and blocks his path.

"No need," he says.

I turn to him. Odin is about eighteen now, three years older than his sister, Madelena. He's almost as tall as me but thin, like he hasn't quite grown into his height yet. He takes another step. I notice the limp, the tightening of his lips. Pain. Was he limping before tonight? I don't recall.

"She'll do as she's told when the time comes," he says.

"Get out of the way, boy," the older De Léon says, but Odin doesn't. He draws himself to his full height and, still blocking the door, looks at me—not his father.

"It's been a hard day for her," he says in an appeal to protect his sister.

I study him. No love lost between father and son, but he does love his sister. Noted.

"She was very close to our uncle," he adds.

My gut tightens. I knew she was close to him. So was Odin. Their uncle was the last link to their mother. If there was any other way to do this, I would do it. The girl is fifteen, and I'm not that much of a monster. "It can't be helped," I tell him, because it can't.

"Boy," the father warns, making a move to come around the desk.

Odin sets his jaw. "No."

I open my mouth, but before I get a chance to speak, the door opens. We all turn to find Madelena De Léon standing like she'd had her ear to the door all along. Her hair is wet, and she's wearing different clothes than she'd worn to the funeral. She looks like she's been crying for days. She glares at her father, then, without any hesitation, she shifts her gaze to me and holds mine. And I know in that instant, in the look in those eyes, that this girl will not bow meekly and do as she's told. Not now. Not ever.

Odin steps toward her. "Maddy," he says through his teeth. "I told you not to come down here."

He's protective of her. I would be the same if I had a sister—and there's no way in hell I'd let her sign a contract like the one Madelena will be made to sign tonight.

"It's fine. I'm fine," she tells her brother.

I watch the two of them together. I know what she looks like. I've seen her before, although not often. Where we used to be the scum of Avarice, now Augustines and De Léons socialize in the same circles. Who'd have thought it? But all it took was one fuck-up. It had been inevitable. We only had to be patient. Because Marnix De Léon fucked up big. I know the cost of that sort of mistake well and he will pay.

She takes in the room while I take her in. Dark hair, sad eyes. Anger. Just behind it, there's fear. I see it, smell it, even as she tries to mask it. But it would be stranger if she wasn't scared. Standing in a room with the Augustine family can be a frightening experience, especially when you're a De Léon. But like I said, I'm not a monster. And she is fifteen.

I hold out my hand, palm up, and beckon her with a curl of my fingers. No need to drag this out.

Odin takes hold of her wrist, but she looks up at him. A silent communication passes between them before she shakes her head and frees herself. I notice she's barefoot when she steps toward me. It stands out, that little detail. The vulnerability of her pale feet. The vulnerability of her.

When I look back up, she's near enough to take my hand. She studies it. This close in the dim light, I see the remnants of eyeliner hastily wiped away, the smudges of black on one temple. Finally, when she shifts her gaze up to mine, and I see the pain inside her copper eyes, I decide something. It's not a conscious thought, but it's decided all the same.

Her father should protect her. It's the way it should be. But sometimes fathers don't protect daughters. I know that well. Even though I will do what I am about to do, I decide that where her father has failed her, I will not.

She blinks, as if this thought, this oath hanging on the one we are about to make, has somehow communicated itself to her. As if the weight of it, of my protection, has been draped like a cloak over her too narrow, too delicate shoulders.

I gesture once more for her to give me her hand. Our eyes remain connected as she slips it into mine.

Her skin is cold to the touch, and I don't miss the slight tremble of her small hand in mine. I hate that I have to do what I have to do.

My father clears his throat. There is no way around it, and she will survive. Hell, she has survived being a De León this long, I tell myself. She's been through worse.

She walks at my side as we take the final steps to the desk together. There's slight resistance, but she, too, knows that neither of us have a choice.

"Forgive me," I tell her quietly. Her forehead creases in confusion, but before she can see what is coming—before she can be afraid—I slip the switchblade from my pocket, snap it open and slice a line into the palm of her hand.

She cries out and tries to pull free as tears fill her eyes. I hold her hand over the contract and, using the same knife, slice my own palm so that our blood drops in unison onto the sheets of heavy parchment.

"Blood joins blood," my father says as I smear our thumbs through the deep red, hers and mine. I take the handkerchief from my breast pocket and press it into her palm. I'm not sure if her gaze is on the blood or the ring on my finger bearing the Augustine insignia.

Keeping hold of her hand to staunch the bleeding, I step away from the desk, taking her with me. We watch the two witnesses, one from each family, sign their names to the contract before our attorney applies the final seal. Once that is finished, my father stands back and, with that victorious smile playing on his lips, he looks at us. At me, at her, at Caius and finally at De León, his forever enemy. "It is done," he declares.

I turn to the girl who is wiping tears from her face with her free hand.

"You belong to me now. Do you understand?" I tell her in a low voice so only she can hear.

She wrinkles her forehead, her lips trembling as she draws a breath.

"Do you understand?" I repeat.

She nods once.

"Good. Don't forget it."

The instant I release her, she runs from the room. I wipe the blood off my hand with a handkerchief Caius hands me as our attorneys collect the contract, briefcases snapping shut. My father gives me an approving nod and leads the way out. Our footsteps echo as we make our way toward the front door of the De Léon mansion, but before we reach it, something draws my gaze. It's an irresistible pull and when I glance over my shoulder, I see Madelena standing at the top of the stairs, nursing her bleeding hand. Her eyes are locked on me and if looks could kill, I'd be dead.

I give her an infinitesimal nod and I swear her eyes narrow.

At least she'll be safe for now. From me, for the next five years. From my family. From her own. Trading the house of one monster for the house of another.

But destiny is destiny. Fate is fate.

The Augustines have waited a long time for the scales to be leveled… for fate to finally give us our due. Each of us must fulfill our part as it is written—whether we like it or not.

Madelena De Léon's destiny is sealed. She is to pay what is due.

And my destiny is clear. I am to ensure that payment is collected in full. No matter the cost.

2

MADELENA

I watch the bastards walk out of the study. Odin told me to stay in my room, but it's not like that would have changed anything. I knew what my father had agreed to in order to save his neck. I'm pretty good at being invisible, lurking in shadows and listening. It's easy with my father because he wishes I was invisible. Wishes I'd never been born.

He's another bastard just like them. Worse, if he can sell his own flesh and blood and on this day of all days. We buried my uncle, Jax Donovan, today. He was my mom's brother and the last link to her.

Santos Augustine stops on his way out. As if what we just did—that shared spilling of blood—somehow bound us, creating an invisible tether between us. He turns and looks up at where I am lurking in the shadows of the second-floor landing. His eyes meet mine. Even at this distance, they send a shiver along my spine.

I narrow mine and send all the hate I can muster his way because maybe he can see what's inside of me too.

"You belong to me now... Don't forget it."

What the fuck does that even mean? I'm fifteen. He's ten years older than me. What can he do to me? Nothing. That's what.

We stare at each other for a long minute before he gives me an almost imperceptible nod and what I swear is a smirk before he and his family walk out of my sight. Out of our house.

My brother appears at the bottom of the stairs. He pauses to look up at me, and I see his face contort with pain as he begins to climb. My father glances at us, then disappears back into his study. He can rot there for all I care.

"I told you to stay upstairs," Odin says, taking my hand. The handkerchief is sticky with blood, but he peels it away. I suck in a breath. "He didn't have to be so fucking brutal about it."

"I'll be fine," I tell him.

"Let's go get this bandaged up." He looks at me with that pitying expression. Why, I don't know. He's the one with the fucking limp.

My eyes fill up. It's bad this time. He's never limped before.

"Are you okay?" I ask him as we walk through my bedroom into the bathroom we share. It's a jack-and-jill. The second bedroom wasn't supposed to be Odin's, but he's been there for as long as I can remember.

"I'm not the one with a cut in my hand. Sit."

I perch on the edge of the tub while he rummages beneath the sink for the first-aid kit. Once he has it, he sits on the closed toilet seat and drops the handkerchief into the trash can. He proceeds to clean the cut. It stings, but I hold my breath and don't make a sound, watching him work as he carefully bandages it.

Once he's finished, he throws away the cotton swabs and washes his hands. "It'll probably scar. I'll see if I can get you a cream."

"I don't care about a scar," I tell him, watching blood stain the bandage. It hurts. But weirdly, it gives me something to focus on.

Something to time my breath to.

You can feel your heart beat to the throbbing of pain like this. It's a strange sensation. Grounding in a way.

"Here," Odin says, taking two aspirin from a bottle in the cabinet and holding them out to me.

I take them and watch him swallow two himself.

"The limp isn't better," I tell him, as if he didn't know.

"It'll be fine. Just needs some time."

I follow him into his bedroom, where he drops onto the edge of his bed like he's exhausted.

I sit beside him and lay my head on his shoulder. "You shouldn't let him do it."

"I'd rather he beat me than you," he says and guilt washes over me even though that's not his intention.

Our father is an asshole and a drunk. And Odin has stood between him and me too many times.

"I wouldn't." I look up at him.

"Well, sis, you're safe now," he says with a dark smile on his face. "You belong to Santos Augustine. I don't think he'll take it well if our father lays a hand on you."

"Is that like the silver lining or something? Because it's a crappy silver lining."

He chuckles and scoots back to lean against the headboard. He studies me. "What did he say to you? Before he did it?"

I cross the room, push the curtain aside to look out into the dark street. I'm not sure if the lights I see in the distance are the tail lights of the Augustines' cars.

"Forgive me," I say, turning back to Odin.

"Hmm."

"And then the ominous, *'You belong to me now... Don't forget it.'*" I mimic Santos Augustine's low, dark voice. "Asshole."

"You do, though. You understand that, right?" Odin asks seriously.

"I understand that he's a jerk and a bully. I understand that our father fucked up and what they should do is punish him."

"They are."

"No, they're punishing all of us."

"These things are complicated. There's history between our father and Brutus Augustine."

"What history?"

He shakes his head. "I'm not sure of the details, but Santos's aunt, Brutus's older sister, used to work for The Club. Something happened with her and dad."

I feel the blood drain from my face. "He hurt her?" I know what he's capable of.

"I guess. It doesn't matter for you. It was a long time ago. What matters is that you take this seriously."

"It's not the middle ages. Women don't belong to men anymore."

"People don't sign contracts on parchment in blood anymore either. This is real, Madelena."

"Don't call me that." He only uses my full name when he's either angry at me or I've done something stupid. I can't stand the former and the latter, well, whatever.

"I mean it. Just be careful."

"Odin—"

"Promise me," he says in a tone I don't like, one that is too serious. When I don't answer right away, he raises his eyebrows.

"Fine. I'll be careful, whatever that means." I pick up the framed photo of Uncle Jax, Odin, and me. We took the picture last year at the amusement park. We had such a great time.

"Are you okay?" he asks.

I shrug a shoulder and put it down. "I'm going to miss him."

"Me too."

He reaches over to open the nightstand drawer

where he keeps a small flask. He twists the cap off and holds it out to me.

I mock gasp and touch my hand to my heart. "Odin! I'm fifteen!"

"I think we both deserve a little tonight."

I take it and drink a big swallow, expecting but still wincing at the burn as it slides down my throat. I hand it back and watch Odin drain the flask.

"You're going to get wrinkles if you keep looking at me like that," he says, closing the flask and putting it back in the drawer.

"You're in pain. I see it."

He touches my hand. "You and me both. Go to bed. I want to forget today."

I nod because I want that too. I kiss him on the forehead and switch out the light on the nightstand, leaving the door open a crack. On my way to my bedroom, I take the destroyed handkerchief out of the trash can. I'm not sure why I do it, but I do. I bring it to my nose and inhale the subtle, lingering scent of aftershave beneath the metallic one of blood. In my room, I shove it into the recesses of my bottom dresser drawer and change into pajamas before slipping into bed.

I don't sleep right away, though. I lie wide awake, staring up at the ceiling, and think about what happened. About how Santos Augustine said those two words before he cut me—like he wasn't going to enjoy what he was about to do. Like he didn't want to do it.

But that is a bunch of bullshit, I tell myself, and roll

onto my side. If he didn't want to do it, he could have not done it. He's an asshole. I know that. All the Augustine men are assholes with too much money, too much power, and absolutely no qualms about getting their hands dirty. I've seen Santos out on a few occasions. He always has some beautiful woman on his arm, and he's always dressed impeccably. He's also a man people give a wide berth to. That's subconscious, I think, and pathetic. I know more about him than he might realize.

And I know Odin is right. What he said about me belonging to him, it was a warning.

One I won't forget anytime soon.

3

SANTOS

We get home an hour later. My father purchased this property five years ago. When the original family who owned it, one of Avarice's finest, lost everything, the bank had taken it over. That had been more than a decade ago. The house had then been left to rot, the grounds turning into a forest of weeds. It's a beautiful, gothic structure my father has rebuilt, putting thought into every detail and sparing no expense.

Soft piano music comes from the living room, where I can see a fire is lit.

"Evelyn," Father calls out to our mother as Caius and I follow him toward the living room.

"You're late," Mom says, heels clicking as she comes around the corner. She's dressed as if she's been out, which she probably has, with a martini glass in one hand and the other reaching to wrap around our father's neck. She kisses his cheek. "How did it go?" she asks, glancing at us.

"As expected."

"It's done?" she asks, her gaze falling to the handkerchief I'm still clutching even though my hand has mostly stopped bleeding.

"It's done. Get me one of those, will you?" he asks, gesturing to the martini glass in her hand.

"Of course," she says.

"Santos. Come, we'll celebrate," Dad says.

"I'll be right there. I'm sure Mom doesn't want me bleeding all over the furniture."

"You're right, I don't," Mom says and watches as Dad glances to Caius, then walks into the living room without another word.

I look at my brother, too. Is he disappointed?

"Caius," Mom says, walking toward him to take his hand. "You should come too. I'll pour you a whiskey."

"I'm fine, Mom," Caius says. "I'm actually heading out anyway."

"At this hour?"

He checks his watch. "I have a card game."

"Hmm."

"Go take care of Dad."

There's a beat where she doesn't reply. I watch the moment, this silent interaction between them. Caius and I share the same mother, but we don't share the same father. Mom was a single mother when Dad met her.

"All right," she says, then turns to me. There's

another moment, an empty one, until she smiles her brilliant smile. She is a beautiful woman, our mother. Younger than Dad by ten years, she spends her time taking care of herself since Dad refuses to let her work. "Santos, go get cleaned up. You're right. I don't want you bleeding all over the living room. Usual drink?"

I nod. My usual is a club soda. No alcohol for me. I've seen what it does both to others and to myself. I can't afford to lose control like that.

"I'll be there in a few minutes," I tell her. She brushes something off my shoulder then returns to the living room, humming quietly as she sips her martini.

"You want to come with me?" Caius asks once she's gone.

"Nah. Not tonight." I study my brother. He's two years older than me. I was an unexpected but happy surprise, according to Mom. She never expected to have more kids. Something had gone wrong when she'd delivered Caius, and she'd been told she couldn't have any more. "Don't let Dad bother you. He's just caught up in the moment. He's been waiting for this for so long."

Caius studies me back, and after a moment, a smile spreads across his face. He pats my back. "No worries, brother. I'm a big boy. I can take a little rejection." He checks his watch. "Besides, I think I'll be having the better night."

"The Club?"

"Augustine's," he says with a wink. Augustine's

was formerly known as The Club. It was, and still is, an exclusive, invitation-only club for the elite of Avarice.

My aunt, Dad's older sister, used to scrub the toilets there. She died when I was too young to remember her. But our father tells me about her at every turn. Dad bought out the owners a few months ago after they repeatedly denied his applications for membership. He finally got pissed enough to do it. It's how money works. It's how the Augustines work. Would I have done it if it had been me? Probably not. Why be around people who look down their noses at you? But for Dad, it was personal, and he passionately insists on calling it by its new name. He's never been one to take no for an answer lying down.

"Enjoy," I tell Caius, then head up to my room to clean and bandage my hand. I think about the girl as I go. Madelena De León. I didn't like hurting her, and I won't forget the way she looked at me afterward. But it's done now. She belongs to me, and once the Augustine and De León families are united in holy matrimony, we will be unstoppable.

The Augustines are already that, to a point. But the legitimate connections we will make once Madelena is of age and we're married will solidify our place in social and political circles in Avarice and beyond. It will pave the way for the Augustine name not only to become a fixture of high society, but to own it outright. Those who snubbed us will bend a knee. Those who refused to do business with us will clamor for any crumb we throw their way. Those who openly opposed us will be cut out.

In my bathroom, I take off my jacket, remove my cufflinks, and roll up my shirt sleeves to wash my hands and my face. Remnants of blood stain the towel I use to dry my face as I take in my reflection. At first glance, I am respectable—a well-groomed man in a bespoke suit. Good looking. Promising. The Augustine heir.

But there are signs pointing to what I really am, what I come from. On my face, there's a scar that splits my right eyebrow from a fight with Caius when we were kids. In my eyes, determination. Or, to the keener observer, ruthlessness.

I set the towel down and look at my hands, back and front. The cut across the center of one is not so out of the ordinary. My gaze travels up my arm to where the edge of one slash is visible. I push the shirt sleeve higher to see the rest. Forty-two slashes dug deep and healed roughly. All a part of my makeup now. Maybe one of the most defining things about me.

That thought brings on another. One of Commander Avery, or the Commander as we came to know him. Of what happened five years ago that irrevocably changed the course of my life. Of all of our lives. Ultimately, we came out on top. But the cost was brutal.

I draw a deep breath to steel myself.

I am an Augustine.

No, not only that.

I am the Augustine heir.

We are criminals. Killers. Just like the Commander. As much as our family may appear to be moving away from its roots, at our heart, we are a crime family through and through.

I wonder if Madelena saw the shadow of my past in my eyes when she laid her small, unblemished hand in mine.

"Santos."

I startle at the sound of my mother's voice. I blink, shifting my gaze to hers in the reflection of the mirror. She stands in my bedroom, leaning against the door frame, watching. How long has she been standing there?

Clearing my throat, I push the shirt sleeve down over the scars. I turn to her.

"Your father is waiting," she says. She brushes a length of hair down over the right side of her face. I think it's subconscious. She has a scar there, a burn she sustained when she was a teenager. She's always careful to hide it under long bangs.

I smile, move to walk past her. "I'll be right down," I tell her, but she steps in front of me to block my path.

"Are you all right?" she asks, adjusting my tie.

I take in the blood red fingernails. Why do women do that, grow nails like claws? Although maybe she needs her claws. With a husband like Brutus Augustine, it makes sense.

She meets my eyes once she's satisfied with the tie and smooths out the shoulders of my shirt. I look nothing like my mother. Nothing. I am wholly my father's son. Where she is blond, I am dark. Where she is pale, I am olive-skinned.

"You did what you had to do," she says with a reassuring smile.

"She's fifteen," I say.

"She won't stay fifteen forever. Remember how they snubbed us for years. And never forget what they did to your aunt."

"I won't."

"It's for the family, Santos, and as your father's chosen heir, the responsibility falls on your shoulders."

I draw in a tight breath. I want to ask about Caius, about how he feels about that. I want to know how she feels about her first-born being set aside.

But I don't get a chance to ask before she takes my bandaged hand, making me wince when she squeezes. "You have five years to get used to the idea of her, and she has five years to get used to the idea of you. Don't disappoint your father. You know him." I don't understand her meaning but she smiles a wide smile and relaxes. "Let's go. We shouldn't keep him waiting."

4

MADELENA

2 Years Later

"Did you see her?"

"What is she wearing? I mean, Morticia Addams much?"

I recognize the voices. One is Jane Smith, a generic girl with a generic name and a generic life. The other is Ana Hollis. I've known Ana since we were six. I met her in first grade, and we'd been best friends for just shy of ten years.

"I bet her weird brother gave it to her for her birthday. She just turned seventeen."

"You remember her birthday? Is it that important to you?" Jane asks Ana, and I'm surprised Ana remembers it, too, even though she was always good at those things.

"Oh, I just saw the date on the roster. *Mad Elena* strikes again this time as Morticia Addams, right?" Ana says as the two giggle. Well, I guess she did come up with this particular inflection of my name and told the stories to back it up.

Madelena. Let's be real; the name lends itself to ridicule. I've heard Mad Elena so often in the last two years that I'm sometimes not sure if it's real or in my head. It's real now though, very real as I sit with my legs drawn up on the closed lid of the toilet in the gym's locker rooms. It smells like dirty socks, chlorine, and shit in here. I hold my breath as I listen. I'm dead quiet. Invisible.

"I can't believe she actually has a date," Ana says, and I can just see her leaning toward the mirror to reapply lip gloss through the crack of the stall door. "And with Jason. Aren't you mad?"

"Well, it's not *exactly* a date—"

What?

Jane stops talking when a toilet flushes and a girl stumbles out of the farthest stall.

"Don't mind me," she tells them, slurring her words, clearly having had a drink or two too many.

Ana and her friend wait, though, probably giving the girl dirty looks as she washes her hands then uses the air blower to dry them. Why do people use those things? They just literally blow shit around. It's disgusting.

Once she finally leaves, Ana's friend—and I use that term loosely because these girls don't have the capacity to be or even know what a friend is—leans closer to Ana and whispers loudly.

"It's a bet."

I hear the words, but they don't register right away, not in my brain at least. Although, something in my belly feels it, and in my chest. My body's response is in the idiotic way my eyes water.

"What?" Ana asks, and I am pretty sure I imagine the moment of hesitation, because she's probably salivating for this, eager for it, because what she did wasn't enough.

I don't move as a tear slides slowly down my cheek. Instead, I listen.

"The guys were standing around talking about her one day, and I don't know. I mean, I guess under the crud on her face, she's not hideous or something, at least to them. But you know how men are."

Not hideous. That makes the tears stop. Thank you, bitch.

"Jason too?" Jason is, or had been, Jane's boyfriend. And I swear I hear a hint of glee in Ana's voice as she asks about him. Bringing Jane down a notch?

"He was just going along with them, you know. It's been really hard on him, us pretending to be broken up and all," Jane says quickly.

Pretending?

"What?" Ana asks.

Jane gives a self-satisfied smile that makes me want to puke even for the little bit I see through the crack in the door. "And I mean, those outfits she wears are just begging for a certain kind of attention, if you know what I mean."

No, I'm not begging for a certain kind of attention. I'm begging for you and your fucking idiotic boyfriends who have clearly taken too many hits to the head to leave me the fuck alone.

Although I guess I'm not, if I'm being honest with myself—and I did promise to be honest with myself going forward, didn't I? I'm at prom with Jason Cole, after all. Why on earth did I say yes? Why did I think he was seriously interested in me? *Me?* No one in their right mind would be interested in me. Don't I know that?

Jason is my lab partner. He was also, or according to Jane, still is, Jane's quarterback boyfriend. Star of the football team. He's not very bright but usually sweet to me. He's one of the only ones who is. But maybe he's only sweet so he passes because I've been helping him along. Well, more than helping. I've been letting him cheat off me.

"Anyway, you can't say anything until the night is over," Jane continues.

I'm imagining a Carrie moment, pigs' blood included. Idiots.

"What's he going to do?" Ana asks, actually managing to sound concerned.

"Just take some pictures. It's all just fun, you know? Teach her a lesson. Teach her not to flirt with another woman's property," Jane finishes, the venom in her voice turning it ugly.

"What kind of pictures? That's not really—"

"Why do you care?" Jane snaps. "I didn't think you two were friends anymore."

"I don't! We're not! She's crazy."

Fuck you, Ana. I dig my nails into my palms so hard I draw blood hating the fact that Ana still has the power to hurt me.

The bathroom door opens then, and a group of girls stumbles noisily in. It forces Ana and Jane to leave, thank goodness, and I wait just another minute before slipping out of the stall and returning to the prom to find my date.

The good news is that this isn't new to me. For almost two years now, I've been essentially on my own. Not even bullied really. They're scared of me because I'm not some meek little coward who will lick their asses. I'm too angry for that.

I remind myself of it as I dig my nails deeper into my palms. People clear away from me, sensing whatever this is coming off me. Good. The stares and whispers I can't do anything about, but what I can do is not give a fuck. I can not give them the satisfaction of knowing how much it hurts me when I hear the way they bastardize my name and make it into *Mad Elena*.

The music is loud, and the gym decorated for a high school prom. Junior year. It's, as expected, shitty. Although that's probably my attitude. I shouldn't have come. I should have known better.

The dance floor swells with the popular kids dancing in groups, one so similar to the other, it's a wonder anyone can tell them apart. I see Ana among them and when our eyes meet, it slows me down for a minute. It stops her dancing, but she's quick to look away. She has new and improved friends now. A new and improved life.

I look down at myself, at what I'm wearing. A black floor length dress of intricate lace, with long sleeves and a high neck. I paired it with my usual chunky boots and my hair is loose down my back. Freshly dyed black. I dyed it for my stupid date. For this ridiculous night.

God. What am I doing here? I don't belong here.

I turn to go then, but I hear my name. "Maddy." A hand wraps around my arm, stopping me.

I look at it, then up at Jason as he spins me around to face him, tugging me so hard that I crash into his chest and bounce backward. "Don't call me Maddy," I snap and pull free.

"Sorry. Thought you preferred it to Mad Elena."

Does he say it the way the girls do? Or am I hearing that? Is it even true what Jane said? Jason hasn't been cruel to me.

Not yet.

But the term is just about over. He'll pass science. He doesn't need me anymore.

"You look pretty," he says, brushing my hair over my shoulder. "Did I tell you that already?"

"No, you didn't," I say when he leans close. I smell cheap liquor on his breath.

"Well, you do. Real pretty."

I put my hands on his chest to keep some space between us while I think.

"Something happen?" he asks, studying my face when I'm silent for too long. Something I'm probably mistakenly translating as concern wrinkles his perfectly smooth forehead. He pushes his hair back. It always flops into his face. He gives me that smile with the dimples that makes him look so innocent, so not like the rest of them. And I admit that there's a part of me that doesn't want to believe what I overheard. I don't want to believe it's true because I thought Jason and I were friends on some level, at least. As much as I hate to admit it, there is a part of me that wants a friend. Someone to cushion the loneliness.

A group of his friends passes noisily by, one shoving Jason's shoulder as another makes a cat call. Jason grins, a gleam in his eyes as he meets theirs. And I know. I get it. Jane wasn't lying.

I force a smile when he turns back to me. I stand up a little taller. It takes effort but I do it.

"No, nothing's wrong. I was just looking for you, actually. I'm so happy to be here with you." I say, throwing up a little in my mouth as I do. I step closer to him, set a finger on his lips and tilt my head, sticking my chest out. This dress definitely presents my breasts at their best. Maybe Jane was right. Maybe I am trying to get *that kind* of attention.

Jason looks eager as he drags his gaze back up to mine. "We should go somewhere private then," he says with a glance at the dance floor, where I can see Jane watching us with daggers in her eyes.

"Yeah, let's do that," I say, still not sure of my game plan. Maybe lead him on and get him to strip naked then disappear with his clothes? As I think it, the perfect idea forms—because I need to do something.

I need to send my own message, and they need to be punished.

So I take hold of his tie and lead the way through the gym, heading toward the exit that will take us toward the classrooms.

I make sure to slip into the shadows, aware of where all the chaperones are throughout the gym. I shift my grip to his hand when he knocks into one of the tables of food. How much did he drink? I almost feel sorry for him.

Almost.

With a backward glance, I open one of the side doors and slip out of the gym and into the dimly lit hallway. A couple of kids loiter here, making out in the shadows.

"Where are we going?" Jason asks, tugging me to him and shifting his grip to my ass.

I grin and pull his arms higher to my waist. "Somewhere more private," I tell him as I push through the door into the stairwell.

"I like the sound of that."

Jason follows me up the stairs like a good little dog. Once we get to the science hall, he slows down. "They'll be locked," he says.

I pull him along. "Nah. I know where Henderson keeps the key." Mr. Henderson is a functioning alcoholic. To each his own, but I'm pretty observant, and I know once he locks up, he tucks the key up onto the top of the doorframe.

"Good girl," Jason says approvingly as I stand on tiptoe to retrieve it, then unlock and open the door.

"After you," I tell him, swallowing back my distaste of being called a *good girl*. Are all men assholes? My brother isn't. Not to me, at least. Dad, yeah, pretty easily falls into that category. All the ones from school do too. Jason just confirmed that. So maybe it's true and my brother is the rare exception.

We enter the lab, and I shut the door behind us. I take a moment to make sure no one followed us before drawing the little curtain closed on the window.

Jason is very handsy as I push him backward toward our table. His lips are disgustingly moist, and I manage to turn my head just out of the way of his kisses. It's not that hard, and I almost feel sorry for him.

For what I'm going to do to him.

"Let's get a pic," he says, taking out his phone and raising it over his head.

"No," I say, but it's too late. He's snapped one, although I'm a dark blur as I turn my head away.

"Come on. We're making memories, right?"

I smile, take his phone, and set it aside. He takes off his jacket and tosses it as I strip off his tie. I slip it around him to bind his hands behind his back. "After,"

I say, as I pull the tie around his wrists and his smile grows so huge, it's almost blinding.

"Kinky. I like it."

I make a knot. I'm pretty sure he can get out of it if he wants, but he lets me unbutton his shirt. It's no easy task as I try to dodge his wet kisses. Really, this is why Jane wanted to humiliate me? Is she that jealous that this boy, and his buddies, might have looked at me once too often? Pathetic.

I shove his shirt off his shoulders and let it hang there before reaching for his belt.

"Wait, wait. Let me see you. Take off your dress."

"Not yet," I tell him, undoing his belt and slacks and pushing his pants down around his ankles before picking up his phone and turning it to him so face ID unlocks it. "Let's get a pic first."

"Hey! What the—"

The flash is momentarily blinding and it's hard to suppress my smile when I see what he looks like with his pants around his ankles, erection pressing against his tighty-whities.

"Ooh," I make an embarrassed face. "Not as impressive as I'd hoped." I stand back to study him, biting my lip in faux concentration. "It is a sad little thing."

"Hey man," he says, all serious as he straightens, wriggling his wrists free of the tie. I step backward to get another photo, and he trips over his pants as he tries to get to me. "Stop. What are you doing?" He bends to pull up his pants, does up the button, and I get one more picture before he grabs my wrist roughly and takes the camera. "What the fuck, Maddy?"

"I told you not to call me that," I say. He tightens his grip around my wrist, and I watch him delete the photos. Once that's done, he pulls me toward a lab table.

"You like dirty pictures?" he asks, shifting his grip to my arm and holding me tight as he snaps one of me. "I like dirty pictures too." He traps me against the table with his chest, a fucking quarterback and me at a hundred and ten pounds, and grins down at me. He presses his little cock against me.

"Get off me, asshole."

"What did you say? Not impressive? It'll feel pretty impressive when it's inside you, fucking Mad Elena."

He sets the phone down behind me and grips my ass, kneading my cheeks hard.

"They're right to call you that, you know? You're a fucking weirdo."

"Fuck you! Get off me or you'll regret it!"

"I'll regret it? How's that? What are you going to do besides get on your knees and give me what I want while I get it all on video for posterity?" He shifts one hand to my shoulder and picks up his phone with the other.

"I don't think so, asshole," I tell him and bring my knee up fast and hard between his legs. There's an instant of silence, a heavy, weighty moment. I watch his face as pain registers and feel his fingers dig into my shoulder.

"You. Fucking. Bitch," he hisses the words as his face turns beet red. He curls up a little, not letting go of me as he processes the pain.

I try to shove past him, but he only tightens his grip and uses his bulk to keep me pinned.

"Get off me!" I scream as he straightens, a dark, angry look on his face. He is so much bigger than me. So much stronger. And the way he wants to hurt me right now, it's not just to humiliate me. It's worse. Much worse.

"Or what?" he asks through clenched teeth.

"Or you deal with me, asshole," says a voice I know. A voice that makes time stand still and sends shivers along my spine. A voice I haven't heard for two years but one I'll never forget. One that's darker and more violent and powerful than pathetic Jason Cole could ever be.

5

SANTOS

I can't fucking believe what I'm walking into.

I received the call an hour ago telling me Madelena De Léon is not in her bed where she's supposed to be—tucked in safe and sound and *mine*. It wasn't hard to track her to prom. Fucking prom. I almost forgot how old she is. Seventeen now. I haven't seen her in two years. Pictures when I've looked for them, but not once in person.

The woman standing before of me now—because she is a woman, no longer a girl—looks very different from the one I signed a blood oath with. Except the eyes. They're the same. Angry. Not what I'd expect to find considering the predicament she's in.

"What the fuck?" the idiot quarterback says, looking over his shoulder at us.

I'm here with two men. No more are necessary. I didn't want to scare the kids of Avarice High at their little dance. "What the fuck?" I echo, closing a hand around his arm and jerking him backward off her.

Madelena stumbles forward but catches herself.

"I'll deal with you in a minute," I tell her. "Don't move."

She turns wide, shocked eyes from the idiot boy to me and for a moment, it's me who's stunned.

I look her over.

No. Definitely not a girl anymore. Not in that dress. Not with those curves.

I clear my throat, focus on the task at hand. Her dress is still mostly intact, except for a little tear at the shoulder. Her hair's messed up, too, and her makeup is smeared, but apart from that, I got here in time.

The idiot boy tries to get free of me. He requires all my attention, which annoys me because I want to look at how she's grown. I turn to him. His shirt is half off, and his pants are held up by a single button.

I shove him backward against a lab table, following him.

He stumbles, tripping over his own feet. He's a big guy, but he gets his muscle from the gym. I'm pretty sure the entitled little prick doesn't know how to fight.

"Look, I don't know who you are. I didn't know she..." he glances at Madelena. "Didn't know she had a boyfriend."

I chuckle, shove him again. "Oh, I'm not her boyfriend."

"Oh. Well. Fuck." He smiles, and two stupid

dimples form on his stupid face. Christ. "Look man, whatever, I didn't know. She was coming on to me."

"Yeah, I heard that a minute ago. How old are you anyway?" He looks older than the average junior in high school.

"Nineteen. Almost twenty," he says like he's fucking proud of it.

I raise my eyebrows. "Held back a time or two?"

He falters, glances at Madelena, at the two men blocking the door. When he turns his attention back to me, I push him against the wall and hold him there.

Idiot.

"What's the matter? Don't they teach you English here? Because the words *get off me* are pretty fucking self-explanatory even to me, and I'm not college educated. Barely scraped by in high school, if I'm being honest."

Madelena snorts.

I turn to her, and her gaze shifts from the idiot boy to me. And now I see it: the fear behind the anger, the girl inside the woman.

"He hurt you?"

She shakes her head.

"But he tried to."

"Whoa, whoa, whoa." The idiot boy's voice grates on my nerves. "No one was hurting anyone. Mad Elena and I, we were just fooling around. Having a little fun. Taking some pictures, isn't that right, Maddy?"

"I told you not to fucking call me Maddy," she snaps at him, suddenly animated.

"Mad Elena?" I ask, looking from him to her.

"It's nothing," she says, neck and cheeks flushing red. She's embarrassed and unable to hold my gaze. She takes a step toward the door, but I block her path.

"I told you I'd be with you in a minute," I say, lifting her chin with one finger to make her look at me. I search her face, studying it. She's wearing a shit ton of makeup, and I get the feeling it's armor. Protection. "You don't need all this," I say, though I don't know why.

She blinks, the whites of her eyes pink and damp.

"I'm going to go," the idiot boy says, interrupting again.

"You're a fucking nuisance," I tell him, gesturing to one of my men to keep him where he is as I turn back to Madelena. "You sure he didn't hurt you?"

"I can handle myself."

"Clearly."

She sidesteps to get around me, but I block her path.

"Let me go," she says.

"Do you remember what I told you the night we signed the contract?"

She bites her lip, and the act draws my attention. Little white teeth against dark red lips. It takes me a minute to drag my gaze back to her eyes.

Gold, like a fucking wildcat.

"Do you remember, Little Kitty?"

Her forehead creases. She licks her lips, clears her throat, then nods.

"Tell me. Say the words."

She blinks, looks over my shoulder either at the idiot boy or my soldiers, then back at me.

"Say them."

"I belong to you."

"And?"

"Not to forget it."

"So you didn't forget. You just chose to disobey."

There's that biting of her lip again, and I see how her hands turn to tight little fists at her sides.

"Your friend here—" I start.

"He's not my friend," she cuts me off.

"Glad to hear it. He's going to be punished for touching what's mine. But that doesn't mean you're off the hook." I step closer to her, my gaze sweeping over the swell of her breasts.

Idiot boy makes a squeaking sound. Neither of us bother to look.

Madelena licks her lips, that flush back in her cheeks. I get the feeling it's for a different reason than moments ago, though.

"Tell me how I should punish you," I say darkly, the question more seductive than I intended when I walked in here.

Her mouth opens, and she's taking the shallowest of breaths. I wonder if she's aware of the way she's looking at me.

"Tell me," I whisper before coming close enough to inhale her scent. As soon as I do, I stop, surprised to find something familiar. Confused, I lean closer and she gasps when the tip of my nose touches the skin of her neck as I breathe in deeply, then draw back.

Madelena's cheeks burn now, and she can't hold my gaze. I don't say it, though. I'm not here to humiliate her. I'm just here to protect what is mine. But what I smell, strangely, is my own brand of cologne. Is it on purpose? How would she know the scent? It's custom made for me, not one you can buy at the fucking mall.

Then I remember the handkerchief I pushed into her hand the first night we met. I guess the scent of it would have lingered beneath that of blood. Did she research it? Have it custom-made for herself? No. Surely I'm overthinking this.

I clear my throat and wait for her to return her gaze to mine.

"Tell me. How do I punish you?" I ask, voice low and deep and just for her.

"I..."

"Do I take you over my knee? Spank you?"

Her eyes grow huge, pupils dilating as she exhales audibly, then falters. I swear I see her nipples pebble beneath the dress. And, frankly, saying the words out loud makes me feel it deep in my gut too. I'm old enough to control my dick, but I can't deny that I feel it.

"How old are you now, Madelena?" I ask even though I know.

"Seventeen."

"Hmm. That's too bad," I say, letting my gaze drop once again to the swell of soft breasts. "Too young. But I tell you what." I brush her hair behind her ear. "I'll put a pin in it. Make a note to remember what I owe you."

She swallows so hard I hear it.

"Val, take Madelena home, will you?"

"Sure thing." Val is my most trusted man.

"By the time you're back, we'll be finished here." I glance at the idiot boy.

"Yes, sir," he says and gestures to Madelena to go ahead of him.

She glances from me to idiot boy and back. "He didn't hurt me," she says, probably aware of what will come once she's gone.

He would have, I don't say. "Noted." I touch a finger to her jaw so she looks at me, not him. "You belong to me. Do you understand that better now?"

She nods, but I'm not sure the message has hit home.

"Say it."

She tenses her jaw, like the night in her father's study. She's defiant. My palm itches to spank her little ass and make sure she feels the truth of that statement, but like I said, she's too young for me to be doing that just yet.

"Say it."

"I belong to you," she says through gritted teeth.

"Good. Go home, Little Kitty. And don't let me catch you with another man ever again."

6

SANTOS

One year later

"Ready?" Caius asks from the doorway.

I turn to glance over my shoulder. "I'll be right there."

My father squeezes my hand, and I look back at him—at what is left of him. He's been sick for years and never told a soul, just carried on while the cancer ate him from the inside out. It's amazing how quickly everything has changed, how remarkable the decline of a seemingly healthy man is.

I hear Caius descend the stairs. My father's gaze is just beyond me to where my brother just stood. When he drags his eyes back to mine, I see how dull they've grown. I inherited the forest green, but the shades are a world apart now. Like he and I will soon be a world apart.

"You watch your back. Always. You hear me?" he asks.

"I know that, Dad." I don't like how he talks about Caius some nights and it gets worse, he becomes more paranoid, as the cancer that's killing him progresses. "We'll miss you tonight." It's the first big social event he won't be attending with us.

He inhales deeply, then lays his head back against the pillow as the nurse returns from the other room with more medication. They wanted him at the hospital by this point, but he wants to die in his home. As much as I hate the thought of him being gone, I want him to be as comfortable as possible, so he now has a full team of doctors and nurses who take shifts around the clock.

"I have the morphine, sir," the nurse says.

"Get out," Dad tells her. He's never been a patient man, but it's even worse now.

"Give us a few minutes," I tell the woman. She nods and steps outside, closing the door behind her. "She's just here to help you," I tell my father.

He waves it off and points to the glass of water on the bedside table. I bring it to his mouth and push the straw between his lips. He takes a sip, and I set it aside.

"The will," he says once I turn back to him.

"What about it?"

"You should know."

"Know what?"

"I changed it."

Surprised, I wait, eyebrows furrowing. As far as I know, our mother is taken care of, and Caius and I split everything down the middle. Any details beyond that, I don't care about.

"Caius isn't my son."

This again. "He is your son. Maybe not by blood, but you adopted him as yours. He carries your last name. He's been good to you. And he's a brother to me."

"He's not blood."

I grit my teeth. How many times will I need to hear him talk about my brother this way? "What did you change?"

"It all goes to you. Everything."

Shock makes me stop. "What?"

"There's a small allowance for Evelyn. One for Caius. But the bulk of it, control of it, it's all yours."

Fuck. "Does Mom know this?"

He starts to talk, but a coughing fit takes over. I give him another sip of water before he continues, "She knows the Augustine legacy can only be carried on by a true Augustine."

"Caius is a true Augustine. Hasn't he proven that?"

"I'm not his father."

"Dad—"

"And it's because of him you..." Another coughing fit takes hold. "Your mother will understand why I did this. She won't like it, but she'll know," he says bitterly.

The doctors warned about the paranoia, but some

days, it's so bad it's hard to watch. They said to try to keep him calm. "Very smoke and mirrors, Dad," I say. Before I can continue, we're interrupted by a knock on the door, and my mother enters without waiting to be invited in.

"Santos, we're going to be late." She looks at my father, walks over to him, and touches a hand to his cheek. "Sweetheart. Let the nurse give you your morphine and sleep."

I watch them together. She looks so alive and vital. He looks closer to death than life. There's only a ten-year difference between them, but what a difference that is when one is sick and the other healthy.

"I'll be sleeping soon enough," he tells her and brushes her hand away. "I need to talk to my son. Go."

She smiles but there's nothing warm in it. I get it. He's pushed her and Caius away and she is very protective of Caius. Always has been.

"Mom, I'll be right there. Caius is downstairs."

She looks at me, straightens my tie and smiles. "All right. Just another minute though. He needs his strength."

Dad snorts and watches her leave, watches as she closes the door behind her, and only then turns back to me. "If you forget everything else, remember this one thing. You can only depend on yourself. No one can be trusted. No one. Do you understand, son?"

"You trust me, don't you?" I want to make light of this, not liking what he's saying. It's the meds or the disease talking.

"But you'll be alone once I'm gone."

"Dad—"

He starts coughing again, and I call the nurse. She administers the morphine, and Dad settles. Rather than having gone downstairs, Mom is waiting in the hallway, expression unreadable. She watches him before turning to me.

"Come, Santos. We need to attend this event. It's important."

I kiss Dad's forehead, but he's already asleep. I walk out into the hallway, down the stairs, and out to the SUV. Caius is already inside waiting for us, and the two of them start talking as we head out.

"Aren't you anxious to see your soon-to-be-fiancée?" Mom asks.

I shift my gaze out the window without answering her.

I haven't seen Madelena in a full year. She's eighteen now. I should be putting my ring on her finger, but I didn't realize I'd be saying goodbye to my father in the middle of all this, and it's taken all my attention.

I still remember our last meeting in that science lab —still remember every detail of the night, and what I learned from the idiot boy once she was gone.

Mad Elena.

It's the nickname they'd given her after a rumor was started by her one-time best friend. From what I'd gathered, she'd essentially been shunned by the same idiots who have their fifteen minutes of glory over and done with before they can collect their diploma and toss their graduation cap. The same ones who end up working for you later in life.

But when, as a teenager, you're in the thick of it, when you're ostracized for years, friendless for years, that's not where your head is. And I feel for her.

It didn't help that she came from two of the most powerful families in Avarice and power breeds enemies. That kind of wealth and influence doesn't come from above board dealings. Not entirely. And every single member of the high society of this place has skeletons in their closet. The fucking town is full of pariahs.

Ana Hollis, Madelena's 'best friend,' is the daughter of Brendan Hollis, a man Marnix De Léon took down hard. Ana just made Madelena pay the price for it.

No, the irony is not lost on me.

The car slows as we near the gates of Augustine's, which is set along the cliffs that make Avarice's landscape so strikingly beautiful.

Security stops our SUV at the gates. The first man sternly asks for identification as he holds onto his clipboard. We're going to need to get the club up to date. The computer systems they use are beyond old. Before Caius has to open his mouth, a second guard sets a hand on the first one's shoulder and draws him back.

"Good evening, Mr. Augustine," he says to me first before acknowledging Caius more casually by his first name and nodding to our mother. I don't miss the irritation on Caius's face.

"Evening," I say. I just want to get this night done.

Even though the club transferred ownership several months ago, it's our first time attending as a family since my father got sick and no matter what, we aren't welcome. We bought our way in. There will always be whispers.

My marriage to Madelena De Léon is all a part of legitimizing us, because even though our name is carved into the stone above the grand front entrance, we are not born society members.

Tonight, we're attending a lavish ball hosted by Marnix De Léon to raise funds for a charity to which the Augustine family has donated a large sum. That fact just may keep their tongues from wagging for at least one hot minute.

The guard waves us through, and I wonder how many members will know Caius. He's been here several times and has been inserting himself without much care about the whispers. I think he might even like the gossip in his wake. My brother is charming. Me? Let's just say people break ranks when I walk through a room. But Caius is no less dangerous. He's just quieter about it.

The SUV comes to a stop, and the driver opens the door. I climb out and extend my hand to help our mother out. Caius follows her. We stop to take in the opulence of the beautifully lit gardens.

Mom pastes a smile on her face. Caius doesn't bother. We all know that a few years ago, these people would have wiped their feet on us. None of us will ever forget that.

A man approaches, and I get the feeling he was waiting for us. Well, for Mom, when I see how he looks at her.

"Evelyn." He takes her hand, leans in to kiss her cheeks. "You look lovely."

My hackles go up. They know each other, obviously, but that's not too surprising. She's been doing charity work for years, and the last few months, it's been centered in Avarice. But there's something in his look that's not right. She is still a married woman even if her husband is on his deathbed.

I study him. He's younger than Dad, and a hell of a lot healthier.

"Lawrence, you remember my son, Caius." Caius and Lawrence shake hands as if they have already met. "And this is Santos, Brutus's son." Odd introduction, I think, but I extend my hand. "Santos, this is Dr. Lawrence Cummings. He's one of the members who founded the original club."

Ah. So we have history. I recall now how Dad talked about Lawrence Cummings.

"Dr. Cummings," I say, shaking his hand because it would be too awkward not to.

"Brutus's son," he says and openly looks me over. "I can see it."

What an asshole. "Dad mentioned you a time or two. I didn't realize you'd kept your membership."

He clears his throat, then glances at Mom. "We worked it out. How is your father?"

"Fine," I say flatly, my expression daring him to say another word to me.

"Yes, good to hear," he says awkwardly before turning to my mother. "May I escort you inside, Evelyn?" Lawrence holds out an arm.

"Thank you, Lawrence," she says, and I don't like it. I don't like the tone of it. I don't like the familiarity, the ease with which they walk a little too closely, if you ask me.

I look over to Caius to find him watching too. His expression matches mine. "What's that about?"

Caius takes a breath in and shrugs a shoulder. "Mom doing her part for the family, I guess."

"You know who he is?"

Caius nods.

"I don't like him."

"Join the club," he says, then pats my back. "Although I guess you own it."

"*We* own it," I clarify. Fuck. My conversation with Dad replays. Caius can't know about the change to the will, can he?

"Fine, brother. Let's go in. I need a drink."

We enter the mansion that houses the club, and if the gardens were impeccable, this is something else entirely. Soft music and the hum of conversation and laughter spill from the ballroom as we enter. My brother and I stop to take in every detail from the chandeliers that cast soft golden light from above to the sconces that flicker along the richly paneled walls. Tables that have been draped in the finest linens and set with so much silver and crystal it's almost blinding. Not to mention the flower arrangements that must cost more than most people earn in a year.

Well, not these people. Ordinary people.

My mother is a few steps ahead of us. She laughs at something someone says. Caius walks toward the nearest bar and returns a moment later with a club soda for me and a whiskey for himself.

"Thanks," I say.

"Bunch of pretentious pricks if you ask me," Caius says. We're watching our mother being introduced to a group by Cummings. There's a delay before the smiles appear and those smiles aren't quite welcoming, not quite warm. Fucking elitists. Sometimes I wonder why Dad wanted this. Why want to be a part of something that doesn't want you?

Although that's hypocritical.

"Caius," our mother turns to beckon my brother, who downs his drink and pastes a smile on his face. "Come meet…" her voice fades out because, as if fate heard my thoughts, my attention is drawn to the far corner of the room. It's not a movement or anything I can put my finger on that catches my eye. I'm simply drawn to look.

It's her, Madelena De Léon in the flesh. This particular charity is for mental health, a charity her mother was involved in when she was alive. Understandable. Her father has kept it going in her memory.

Madelena is seated on a chaise lounge, and as I watch, she takes something out of her clutch, a bottle of aspirin or something. She pops two into her mouth then, half turning away from the room, brings a flask to her lips and quickly swallows those pills with several gulps of what I'm sure is not water. She slips the flask back into her clutch and turns back to the room. She teeters when she stands, taking a glass of wine from a passing waiter's tray. I sharpen my focus. What were those pills, and how much has she already drank, I wonder.

She pushes dark hair over her shoulder. It tumbles in thick waves down her back, the black satin dress hugging her, fitting like a glove. It drapes to the floor, dragging a little as she moves. The light catches the pale, perfect skin exposed along her collarbones, the split of the dress giving me a glimpse of thigh high stockings. She's quick to cover herself though, and I notice how modest the gown is by the standards of the others here—similar to the lace dress she'd worn to prom had been. She isn't dressing to draw attention, but she does all the same. I see it in how the men around the room glance her way, their gazes lingering just a little longer than I like.

But no man approaches her. That's because of me, I know. Word is out that she is mine. None of the women do either, though, and I remember my discussion with the idiot boy from prom. Remember her isolation. It explains her fight. She's like a cornered cat with her claws out. Always claws out.

As I look on, Madelena rubs a spot on her hip, and when I follow her gaze, it leads to her father standing in a circle of men. He's drinking, probably already drunk. I return my gaze to her to see her walk quickly, a little clumsily even, toward the curtained off exit at her back. Just as she reaches it, someone pushes the curtain aside to enter. She crashes right into him, and the collision sends the contents of her glass all over the man's shirt. Of course it's red wine, and he's clearly not happy about it.

He grabs her arm and forcefully yanks her back toward himself so hard that she stumbles. Fury makes my blood boil. My hand clenches around my glass and I'm surprised it doesn't shatter. I take a step, feeling the eyes of every person present follow me as I cross the room in silent fury.

7

MADELENA

I don't have to attend too many of these events, but the ones I do are excruciatingly painful. My father drinks. I guess he and I have that in common tonight. My brother disappears into the flock of women looking to land a De León. Someone should tell them they're out of luck.

Me? With the news of my impending engagement, I'm usually left to my own devices. I guess that's a win. No man comes near me because they know I'll be engaged to the Augustine heir, and no one in their right mind wants to fuck with the Augustine family.

But tonight is different. Tonight, it seems someone does want to fuck with them —because the man I just bumped into has a vise-grip on my arm.

"It was an accident, and I apologized. What more can I do? I tell you what, I'll give you my address so you can send me your dry-cleaning bill," I tell him, teetering on my heels, the room spinning a little. A consequence of the drinks and pills I've had tonight. In my defense, I needed them after what happened. Odin wasn't home when our father went on his rampage. He can usually calm him down, not always, but often enough. Me not so much.

As much as it hurts, though, I'm glad it was me and not Odin to take it.

Odin's empty flask is in my clutch, plus a couple of painkillers. It's nothing too strong, but the combination is what's amplifying everything.

The man who has hold of me looks me over—my face, my mouth, then the swell of my breasts. What is it with men and boobs?

"I'm not sure that apology was heartfelt. Did you think so, Leo?" he asks his friend, the grinning jackal flanking him.

"I'm thinking it could definitely be more heartfelt," Leo Cummings says. The two walk me backward. I look to where I just saw Odin, but my view is blocked by the throngs of people. Although we're in a public place, although there are hundreds of people here, I feel the aggression of these two, and it's a little worrying.

I breathe deeply, remind myself I can handle men like this. I have before. I will again.

"Why don't we go up to my place, and she can make things right," Leo says suggestively, producing a key.

I open my mouth to respond, to tell him *when hell freezes over*, but before I can get a single word out, a hand lands on each of their shoulders. Hands I know. In fact, I'd know them even without the ring bearing the Augustine insignia of a heart pierced by two swords.

"Is there a problem here?" Santos Augustine's voice sends a familiar chill along my spine, making me shudder. It's been a full year since I've seen him—a full year, and even so, just the sound of his voice has my body reacting.

Leo and his friend part and turn to look at Santos. When I meet Santos's eyes, they capture and hold mine. It reminds me of our first meeting, of how he'd looked at me then. It's a strange sensation, like a cloak draped over my shoulders.

His eyes are a rare shade, dark and endless, like an evergreen forest in winter. He's wearing a custom-made three-piece-suit. Black on black on black. No tuxedo for him. He doesn't conform to any rules.

He's an Augustine. He doesn't have to.

I swallow hard because I remember other things too—like what he'd said to me the first night. What he'd had me repeat the last time we met.

The spanking he'd threatened me with.

That part sends a flush of heat spreading from my core outward, all the way up my neck to warm my cheeks. I struggle to hold his gaze, afraid he can read my mind

Another man joins us, coming to Santos Augustine's side. It's Caius Augustine. He's two years older than Santos. I haven't seen Caius since that night in my father's study, but he hasn't really changed. They still look so different, dark and light, but I know deep in my heart how dangerous both of the Augustine brothers are.

"Making friends, brother?" Caius asks, voice low and deep, as much a growl as his brother's.

Santos's eyes hold mine. He doesn't answer Caius but when he shifts his gaze to the hand on my arm, I remember what happened to the last person who touched what belonged to Santos Augustine. I get the feeling the man holding onto me now feels the danger emanating from the Augustine brothers, because he drops his hand and steps backward, away from me.

Leo isn't as smart though.

Santos turns to Leo. "No, not making friends," he says.

Leo glances at his buddy, I guess for backup. He's not going to get it.

"Get out of here," Caius says casually to them.

They nod, but Santos blocks Leo's path. "What did you say to her?" he asks. "Something about taking her to your place to make things right? What did you mean exactly?" He steps so close that Leo, who is a good head shorter, has to crane his neck to hold eye contact. Aggression is practically vibrating off Santos. I feel the waves of it, know the danger he poses. Is Leo Cummings so oblivious he doesn't sense it? "How would she make things right exactly?" Santos finishes.

"Brother." Caius closes a hand over Santos's arm.

I know I need to defuse this now, before history repeats itself, although I wonder how many other women they've cornered like this. Maybe I should let them deal with the consequence that is Santos Augustine. They're jerks. But the image of Jason Cole the day he returned to school after prom is still so vivid in my memory that I can't.

"They didn't mean anything. They were just being stupid," I say to Santos—only to Santos. "And they were leaving."

He turns his gaze to me, the green dangerously bright. "Were they? It didn't look like that to me."

"Santos," Caius says cautiously to his brother. "We're drawing attention." I notice how much quieter the room has grown. How, even though the orchestra is still playing, conversation has died down.

Santos's jaw tenses, and his eyes narrow. It takes him a full minute to draw in a slow, deep breath before smiling a smile that I can only describe as terrifying, more so than anything Leo Cummings and his friend could threaten me with. He steps backward, and Caius's shoulders relax.

Santos takes out his wallet and looks at the man who's wearing my wine. He pulls several hundred-dollar bills out and shoves them into the man's chest. "That should cover the cost of a new shirt and then some," he says.

The man closes his hand over the bills I think more out of instinct than anything else, and I have Santos's full attention again when Caius puts an arm around each of the men and walks them away, leaving us alone.

My heart hammers against my chest. Santos's eyes remain locked on mine and there's a palpable shift in the air around us, the dangerous zapping of an electrical current that can't be denied. I've never felt so drawn to any man as I do him. It's as though there's an invisible thread tying me to him, binding us. It's impossible to ignore, and I know how dangerous this attraction is.

"You seem to find trouble, Little Kitty," he says.

Little Kitty. "I think it finds me. I don't like that nickname."

"No?"

I shake my head, and we stand staring at one another. I swear the scar on my palm throbs, as if sensing he's near.

"That's too bad," he says.

I'm the first to break eye contact. I'd like to say it's because I see Odin across the room, but the truth is, he makes me nervous and I can't hold his gaze.

Odin is standing beside my father, who is glaring at me or Santos or, most likely, both of us.

The music picks up pace as if the orchestra was just told to distract the crowd. The noise level rises again as people return to their conversations.

"I need a drink," I say and attempt to walk past Santos, but I trip over nothing. He catches me and quickly positions me so that it looks like we're about to join the dancers—one arm around my waist, the other holding my hand, my body against his.

The racing of my heart intensifies. I feel like it's going to beat right out of my chest. My skin burns where he's touching me and it takes all I have to look up at him.

"I think you've had more than you can handle," he says as if he was giving me time to muster up the courage to look at him.

I snort, wanting to sound casual and unaffected although I'm pretty sure I'm not fooling him. "I don't think you know what I can handle."

"Not to mention the pills," he adds. Before I can begin to wonder how he knows, he drops the façade of the dance and releases me as he takes my clutch and opens it.

"That's mine," I say, trying to take it back.

He holds it just out of reach. "Be still," he commands, and I swallow as my body obeys. *It fucking obeys.*

But what am I going to do, run?

From inside my clutch, he lifts out my flask. He's got his back to the room so no one but I will see. He lets go of that and takes out the small, now empty bottle where I'd kept the pills. No label.

"What were they?" he asks, focusing on my eyes. Is he checking my pupils? Is that why he's been looking at me so intensely?

"Just painkillers. I had a headache." It's only half a lie.

"Headache? Hmm." He puts the bottle back before closing the clutch and handing it to me. "Let's go." He wraps a possessive arm around my lower back, his big hand curling around my waist and turning me toward the curtained exit I'd been hoping to make my way out of earlier.

I move because I don't have much choice, but being this close to him, touching him, it's got my insides knotted up. We walk down the corridor and toward the front entrance, where a large reception desk stands. The ballroom is housed in the old mansion and behind it is a more modern building of about twenty luxury residences. People mill about, and I don't miss the looks they give us as we cross to the elevators. We bypass the ones that lead to the apartments on all but the top floors, and I watch him take a key card out of his wallet and scan it.

The elevator doors slide open, and with just the slightest pressure at my lower back, he signals for me to enter. I do and stand as far away from him as possible, clutch tucked under my arm, arms crossed over my chest. He scans his card again and pushes the button for the top floor where the most luxurious residence is. There are two, and they take up the uppermost floors. I've never been to them, but they're supposed to be stunning. I have no doubt they are.

Santos types out a text as we ride up, and I watch the back of his head.

Once the elevator doors slide open, he looks my way and gestures with a nod of his head for me to step out. I'm not sure if I'm grateful or not that he doesn't touch me.

"Straight ahead," he says.

I walk toward the double doors, where a man stands guard. He's a soldier. Same as the ones who accompanied him to prom. I know it in my gut. This is no simple bodyguard.

Soldiers.

This family employs actual soldiers. It's why he wants me, though. Because legitimate businessmen don't have soldiers.

No, this isn't about *me*. I need to keep that at the forefront of my mind. It's why he wants a De Léon. If I had an older sister, he'd have taken her. The De Léon family is an established, permanent fixture of Avarice. My ancestors are a founding family, in fact. A union between us will legitimize the Augustine name. They may not quite be embraced by high society, but they'll at least be tolerated once our families are joined.

The soldier nods in greeting. Santos's hand hovers at my back. I'm not sure if it's the painkillers, the combination with the alcohol or just proximity to him, but even though his hand isn't quite touching me, I feel the heat of it on my skin.

"Go on," Santos says once the soldier opens the door. I enter, my heart racing. It's quiet up here, so completely still. I look around the large living room, open kitchen, and floor to ceiling windows. The views of the cliffs and the wild ocean are amazing, when you can stand to look at them.

The beacon of the lighthouse pans over the black waters of the Atlantic, and I'm momentarily transfixed. My heart races as I see the great white structure in my periphery. The lighthouse stands tall and menacing on the farthest point of the cliff.

The official name is Avarice Point but what the locals call it is much more accurate.

Suicide Rock.

I go to the windows, equally drawn and terrified, and set the tips of my fingers against the cool glass. A mist is moving in over the water. My gaze is dragged toward that lighthouse, but I catch myself in time, looking down instead—which is a mistake. Not for the height, although it's quite a distance to fall, but because of the cliffs themselves. They terrify me, and I find myself stumbling backward, suddenly dizzy.

Santos is at my side in an instant. He steadies me. He must have crossed the room when I had my back to him. He's a good head taller than me, more than that if I take off my heels. This close, I can see the few gray hairs in his permanent five-o'clock shadow and the specks of gold in his green eyes. I can smell the familiar scent of him, too, and it's a strange, wrong comfort.

He narrows his eyes and tilts his head slightly as if studying me. I wonder—not for the first time—if he can read my mind. More likely, he can read my face. He's much more aware and pays a lot closer attention than most people.

"Steady?" he asks, drawing me out of my thoughts. It's a good thing.

"Fine," I say, purposefully sounding irritated as I remind myself what he is to me.

What I am to him.

He nods, closing off his face to me again. It's when I realize he was letting me see him momentarily. He releases me and takes my clutch from my hand. Opening it, he pulls the flask out again.

My heels click as I move away from him to plop down on the edge of the sofa, tugging the slit of my dress closed when it slips open. I sit with my back to him as I try to force my vision to steady.

He must open the flask and smell or taste what's left because he asks, "Whiskey?"

I shrug. "What are we doing up here?"

"Remind me how old you are," he says, coming to stand in front of me. He's close enough that the toes of our shoes are almost touching, and I need to crane my head to meet his eyes. I should stand up. He already has the upper hand in every way when it comes to us. But my limbs feel weighed down.

"You ask me that every time we meet," I answer. "Math not your strong suit?"

"Eighteen. And you're drunk on whiskey. Not to mention the painkillers, which I'm guessing aren't aspirin."

"I'm not drunk." I don't address the aspirin comment.

"No?"

"No."

"Stand up."

I close my eyes and shake my head as if I'm irritated.

"Do it. Or can't you?"

I roll my eyes and manage to force myself up. It takes effort.

"You're going to stop rolling your eyes at me. Now walk a straight line."

"What are you, the police? I'm not driving. I just had a little whiskey."

"Not a little if this was full. Was it?"

"I don't remember."

"Of course you don't."

"I'm tired," I say, walking past him toward the door. "If you're through interrogating me, I'd like to go home."

I expect him to stop me but when he doesn't, I pull the door open. I know why he didn't bother telling me not to because the same soldier who just let us in blocks my path. He looks to Santos for a signal. He must give it because the man folds his arms and remains where he is. He's built like a fucking tank. So, I close the door and turn back to Santos and wait, hoping the look on my face tells him how much I dislike this and him right now.

"Come," he says, holding out his hand.

I shake my head.

"Do you understand, Madelena, what it means to belong to me?"

"Do you hear how that sounds?"

"It means I take care of what's mine."

That is not the answer I am expecting, and I'm struck mute.

"Come," he repeats, gesturing for me to take his hand.

I look at it. I see the scar in his palm, the one that matches mine. It reminds me of the first night I met him. I shift my gaze up to his. "Why? Do you have a knife on you somewhere?" I ask to turn things around. Because he and I cannot be, will not be. I may have no choice in a marriage, but I can choose my emotions. I can choose if I give him more than he takes.

And I've already decided that I won't.

He lets out a short exhale. "I didn't want to do that to you, but it had to be done."

I raise my eyebrows at that. "Did it?"

"Come, Madelena. You need to sleep. That is all."

My heart skips a beat then goes into double time to make up for it. "I'm not sleeping with you," I blurt out before I can stop myself.

He chuckles. Literally, he chuckles. I'm not sure if I'm offended or embarrassed. Okay, the latter. He steps toward me. "Is that something you think about?" He brushes the hair back from my face, running a knuckle over my cheekbone, my jaw, while his gaze moves to my mouth.

I bite my lower lip so it won't tremble beneath his gaze and I swear his eyes grow darker when I do. My heart thuds so hard against my ribs he must hear it.

His grin is wide when he returns his gaze to mine. "Is it, Little Kitty?"

"No."

"Do you wonder what it will be like?" he asks, walking a slow circle around me. He's so close I feel his breath with every word. It makes the hair on the back of my neck stand on end. "How long have you been imagining it?"

I make a move to pull away, to tell him to fuck off, but he catches me and, with a finger against my chest, traps me at the door.

"Since I told you I'd take you over my knee?" he asks.

I try to ignore the heat that burns my neck and cheeks. I press my thighs together as his finger glides toward my collar bone, traces it. God. This is not happening.

"Because I admit, I felt it too. Wanted it," he continues. He's playing with me. I know he is.

"Stop."

"I'm right, aren't I?"

I shake my head.

He laughs outright, and my shoulders curl in defensively when I should be shoving the arrogant asshole away because of all things, I feel hurt. Fucking hurt.

"I can read you like a book, Little Kitty."

"You're a fucking jerk."

"Maybe. But I never said anything about sleeping together. I just said that *you* need to sleep. You have a dirty mind." He taps the tip of my nose and makes a clicking sound with his tongue. He draws away from me, looking satisfied. I think he's telling the truth about reading me like a book, and that's terrifying—that, and the fact that he is so much more experienced than me.

"I don't think I'm your type anyway. Don't you like them tall and blond?" I retort.

The grin shortens, and one eyebrow rises—the one with the split in it, an old scar.

"You haven't been googling me, have you?" He's amused. So fucking amused.

It was a stupid thing to ask, because I have been doing just that. I've seen the women he is usually with, and they look nothing like me.

He leans in close again, brushing the hair from my ear, and I can feel his lips along the shell of it. I can't help my ragged breath because what he's doing is sending raw electricity through my veins. "You shouldn't believe what you see on the internet, sweetheart," he says seriously, the word sweetheart catching me off guard. "Truthfully, I prefer brunettes." He draws back. I turn my head to look up at him. "And I find myself more and more interested in a certain little kitty with a rebellious streak."

Is he making fun of me again? I can't tell because unlike me, he's unreadable.

He sets two fingers on the raging pulse on my neck and I know it's to show me that he can read me. He knows just how hard my heart is beating, knows what his being so close is doing to me. Most importantly, he knows he holds all the power.

I steel myself, force myself to look him straight in the eye. To try to separate my body from my mind. Seeing him this close is different than looking at photos in the society columns. He's sort of beautiful in this dark, cruel way. I already knew that part. But beneath that cruelty, there's a sadness inside his eyes. That's the part the camera doesn't catch.

I blink, and before I can think, I'm touching the scar that divides his right eyebrow.

Santos grins and takes my hand, and he's gentle as his finger traces the scar he put on my palm. It's strange because there is nothing gentle about this man. I know this. He is dangerous.

"Come, Little Kitty. Time to put you to bed."

Without a word and without me expecting it, he lifts me up and carries me down the hall. I hook an arm over his shoulder. It's all I can do as my mind processes what is happening, what I *should* be doing, and what my reaction *should* be. But it's a mistake because I find my grip tightening on the hard muscle of his shoulders, his bicep, feeling his strength beneath the barrier of clothes.

Santos Augustine is all man… and I like it.

He doesn't say anything. I'm sure he's humoring drunk me. He opens a bedroom door, sets me on the bed, and crouches to slip my shoes off. I watch his dark head and feel his big hands cup each foot. He remains where he is, crouched down, and looks up at me as he slides his hands along one calf, knee, thigh. I fist the bedsheets, and it takes all I have not to whimper as I hold his gaze.

His grin is back, darker this time, dirtier. My throat goes dry as his fingers hook around the elastic of the thigh high stockings, anticipating. His gaze never drops mine, never releases me. I can't look away as he drags my stocking down over my leg and cups my heel as he slips it off.

My body is aflame, every nerve ending alive. I've never been so attracted to a man in my life. Never. Boys I found cute in high school are nothing next to Santos Augustine.

He straightens, shifts my position so I'm lying against the headboard, and when he reaches to do the same with the other stocking, I let myself close my eyes just for a minute, just one single moment, to feel this. Just feel this foreign sensation.

But when I open them again, I realize my mistake... because he's not looking at my face anymore. He's looking at my legs, at what he can see where the skirt has split open. And his face, *fuck*. His face has turned to stone, his mouth into a hard line, his eyes impossibly dark—so dark the green is all but obliterated.

With trembling hands, I reach for the two sides of my dress and pull them closed as he lifts his gaze to mine. A moment passes, silent and heavy, before he shifts his gaze to my hands, covers them with his, and draws the dress apart again.

"Stop. Don't," I say, desperate for him not to see, because how could I be so fucking stupid?

He doesn't stop, though. He pushes my hands away, and there are too many bruises, too many still angry welts. His hands tighten, like he's flexing a fist as he moves the dress farther over and sees more. More. So much more.

I can hear myself breathing ragged breaths, hear the panic in the rush of blood against my ears. The room spins around us as I try to focus on the top of his head, on the feel of calloused hands softly tracing something else. Something different than the fresh welts. Something older.

My throat closes up and I feel my eyes well.

When he looks at my face again, I can't hold his gaze. It's too much, too overwhelming. He's seen too fucking much.

I hate that nickname he's given me. *Little Kitty.* Wounded, fragile little kitty. Broken little kitty. Little kitty who is alone and pathetic and helpless.

Fuck. Fuck him, I think, trying to steel myself, to swallow down all the emotions.

"Madelena," he says, my name a command.

I raise my gaze to his because I have no choice.

"The cuts are old," he says in a tone that seems barely controlled. "We will discuss those."

We won't. I can't. He won't understand. I barely understand.

"But there's a more pressing matter," he continues,

and I'm relieved for exactly one split second. "The welts, they're fresh. That's why the painkillers."

I swallow. I mean to nod even though he didn't ask it as a question, but I'm not sure I can.

"Who did this to you?" he asks, voice ragged and low and unrecognizable.

I just stare at him, unable to answer, to do anything but stare at this man who is different than I expected him to be. Because what would he do to the man who did this? Who truly did hurt me? Who more than touched what is his?

I've seen what he's capable of, and I have a feeling it's the tip of the iceberg. If he gets his hands on the man who did this, what he did to Jason Cole will look gentle.

"Who did this to you, Madelena?" he asks again in that rough voice, the slightly unhinged one. But still, he's controlled. He's reining it in, whatever he's feeling.

"It won't happen again," I say, not sure why because I can't guarantee that. But there's one more thing at play. He doesn't understand that it could have been so much worse. It could have been Odin, not me. Odin, who still limps after so many years.

I hear him swallow, watch his Adam's apple work. It's easier than looking into his eyes.

"There are two men who had access to you. Your father and your brother."

I flinch.

He stands, hands fists at his sides. "Which one of them did this?"

I look down at the bed, the pretty coverlet with the fleur-de-lis pattern. At my legs, at the chaos the belt left behind. Rage. This is the result of uncontrolled rage. When men lose control, it's dangerous for the women in the room.

"Your brother was protective of you once. I remember that."

I draw my knees up to sit on them, cover them with my dress. It's too hard to look at him. But he takes my jaw with one giant hand and forces my face upward. I'm trembling all over, and I hug my arms around myself. He's silent for a long, long time as that well of tears streams down my face.

"Who hurt what is mine?" he finally manages in a ragged, old voice. A broken voice. "Say it."

"Please..." I shake my head.

"Say. It."

It's a command, a simple, straightforward command. He will not accept my silence. I jerk my head from his grasp. This man can play with me. He can taunt me with his touches, with his looks, but he can be my avenging angel, too. He has been that.

"If you don't tell me, so help me, I will punish them both."

"No!"

"Then say it. Tell me who hurt you."

"Please, leave it. Please. You don't understand. You don't know—"

"Say. It."

I press my hands to his chest to keep distance

between us. He must see that I'm afraid. I'm afraid of him right now. Because he is also a man, and his control is hanging by a very thin thread.

He forces himself to step backward and scrubs his face with his hands, eyes still so dark when they meet mine again. That's the physical manifestation of his rage. He turns to go to the door. He's almost gone when I leap off the bed.

"My father!" I cry out. "Not Odin. He would never... Odin would never hurt me." He'll take my father's punishments in my place. He has.

He stops, back stiffening. He doesn't turn back to me. I watch his hands clench and unclench.

"The cuts?" he asks without looking at me. And thank God for that.

"That's... Nothing."

He glances back at me and I don't know if he understands. I stand wringing my hands, sweat pooling under my arms as my body begins to tremble.

His eyebrows come together. His jaw is tight. But I can't talk about the cuts ... I'd rather take a hundred beatings than talk about that.

It takes him a full moment to move and when he does, I charge after him.

"Wait!"

"Val!" he calls out, and the hulk guarding the entrance to the apartment enters. "She stays in the bedroom. No one goes in. She does not come out."

"Yes, sir," Val says. I open my mouth, but Val turns

his attention to me, standing between me and Santos, blocking my path.

"Wait! What are you going to do?" I call out. He keeps moving. "If you hurt him, he'll hurt Odin!"

At that, he stops. He glances backward, his eyes slits.

"When I'm done with him, he won't be able to hurt anyone."

I feel my mouth drop open and before I can say another word, he's gone. Santos is gone.

Val, the incredible fucking hulk, stalks toward me, and for all my bluster, I find myself backing away. I turn on my heel and scurry back into the bedroom where, before I'm two steps in, the door is closed and locked.

I'm left staring at it, wondering what the fuck just happened. Wondering what he will do to my father. How he will punish him. Because he will punish him. But will he stop at that?

8

SANTOS

By the time the elevator arrives downstairs, Caius is waiting for me. Four soldiers enter the building. They're dressed in dark suits to blend in, but they still stand out. It's the look in their eyes, or maybe it's the energy they give off.

"What's going on?" Caius asks me as I direct the men to enter the ballroom.

"Marnix De León. He still in there?"

"Oh yeah. Guzzling down whiskey like a fucking champ. Remind me again, it's not on our tab, right?"

I'm barely able to see straight through my rage. My fury at her father. Fury at myself. Because how many times can I let this happen? How many fathers will beat their daughters while I stand by like an impotent fool? How many will do worse?

And the cuts. That I don't understand. I file that fact away for now.

"Santos?" Caius puts a hand on my shoulder to stop me just outside the entrance of the ballroom.

I blink hard. I need to stay here, in the present moment. I'm in time. She's not dead. Just fucking covered in welts.

"Brother," Caius says again, getting in my face this time to make me look at him. My brother's eyes are sky blue, like our mom's, and they can look so very different from mine. The darkness inside him—because there is darkness inside him—he's better at keeping hidden.

"He beat her." The words are raw and taut with fury.

Caius's forehead creases.

"Her thighs are covered in welts. Fresh welts." I don't mention what I saw beneath those welts. If I'd looked closer, if I'd stripped her bare and scrutinized every inch of skin, what would I have found? More scars? More cuts? And the welts, how far did he go? I only saw her thighs.

"Her father?" he asks.

I nod once.

He knows what I'm thinking about. He understands my reaction. Caius knows me well, better than anyone in the world.

"Let's go get the son of a bitch," he says.

Again, I nod, because I'm too furious to speak. My brother and I enter the ballroom together, and heads turn. Just like the soldiers, I'm sure we're giving off a particular energy.

One of aggression.

Of violence walking.

It takes all I have to unclench my hands, and I have to keep my arms stiff at my sides as if a marching soldier as I scan the room and find him. Marnix De Léon. He's in the same place he was earlier—holding fucking court, laughing. Drunk.

His boy, Odin, sees us first. He doesn't make a move to warn his father, or maybe he just doesn't have time. When we get to their circle, our soldiers close in enough to make an impression but not so tight that we draw too much attention.

"Excuse us," I say. My eyes are locked on Marnix, but I'm speaking to the people gathered around him.

"He needs a word with his future father-in-law. Just hammering out some wedding details. Bridezilla and all," Caius says in that way of his like he's relaxed and so casual. So charming.

"What's this about?" Odin asks as Marnix swallows the whiskey in his glass.

The group dissipates.

I don't look at Odin. I don't take my eyes off Marnix. "You and me have something to discuss."

"I don't think we have anything to discuss—"

"Let's go." I gesture to the soldiers, one of whom knocks into Marnix from behind to nudge him.

"I'm guessing we'll need some privacy," Caius says to me. "I know where we can go."

His coming here as often as he has been is paying off. Caius leads the way, with Marnix, Odin, me, and the soldiers trailing him. We use a door I hadn't noticed before to leave the ballroom. It's one servants might have used to come and go unseen.

Caius really has taken to getting to know the layout of the place. We are in a deserted corridor, where we pass half a dozen closed doors, but Caius heads to the one at the far end. He produces a key and unlocks it, then steps aside. "After you," he says to Marnix.

Marnix glances at the stairs leading down, then back at Caius. "What the hell is this about?"

I walk around to face him. I've managed to get myself at least a little bit under control. I glance down to his belt, then back up. "Is this the belt you used?"

Marnix De Léon, my soon to be father-in-law, goes white as a ghost before my eyes.

I see Odin's face in my periphery, see his confusion, then a too-quick understanding that leads me to believe this isn't the first time this has happened.

"Where is my sister?" he asks me, suddenly panicked. He turns to walk back into the ballroom. I gesture to a soldier, who stops him. "Where is my sister?"

"She's safe. No thanks to you." I turn back to Marnix. "Down. Now."

No one waits for him to move on his own. The soldier closest to him grips him by the shoulder and marches him down the stairs.

"It's not the fanciest space, but I am thinking the way you look, you're more concerned with privacy and good sound proofing," Caius says as we follow him down. One soldier stays upstairs to guard the door. We're in a cave-like space, a wine cellar. It seems to span the length of the building based on the lights that go on one after the other, probably on sensors. The floor is dirt, while the walls are carved stone, and shelf after shelf is stocked full with bottles collecting dust. The building itself is built on a cliff so I guess this was carved out of that rock. "Had a tour," Caius says to me. "There's about fourteen thousand bottles down here. Can you believe it?"

"I can, actually."

"Good stuff, too. I sampled."

I would chuckle if I wasn't so preoccupied.

"No one will hear a sound," he adds to Marnix De León's discomfort. "And although it's a little chilly, getting blood out of carpet is hard work. Housekeeping will thank you."

I let out a short exhale. I appreciate my brother's ability to hold onto his sense of humor no matter what. I'm too fucking serious for that.

"What did you do?" Odin asks his father, who brings his nearly empty whiskey glass to his lips to drain the last drops then sets it on the stone table slab in the center of the room. It has a four-inch wooden chopping block cut to fit on top. He's right-handed. I make a mental note.

"Yeah, old man. Tell your boy what you did."

Marnix looks at me with hate-filled eyes. He's terrified, I can see that. He may have hired crooks to do his dirty work for him before, like he unknowingly hired us to take care of his enemy, but he's never crossed a mafia family. Does he realize yet that the shit in the movies and the books is real? Does he get that we don't fuck around?

After tonight, he will, and I can already see the wheels turning.

"We have a contract," I start when he doesn't speak. "One that binds your daughter to me. That says she belongs to me."

His eyes narrow.

"She. Belongs. To. Me," I say again so as to leave no confusion.

"Not for another two years. Terms are clear."

"Think of it like buying a car. You negotiate an agreement, pay your money, but then come delivery time, you get that car just not quite in the condition you agreed upon," Caius says from where he's leaning against the wall. I see a hammer and nails on the shelf beside him and if I know my brother, he chose that spot on purpose.

"Dad," Odin says. "What did you do to her?"

Marnix scans the room. He glances at the soldiers standing at the stairs. I hope he's not foolish enough to try to run for it. I'm glad to see in the next moment that he's not that stupid, that cowardly. He takes a deep breath. His whole face relaxes then, and he's the man from upstairs, the one holding court.

"The girl needed to learn a lesson," he says to Odin, then turns to me. "She has a big mouth. I should wish you luck with her. Hell, you can have her now if you want her so fucking badly," he tells me, then turns to his son. "You fucking kids are both a disappointment."

My chest tightens and breathing is hard. "You cannot give what is not yours."

"What did you do?" Odin asks him again.

The older man shifts his gaze to the far wall.

"He whipped her. Welts two inches thick across her thighs."

Odin's face looks pained. He turns from me to his father. "Why? Why hurt her?"

"Why not? Isn't she the one who broke us?"

"Mom decided to jump. She was sick. You know that. It had nothing to do with Madelena."

"Like hell it didn't."

Odin's jaw tenses. This is clearly an argument they've had before.

"For your part, you didn't protect her," I tell Odin, because he didn't.

"I didn't know," he says, hanging his head and something in his stance, in the way he looks, it's almost broken, like this was a step too far. It gets to me.

"Get him out of here," I tell a soldier.

"No," Odin says, straightening. He then turns to his father. "I will stand witness."

"Interesting," Caius says, picking up the hammer and weighing it.

I stalk toward the older man who, to his credit, doesn't back away. "I asked you a question earlier. Is that the belt you used?"

He nods once.

"Take it off."

His eyes narrow. I guess he thinks it'll be an eye for an eye, that he'll get off with a belt whipping.

That's not how I operate. He will learn that tonight.

With an almost victorious grin, he unbuckles his belt, slips it from the loops, and dangles it out in front of me.

But I'm going to need my hands free. I gesture to a soldier, who takes it and remains standing directly behind him.

"You do not touch what is mine. You're going to learn that tonight. Put your hands on the block."

"If you're going to whip me, go ahead. I won't move. I'm no coward."

"Put your hands on the block."

"Fine, asshole," he says with a shake of his head and a grin toward Odin. "Good opportunity to teach you how to take a fucking whipping like a man."

I turn to Odin, whose eyes are locked on his father. Given what his father just said, it's not the first time he's hit them, like I had already guessed. I wonder if Odin stood between him and Madelena, but tonight isn't the time for that. Tonight is to teach. "Just know that if I ever have to punish you for going against me, this will look like child's play. You hear me?" I ask Odin.

Odin's eyes are narrowed and still locked on his father, but he nods. Turning my back on them, I walk toward my brother, who grins and hands me the hammer.

"What the hell?" Marnix De Léon says when I turn back around. He draws his hands from the board just as I give a nod to the soldier, who hooks the belt around his throat and crosses it at the back of his neck. He tugs but not too tight—don't want him getting off too easily. But it forces Marnix to clutch at it.

"I told you to put your fucking hands on the block!" I say, rage amplifying my voice. I grab hold of his right arm, force it onto the block, and drive a nail through the back of his hand, pinning it.

Marnix De Léon stills—then, a split second later, he screams.

Did she scream when he beat her? His own daughter, a woman half his size. Did she scream?

I raise the hammer and drive the nail in farther, then raise it again to bring it down on his hand once, twice, three times. I meant to aim for his thumb, but to be honest, I'm not that critical. He just keeps on screaming as I shatter the bones in his hand.

As abruptly as I began, as quickly, it's over.

I slam the hammer down beside his mangled hand. When the soldier releases his hold on the belt, Marnix drops to his knees, the arm of the trapped hand stretching. He's whimpering, still attempting to scream but unable to as he gasps for air.

Odin looks on, fucking witnessing. I don't know what I expect to see in his eyes or on his face but apart from the green of his complexion, I don't see fear or anything resembling it. When he meets my eyes, he swallows down that bile and holds my gaze. He knows his father deserved this and probably much more, and I wonder how many times Marnix De Léon has beaten his son—if his limp is because of the asshole now whimpering on the floor.

"Oh, that's going to be quite the puzzle to piece back together," Caius says, having come over to examine the mangled hand of the man kneeling on the floor. Marnix's arm is stretched up, that nail doing its job and keeping it where I told him to put it.

"Let's go," I tell him and my soldiers. I'll leave it to Odin to get the nail out. We walk to the stairs. Caius stops to pick out two dusty bottles of wine.

"I've had enough of the party," Caius says to me once we get upstairs. "These look good. Shall we?"

I nod, and we head toward the elevators that lead to the penthouse apartment. Although as a rule I don't drink, I make an exception tonight. I drink a bottle of wine with my brother, and I think about the woman in the next room. I think about what could have happened to her... what can still happen to her.

And I decide. Maybe I decided earlier that night, but I know without a doubt in this moment what I need to do. I've been wrong before, and my poor judgment cost me. But I wasn't the one who paid the ultimate price.

"You're lost in thought, brother," Caius says.

I drink the last of the wine directly from my bottle and stand at the window, looking at the fog that's rolled in and at the light from the lighthouse. "I want her out of here tomorrow. She doesn't go back to that house, doesn't see her father or her brother. I want her guarded twenty-four-seven."

"Santos," he says, coming to me when I stand. He takes my shoulders, turns me to him. This is the problem with not drinking. When I do, it makes everything slower, and it takes a moment for my eyes to focus on him. "The past is not repeating itself. Not with her. Wait the two years. It's what you agreed."

I shake my head. "No. Not making that mistake again. Arrange it. You'll take her."

"Doesn't she start school or some shit in a few weeks?"

Art school. Local. I remember. "Fix it. Do what you need to do. I want her out of Avarice. Somewhere no one can find her."

He studies me, sighs. "All right. Fine."

I nod, put my hands on his shoulders and think about what Dad told me tonight, how he changed the will. "I love you, brother," I tell him. That's going to be another problem for another day.

"Fuck, maybe you shouldn't drink," Caius says as he gives me a hug with a pat on my back. "You become a sentimental fool."

I smile.

"That was intense down there. On point, but intense. You're a sick son of a bitch, you know that?"

"Ditto," I say. He was the one who'd handed me the hammer, after all.

9

MADELENA

I must fall asleep at some point, because I wake up when the bedroom door opens. It takes me a minute to remember where I am, what happened. I sit up in the bed, looking around. My shoes are on the floor, along with one stocking, and I'm lying on top of the bed. I have a headache, and my mouth feels like it's stuffed with cotton.

A woman enters, pushing a tray, and I draw the blanket over myself. I smell breakfast. Another two follow her, and I notice they're all wearing uniforms. Two are housekeepers. The other, room service, maybe? Do they have room service here? I've never spent the night, but I guess so. The building is run like a very exclusive hotel.

The two women draw the curtains aside, letting in the bright morning sun. I turn away, feeling like the bride of Dracula as I cover my eyes, then I wipe at the corners of my mouth. A glance at the pillow shows smears of black that have to be eyeliner and mascara. I can imagine what my face looks like.

"What time is it?" I manage hoarsely. There's no clock on the bedside table, and my phone is in my clutch, which must still be in the other room.

"Nine o'clock, Miss," the one taking the lid off the breakfast plate says. I glance into the corridor through the open door behind her. Val is gone, but I don't see anyone else. Is Santos back? What did he do? The way he left here last night, raging, was a little terrifying—and I know one thing for sure. I don't ever want that rage directed at me.

The two women draw the curtains of the other window open. I didn't realize it was a two-person job, but okay. We have household staff, too. We don't need them, if you ask me, but it's a status thing to our father.

"Breakfast is ready, Miss. Is there anything else you'd like?" the nearby woman asks, the three of them standing back once the curtains are opened and the breakfast plates are uncovered.

I'm not sure how many people Santos thinks will be eating, but there's enough to feed me about four times over. Then another thought comes. Is he going to come in here and eat with me? Are we going to have breakfast together?

"Where is Santos?" I ask the woman, because the thought of sitting across a table from him for something as mundane as breakfast makes me a little uneasy.

"Mr. Augustine won't be dining with you. Shall I pour your coffee?"

"Where is he?"

"I don't know, Miss. If that's all..." She trails off and raises her eyebrows at her two helpers. They all turn to leave the room, and I slip out of the bed. I need my phone. The woman almost has the door closed, but I grab hold of it. She doesn't fight me off. I'm not sure I expect her to, but she does seem surprised as I draw it open.

"My purse," I say, although I don't know why I'm explaining anything. I take a step into the hallway but stop dead in my tracks when a woman who looks to be in her late forties steps into view. She's dressed in a tweed fitted suit that looks like it was custom made for her, along with a pair of stiletto heeled boots. Her makeup is perfect, her skin dewy with vibrance. Her blond hair is cut short and falls in a sharp angle, and I notice not a single line forms around her eyes when she smiles the tiniest smile at seeing me.

I look down at myself, remember the smear of black on the pillow, and attempt to at least tamp down my hair. This woman is all elegance and style. Right this moment, I am the opposite.

"Ma'am," the woman in charge of the housekeepers says with a nod to the older woman, who doesn't bother to acknowledge her. Is this Santos's mother? I've never met her, and the photo or two I've seen were older, of when she wore her hair longer in a less severe cut. But her eyes, those are familiar. Like Caius's eyes.

"So, you are Madelena De Léon," she says, entering the bedroom and walking me backward into it. "I hope breakfast is to your liking?" she asks, picking a raspberry off the plate of fruit and popping it into her mouth. She doesn't close the door. I won't run past her, but I'm not a prisoner here, surely.

Last night was different. Last night was... I don't know.

"Where is Santos?" I ask because breakfast is the furthest thing from my mind.

"My son left in the early hours. Business."

"Oh. Uh, I should—"

"Bathroom's there. Start with washing the night off, perhaps? They say you age seven days when you don't wash off your makeup before bed."

I self-consciously touch my face.

"Everything you need should be there. I'll pour you some coffee. Go on. You have a little time yet."

I want to ask her what she means, but she turns back to the tray and pours two cups of coffee. She takes hers to the window, looks out over the rough, gray ocean, and sips. I go into the bathroom, locking the door behind me. This is weird.

The towel I'd used last night after washing my hands is still on the countertop, and I run the tap. I take in my reflection. Jesus. I think Dracula's bride may look better. I've got more of a zombie vibe going.

Bending down, I wash my face. I have to use the hand soap to get the makeup off, but I don't have a choice. Once my face is as clean as it's going to get without proper makeup remover, I search the drawers for a toothbrush and am grateful when I find two sets of toiletries, his and hers, filled with toothbrushes and sample size toothpaste, hand lotion, and a tiny manicure kit. I unpack a toothbrush and brush my teeth, then smear the lotion onto a cotton swab to wipe away the last of the eyeliner that I couldn't get off with the soap. I finger comb the tangles out of my hair. It's a little wavy but not too bad to manage. The dress is wrinkled, but I've definitely looked worse.

I take a deep breath in and hope that maybe she'll be gone before I open the door. No such luck.

She turns to me from the same place at the window. She brushes her hair down over the right side of her face and I realize the skin is damaged there. It looks like an old burn. She smiles. "Now I can see your face. Not too bad," she says, although she is clearly unimpressed.

"Gee, thanks," I tell her, annoyed, and move toward the tray to take the cup of coffee she had poured for me. I add cream and sugar, then sip. I watch her as I do. She seems to have no qualms studying me so openly. She's very much giving off wicked stepmother vibes.

When I clear my throat and glance away, she comes closer and pushes my hair over my shoulder. She touches a long, blood-red fingernail that is just this side of sharp along my cheekbone. "Youth is a gift we all squander," she says. She brushes my hair back and is standing so close I actually take a step backward because she's creeping me out.

"Excuse me," I say, setting the coffee down. "I need my phone."

"Mother, there you are," a voice says when I've barely taken a step to the door. We both turn to look. Opposite how she looked at me, Evelyn Augustine actually smiles. I guess she isn't thrilled to have me for her soon to be daughter-in-law. News flash for her, I'm not exactly jumping up and down for joy at the prospect of marrying Santos Augustine or having the evil queen as my mother-in-law.

"Caius, darling." She goes to him.

He smiles casually, hair still wet from a shower, and glances at me over her shoulder as she kisses his cheek and bids him a good morning. He's wearing a charcoal cashmere sweater and a pair of black slacks. He has his hands in his pockets, and I see on his wrist the deep blue stones on a bracelet that matches the one I've glimpsed on Santos's wrist. Lapis Lazuli, I think. They look like prayer beads, but honestly I can't see either of these men praying.

More like they think they're the gods.

"Mother, I'm not sure Madelena wants to see you first thing in the morning after her first night in Santos's bed."

Santos's bed? This is not his bed. Every drawer is empty. I open my mouth to say that but Caius winks at me.

"Walk of shame and all," he adds.

"I... What?" Is this really happening?

Evelyn looks back at me with clear disdain. "Don't

worry, dear. We know you're not that kind of girl. And even if you were, Santos is not that kind of man. He'll wait until the wedding night. Caius is just being Caius, aren't you?" she says to him, playfully tugging at the hair behind his ear.

I make myself walk toward the door. I mean to get past them. "I need my phone," I say to Caius because he's the one blocking my exit.

He glances to his mother, and they exchange some silent communication. I'm not sure if the brief movement of his head is him telling her to go or what, but Evelyn turns to me with that same empty smile and, without another word, leaves. Caius closes the door behind her and turns to me.

The smile is gone, and I wonder if it was for her benefit. For a moment, he studies me, and I make myself do the same. I can't be afraid. Or at least, I can't show it. They won't hurt me. They need me.

As I study him, I think about how the brothers look nothing alike. Not a single thing. Santos has dark hair, almost black. Caius's is a dirty blond, darker than his mother's but similarly thick, too. Santos's forest green eyes are worlds apart from Caius's blue ones, bright like a summer day.

But there is nothing summery about this man. There is nothing light about this man. I know it in my gut.

Caius Augustine is dangerous.

"Do you mind?" he asks, picking up a strip of bacon.

"Go ahead," I say, sitting on the edge of the bed because I don't know what to do with myself.

"I'm starving. Missed dinner," he explains. "And Santos and I had a little to drink after you went to bed."

I didn't exactly go to bed. I was locked in. I get the feeling he knows that, though.

"Needed it after..." He trails off, his gaze moving over me before returning to my eyes. "Well, let's just say my brother is very protective of you."

I feel the blood drain from my head, and I'm glad I'm sitting down. "What did he do?" I ask cautiously.

He eats another piece of bacon, then butters toast as he speaks. "I heard what your father did. Pretty shitty." He bites into his toast, sending crumbs everywhere. "Good news is, I know for a fact he will never lay a finger on you again," he says with a wide smile as he chews the rest of the toast before picking up my juice and drinking it all, washing his breakfast down. He makes a satisfied sound and sets the glass back on the tray.

"What does that mean?"

He wipes his hands on a cloth napkin then drops it. "Those details aren't for a young lady's ears."

What the fuck is wrong with him? He's enjoying this, without a doubt, and I don't know what's going on.

"Is my father okay?" I ask, scared of the answer as soon as the words are out.

He shrugs a shoulder. "Mostly. He won't hurt

you again. That's what counts." He checks his watch. "You should eat something. We have a few minutes."

Feeling a sudden chill, I hug my arms to my chest. "I want to talk to my brother."

"Oh, he's fine. Odin, right?"

I nod, relieved. Although he could be lying.

"I need to call him. He's probably so worried. I fell asleep. Santos... The man he left, he wouldn't even let me out to get my phone."

"Val. He's very loyal to my brother. Bit of a cement block up here," he says, tapping his head, "but I guess that's what you want in a soldier. All muscle, no brains."

I get up and take a step toward the door because this conversation will go nowhere. Caius Augustine will play with me. That is all. But before I take another, he's in front of me—blocking my path, standing too close.

"Hmm..." he trails off. "There's been a change of plans."

I try to sidestep him, but he matches my movement. "I want my phone."

He shakes his head. "That's not possible." He checks his watch. "In fact, we should go. You sure you don't want anything to eat?"

"I'm fine."

"Well, then, the car should be downstairs."

"I don't need a car. My brother can pick me up." I do drive but we'd come to the charity together. I try once more to pass Caius, and this time, he catches my arm to stop me.

"He's probably occupied," he says.

That makes me stop. "I want to go home." I need to see Odin. Talk to him. Make sure he's really okay.

"Home where your dad beat you?" he asks, no joking in his tone or facial expression. "Home where you're unprotected?"

"I..." I pull free of him, rub my temples because the headache is worse. "What's happening? Where is Santos? I have two more years. I know I have two more years. It's in the contract."

"When your father beat you—"

"Can you not say it like that?" I say, taking a few steps away.

"How should I say it?" he asks, stalking toward me, any joking—even if it was fake— gone. "When he whipped you? When he turned your legs black and blue?" He gestures down, and I cover what he can see. The bruises on my inner thighs are exposed every time I move, and the dress splits now that the stockings are gone. "How else? Any other way to put it?"

I don't respond and he sighs.

"Like I was saying, when your father beat you, he breached the contract. He attempted to damage what was not his. What is ours."

I look up at him, very, *very* aware of the word he just used. I belong to Santos. I know that. My brain has had time to process the insanity of it.

But I do not belong to this man.

"We're taking ownership now," he says.

"What the hell are you talking about?"

His phone buzzes with a text and he lifts it out of his pocket. He types a reply, then puts it away and turns back to me. "Car's ready. I'll take you home to get a few things. We'll have the rest packed up and sent. Your flight is in a little over an hour, so we won't have much time."

"What flight?" Panic has me going along with him when he takes my arm and walks me back into the room.

"You'll want your shoes."

I look down at the discarded stocking, the shoes lying on their sides. I slip them on absently, then follow along as he takes me out of the bedroom.

Evelyn is standing at the window, talking to someone on the phone. She turns her back to us as Caius leads me out the front door where a different soldier accompanies us on the elevator, down to the lobby.

"What flight?" I ask again as we cross it, only a few people milling about. The rest will be passed out in their beds. The ones who are here watch us go. "School starts—"

"I'll explain it all on our way," he says as we exit the building and a man opens the door of an SUV with tinted windows. I climb into the back seat, and Caius follows. The door closes, and the soldier settles into the passenger seat as the man who opened the door for us takes the driver's side.

"Explain what?" I ask Caius, who makes a point of dragging my seatbelt across my chest in a move that feels much more oppressive, much more foreboding, than it should.

"Safety first," he says with a raise of his eyebrows. He puts on his seatbelt too.

"Explain what?" I ask more loudly, really panicking now.

"Turns out you won't be attending the local art school after all. You'll be happy to know I've found a small, but highly regarded school down in Georgia, in Savannah in fact. Very pretty city. Have you been?"

"What the hell are you talking about?"

"I'll assume that's a no?"

"Just tell me what's going on."

Again, he sighs, then leans his head against the headrest and studies me. "Like I said, my brother feels very protective of you. I can guess why, but not sure I agree with his methods. Regardless, I will do what he wants. Like Val, I'm loyal to my brother too." There's a momentary curling of the lip, but it's gone so fast I'm not sure I didn't imagine it. "You'll attend the school in Georgia for the next two years, after which the wedding will take place and you'll come back to Avarice as Santos Augustine's wife. My sister-in-law." He sets his hand on his chin like he's thinking. "Too soon to call you sis?" The last part is said with a questioning look.

I'm struck mute for a moment.

"But... What about my brother?" There's no one

else to ask about. I don't have friends. I don't care about my father. But Odin?

"You'll have to discuss visitation with Santos."

"Visitation? What am I, a prisoner?" It was meant as a joke, but my voice quavers.

He just looks at me like I'm either the stupidest person he ever met, or I've just said the most obvious thing in the world, and I exhale.

Because I am exactly that. Because last night, I was locked in that room. Because I still don't have my phone or any other way to contact Odin or anyone else —not that there is anyone else. They'll lock me away for the next two years until I marry Santos Augustine, then I'll be a prisoner in a different house.

"You can't do this," I say, my voice quiet, as we turn onto our street.

Caius types out a text, his attention on his phone, not on me when he speaks. "We can. We are," he says, and looks at me just as the car comes to a stop. "You'll find when you're an Augustine, you can do whatever you want, whenever you want, to whomever you want." His words sound ugly, his expression uglier.

He climbs out of the car when his door is opened, then comes to my side to open my door. He takes my arm in a grip a little harder than it needs to be.

Once I'm out, he smiles his cool smile. "Lucky for you, you'll soon be an Augustine."

10

SANTOS

1 Year Later

My father hung on a lot longer than the doctors had expected, but still not long enough. The funeral was hard, really fucking hard, and I need to get away.

Just for a night.

"Just about there, sir," says the driver, nearly startling me.

I nod, shift my gaze back out the window, and watch the fading lights of Savannah, Georgia.

I'm not actually sure why I came here. It makes no sense. I won't find comfort here. I know that. I tuck my hand into my pocket and feel the small velvet box there. This is why, I remind myself. It's bullshit, but it's what I tell myself.

I have weekly reports about Madelena's progress at the all-girls private art school where she's enrolled. Like in her various schools in Avarice, she hasn't made friends and isn't trying to, according to the headmistress. The college is a small, Catholic college where most of the classes are taught by nuns. The students all wear the same uniform and attend mass weekly.

I'm not sure why I like the idea. I'm not a religious man. My time with the Commander may even have me repulsed by the idea, but there's something to it, to the ceremony, the ritual. Maybe it's the old-fashioned nature of it. Although the scent of incense makes me nauseous. Too many bad memories. Even today, at my own father's funeral mass, I almost choked on it.

The SUV slows, and I sit up to watch as the large Gothic style mansion comes into view beyond the gates. The mansion is original, and the school itself sits on acres of land enclosed by twelve-foot stone walls. The grounds are gated, the classes given in one of the more modern buildings. The dorms are housed in new construction built to match the old.

Madelena has the best room in the original mansion. I made sure of that. She is also one of the few without a roommate. I knew she'd want her privacy.

A little farther, I can see the hulking shadows of the outer dorm buildings and the chapel. It's two in the morning. The campus is asleep—apart from Sister Catherine.

My phone rings as the SUV slows. I take it out of the breast pocket of my jacket and consider not answering it, consider switching it back off. But what comes next, what comes after the burial, is not something I can put off forever.

I accept the call. "Brother."

"What the hell are you doing?" Caius asks without a greeting. "Where are you?"

The funeral was a few hours ago. It was larger than I'd thought it would be, although I suppose it's not surprising that the good folk of Avarice paid their respects to the newest and most powerful family to join their ranks.

But it was overwhelming in a way I didn't expect and I was unprepared. What I needed most after that, what I wanted most, was to be alone.

"I'll be back tomorrow," I say.

"The will is scheduled to be read in seven hours. Think you can make it by then?"

No, I won't. I rub my forehead, then sigh. He doesn't know what's coming, doesn't know how disappointed he will be tomorrow. I do. I was privy to the details—another gift from a father to his favored son. His blood son.

"I needed to get away, Caius. Just for a little bit. Surely you can understand that today of all days."

"And you left me behind."

"Mom needed one of us. She prefers you."

"Like Dad preferred you?"

"Caius."

"Besides, she doesn't need anyone," he says,

sounding more vulnerable than I've heard him sound in a long time. "Where are you?"

"Savannah."

"Ah." I hear him sigh, then take a swallow of something. It's whiskey, most likely, although he does have a bad habit of drinking good wine straight from the bottle.

"Look, I needed to be away."

"I get it," he says after a long silence.

"You going to be all right?" I ask him, feeling a little guilty for having left him behind.

"I'll be fine. When are you coming back?"

"Tomorrow. Put the reading off until the next morning."

"Fine. But why go see her? What will that do? What are you hoping for?"

"I don't know. It was the only place I could think of."

"Well, if you're expecting a warm welcome, I have a feeling you're going to be disappointed."

That I know. Her letters have told me as much, letters I required of her, but it hadn't been entirely unexpected. I cut her off from her life entirely, from her brother, although I am aware she's had contact with him.

The other girls have cell phones. She's been using one of theirs. As far as her father, I don't imagine she cared much about keeping in touch with him.

I required her to write to me once a month. I don't know why, and I'm not sure what I'd expected—maybe to hear from her that she was all right even if she hated me. It's stupid. I said it on a whim to the headmistress, maybe half-expecting the letters not to come, but they had. Although they weren't exactly letters. They were sketches—self-portraits—of her flipping me off. I smile a rare smile at the memory.

I used to write letters when I was younger, too, with Alexia, the girl who never got to become a woman. The girl who Madelena reminds me of, though not in looks or behavior or anything I can put my finger on. It's just something about them both. A vulnerability. Maybe that they both need protecting from those closest to them because in looks and personality, she and Alexia couldn't be more different. Alexia and I used to write to each other during the summers when she was away visiting family on the west coast. I still have every one of them.

"Look, I need to go. I'll be back tomorrow evening. We'll talk then."

"All right. You take care, brother."

"You too."

I disconnect the call and slip my phone back into my pocket. When the SUV comes to a stop, a light goes on in the foyer. Sister Catherine opens the front door. By nature she's not a very welcoming woman, but she does paste a false smile on. She doesn't like me. Honestly, the feeling's mutual. I don't like her either, and I hadn't from the moment I'd met her.

But by then, Caius had arranged everything for

Madelena, so I just made sure the nun knew my expectations of her where they concerned Madelena.

"Mr. Augustine. Always a pleasure," she says flatly, closing the door once I enter.

"I doubt it's a pleasure at this hour, sister."

Without any more pleasantries, she reaches into her tunic pocket and retrieves a single key on a thin chain.

I take it. She looks at me, and I wonder if she'd say something if I wasn't Santos Augustine, if my money didn't ensure the survival of Sacred Heart College of Art for Talented Young Ladies and keep her very comfortable. But it does. Anyone who thinks nuns don't care about material comforts has never met Sister Catherine.

"Up those stairs. Room 1."

"Thank you. Please go to bed, Sister. I'll see myself out."

She nods, and I wait for her to leave before I head up two sets of stairs to the narrower one that spirals upward to the third floor. It's where the two best rooms are. Madelena has one, and a student one year older than her has the other.

The halls are lit by soft lights, but the corridors are dark. I swear the faint smell of incense permeates the ancient wood here. I breathe through my mouth. But maybe I'm imagining it because the chapel is housed in a separate building far from this one.

I arrive at Madelena's door and listen. All is quiet. I'm sure she's asleep. I insert the key into the lock and hear the click of it unlocking. I turn the old doorknob and push the door open, careful so it won't creak too loudly.

The room is shadowy, but there are two windows where only the sheerest lace curtains are drawn. One of them is open a crack to let in the cool night air. The heavier drapes are left open, and the moon casts enough light for me to take in the details. The desk with its books stacked on one corner, a notebook open with the pen laid across the page. A sweater draped over the back of the desk chair. Textbooks stacked on a chair pushed against the wall.

Two framed photos sit on the edge of the desk, a selfie taped to the front of one. I pick up the first frame to study it. The photo that's stuck to it is printed on plain paper. Odin's arm is outstretched, and Madelena has her head against his shoulder. They're almost smiling. The one inside the frame is a woman and a boy of about three. Odin and their mother. Madelena is a carbon copy of her mother who is heavily pregnant in the photo.

I wonder how much of the events of the day her mother died Madelena remembers. She was quite young. It would be a blessing if she had no memory of it, but I get the feeling that's not the case. The fact that her mother had meant to take Madelena with her—and that the imbecile father blames her for her mother's suicide—must make it all much more complex for Madelena to navigate.

I set the photo down and pick up the second one.

Something twists in my gut to see it. It's brother and sister standing on either side of their uncle, Jax Donovan. They all have big, goofy smiles on their faces, and in the background is a roller coaster. The night she met me, she'd buried her beloved uncle. I'll never forget the look on her face. How she looked like she'd been crying forever.

I put this photo face-down on the desk and shift my attention to the wall where she has a multitude of sketches haphazardly taped up. I recognize her style and have to grin. This looks to be the wall of obscenity. They're like the rude sketches I receive. I've kept them all because strangely, they've made me laugh. The ones here are more serious. Most are self-portraits, while others are line art I can't quite make out in this light.

One draws my attention, and I peer closer. This one is different. It's her and it looks like she had a mirror in front of herself to draw the sketch because her head is resting in one hand, hair like a veil, golden eyes the only thing of color in the sketch. I peel it off the wall, and it rips a little where the tape sticks. I look closer. She's not wearing makeup. And I'm wrong. The gold is not the only color. There is a subtle blue beneath her eyes, shadows like bruises. I try to read the expression in them because I'm not sure why this one has caught my eye. For one thing, it's not her flipping me off, and it's not flattering either. It's too raw for that. Too real. Too vulnerable.

That's it, I realize. That's why.

I fold it carefully and tuck it into my breast pocket beside my phone.

A dresser stands against the far wall with a mirror on top. It's tilted downward since it's so high. The door to the bathroom beyond is left slightly ajar. I walk to it, lean in to see it. It's small with a stand-up shower that would be too tight for me. There's a cracked mirror over the pedestal sink and a toilet. A makeup bag sits open on the edge of the sink. It's smeared with foundation. A tube of lipstick lies on its side, and I pick it up, open it. It's a deep, dark red and it's almost gone. I read the name. Car-crash red. With a shake of my head, I set it down. It's apt, the name. Our lives are like a fucking car crash.

Back in the bedroom, I turn my attention to her bed. It's pushed to the wall directly beneath one of the windows. I go to it and there, beneath a heavy duvet, is the sleeping form of Madelena, her back to me, with hair longer than I remember spilling across the white pillow.

I watch her. I just stand there for a long, long minute watching.

Why did I come? Why here? Why to her?

She makes a sound. I wonder if she can feel my presence, feel my eyes on her. She shifts from her side to her back as I hold my breath. Did I wake her?

No, she stills, and I draw the blanket up to cover her bare shoulder, taking a moment to run the back of my hand over the soft, pale skin of it.

As if she feels the tickle of my touch, she stretches

her arm out and turns her head toward me. She doesn't normally wear jewelry. I noticed that before too. Nothing. Not even to her prom or to the formal charity event.

Her arm is slender, the muscle of her bicep lean, her narrow wrist so small I'm sure if I wrapped my thumb and pinky finger around it, they'd overlap. Her fingers are long, her hand delicate. The bitten-down nails are painted black but have chipped badly.

I give myself one more minute to look at her face while it's relaxed, while she's relaxed. Then I clear my throat.

She startles, eyelids flying open, and bolts upright with a gasp. Big honey-colored eyes stare back at me as her hands clutch the duvet and she presses her back against the wall. "What the—"

"Shh," I say, putting a finger lightly to her lips. "We don't want to wake your neighbor."

She stares up at me, and I see realization dawning as a cloud drifts from the moon and its light shines in from the window. A furrow forms between her brows, but she relaxes a little too, beginning to look more curious than scared. She surveys the room as if expecting to find others, then looks down at herself. I follow her gaze. She's wearing a light pink tank top. It's the first time I'm seeing her in something other than black, and I like it. I like her in color.

But then my gaze shifts to the pebbled nipples of her breasts, and my mind moves in a different direction. As if sensing this, she draws the duvet up to cover herself and shudders.

I clear my throat, walk to the window, and close it. When I turn back to her, she's reaching to the foot of the bed where the ugliest green cardigan I've ever seen is draped over the footboard. She straightens, draws back against the wall when I pick up the sweater and hand it to her.

"What the hell are you doing here?" she asks, taking it, slipping it on and buttoning just the top two buttons. Her gaze moves the clock on the bedside table. "It's the middle of the night."

"Do you always wake up angry?"

"Only when I wake up to strange men lurking over my bed."

"Well, I hope I'm the only man who's lurked over your bed. If not, I'll have to talk with the sisters."

"Oh, don't worry," she says, pushing the duvet back. She's wearing short shorts. I wonder if she's aware just how much of an eyeful she's giving me as she reaches to switch on the lamp on the nightstand. She looks up at me, and I clear my throat for having been caught looking. "You've made sure not a single man came near me for the last four years." She gets out of the bed and crosses to the dresser while I lean against the wall and watch her slender legs, the curve of her ass.

"I beg to differ," I say, distracted. "On several occasions, I've had to rescue you from various men. Just think what would have happened if I hadn't been there."

She glances back, rolls her eyes, and opens a drawer, which promptly gets stuck. She tugs, cursing. I fold my arms and grin because she really has no idea how appealing she is to me right now, all damsel in distress.

It's not that I have a thing for damsels in distress. Just her.

She tries the drawer again, but it doesn't budge. She gives up, bends to open the bottom one, giving me an excellent view of her ass as the shorts ride up. I adjust myself. On her way up, she hits the back of her head on the bottom of the stuck drawer and curses again.

I chuckle, and she turns to glare at me. She flips me off and walks into the bathroom, where she slams the door.

I put the stuck drawer back into place while she's gone, and a moment later, she reappears wearing a pair of sweats. The green sweater is buttoned all the way and her hair is brushed.

"You didn't have to do all that for me."

"I did it so you'd stop gawking. What's the matter? Not enough action from the blonds you like to date?"

"Careful, Little Kitty, or I'm going to think you're jealous." I walk her backward to the wall.

"I'm not jealous."

"Good. Because like I said last time, I prefer brunettes. And besides, I haven't had a blond or a brunette or redhead or anything for the last decade."

That stops her and, quite frankly, me too. Why the hell did I just tell her that?

"Right," she says, her forehead still furrowed in consternation as she studies me.

I touch the line between her eyebrows, rub it. She relaxes her face.

"I like you without the makeup," I say, brushing her hair behind her ear.

She swipes my hand away. "Are you drunk?"

"Am I drunk because I like you without a pound of makeup on your face?"

"Just in general."

"No, I don't drink for the most part."

"Everyone drinks."

"Not me." I pick up a lock of hair. The ends curl around my finger. "I can see you without all that crap on your face. You're very pretty, Madelena."

"You don't have to do that."

"Do what?"

"Fake compliment me. I don't care what you think," she says defensively, clearly uncomfortable with the attention.

"It's not fake. You're pretty. That's all." I let her hair slip from the palm of my hand and brush the line of her jaw with the knuckles of two fingers. Holding her gaze, I slide them down over her throat, her collarbone, to the pulse at her neck. "Are you afraid of me?"

She bites her lip, looking uncertain.

I let my hand wander lower to undo the top button of her sweater.

She grabs hold of my hand to stop me. "What the hell are you doing?"

"I want to see you." She studies me with caution. "Just see." I'm not sure she believes me. Hell, I'm not sure I do.

She swallows audibly as I move a little closer so she can't slip past me as I undo another button. She watches me continue, breathing in short, shallow breaths. When I've undone the top three, she closes both hands over mine and looks up at me.

"Stop," she says, and I see how dark her eyes have gone, how the gold has turned into a deep amber around enlarged pupils.

"I want to see you."

I'm hard. And it's not just her breathing that's ragged. She's beautiful. Maybe not to society's ridiculous standards but to me. But there's more. There's a brokenness inside her. An aloneness. A hurt. And alongside those things, determination. Strength, even. Not enough of it, but it's there, and if nurtured, it will grow. To a certain extent, she seeks a guiding hand. She'd never admit it, but there's a part of her that is searching for it.

Maybe that's what it is, my own selfish need to be that person. I don't know. Hell, after this day, I don't know anything, and that's part of it too. She's clean. She's innocent. She's not part of the ugly world of Avarice. I've rescued her from it. Kept her safe from it. For now.

I shake my head. I feel drunk even though I haven't

had a drop. She does that to me, makes everything so much more. All I know for sure is that right now, I want to see her. Touch her. Feel her beneath me. Right now, I need to be close to her.

When I brush off her hands to continue, she allows it and I peel her sweater open to look at her nipples pebbling against the soft pink of her tank top again. I lean closer to her, bend to bring my nose to her neck and breathe her in, picking up the lingering scent of aftershave. My aftershave.

"You smell like me."

I watch her throat flush red as embarrassment creeps up to her cheeks.

"Don't worry, Little Kitty. I like it."

I cup the back of her head and kiss her throat as I slip my other hand under her tank and hear her intake of breath when skin touches skin. I kiss her jaw, her cheek, then hover my mouth over hers when I weigh her breast in one hand and feel the tight nipple beneath my thumb. I watch her face, her eyes dark now, ringed with a fiery copper.

When her mouth opens, I kiss her, and fuck me, I don't remember a kiss feeling like this or tasting like this. It must be the years of self-imposed celibacy.

I've only been with one other woman in my life, but as I deepen the kiss, as I slip my tongue inside her mouth and taste her, I think how much I want this.

Need it. Need *her*.

I realize that somehow over these years, she's

become a part of me. My oath did more than bind her to me. It bound me to her.

Her hands come to my chest, and she mutters something against my mouth. The words are a jumble I swallow, because right now I need this woman more than I've needed anyone in a very, very long time. Maybe it's the day, the funeral; maybe it's the years that have passed. Or maybe it's what's coming. But right now, I need her every breath, every sound, every touch.

"Madelena," I whisper against her skin. She's soft and warm, and I taste her on my lips. I slide my fingers back down over her belly past the elastic waist of the jogging pants and I breathe in her gasp when my fingers slip into those tight little shorts, the tips just brushing against the hair there when she bites my lip hard and shoves against me.

"Stop!" she cries out.

I step backward as if struck. I touch my thumb to my lip. It comes away red. "What the hell?"

"What the hell? I said stop! What the hell do you think you're doing?" Out of breath, she wipes the back of her hand across her mouth.

I clench my teeth, watch her, see how the wall is holding her up. What the hell am I doing? What was that?

She gathers her strength before my eyes. It's something to see. "You may dictate my life, but I have another year. I know that. Another year before you force me into your bed!"

I shove my hands into my pockets, make fists,

because I don't like where this is going. Not necessarily because what she's saying isn't true, but it's that one word. *Force.* "Your name is on the contract. You offered your hand willingly."

"If I hadn't, wouldn't you have taken it?" I open my mouth to smooth things over, but she continues. "Like you were about to take something else?"

Those final words stop me dead. "What did you say?" I close that space between us and back her into that wall again.

She looks uncertain for the second time this night, but she's more stubborn than smart because she sets her jaw and folds her arms across her chest. "You heard me."

I snort, but I'm furious at her, furious for what she's suggesting. I wouldn't force her or any woman into my bed.

I set my hands on either side of her head and watch her eyes shift left, right, then back at me. That pulse that was racing moments ago is racing again, throbbing against her neck, but this time it's an adrenaline rush of fear. Not arousal.

"Don't ever say anything like that again. Do you hear me?"

"Then don't do anything like—"

I slam my hands against the wall, and she jumps. "Do you hear me!"

She nods fast, hands against my chest again as she tries to keep me back. I glance away, my gaze catching on our reflection in the mirror over the dresser. When I see us, I'm taken aback. I see how her back is pressed against the wall, see how I hulk over her, trapping her there. The beast who very clearly terrifies the beauty.

She's a decade younger than me. A hundred pounds lighter than me. Barely a woman, and a completely inexperienced one at that. What am I doing here?

I shouldn't have come.

I push off the wall and walk away, my back to her as I force myself to breathe in, breathe out. To calm the fuck down.

"Apologize," I grunt without turning to her, because I am pissed. I'm just not sure if it's at her or myself.

"Will you leave if I do?" she asks, rebellion still in her trembling voice. I'm glad to hear it.

I nod once. I'm not welcome here. Coming here was stupid. Giving her the engagement ring was a stupid excuse I fed myself. My brother was right. What the hell did I hope to gain by coming here?

"Then I'm sorry if what I said upset you."

I hear her non-apology and turn to face her, look her over. I shake my head on an audible exhale. Just a little thing, my Little Kitty. Her claws are no match for my teeth, and tonight is not the night for this. I need to leave before I do something stupid.

"Come here," I say, reaching into my pocket.

She hugs herself as if she's cold but steps toward me, never taking her eyes off me as if she could run from me if I pounce. But she comes. I'll give her points for that. I take her arm. She resists at first, but I draw it out, hold her hand. I look again at the chipped, bitten-down nails. I turn it over to look at her palm, tracing the scar I left. One of many to come, I think, even if they are the kind you don't see. The thought weighs heavy on me as I slide the ring onto her finger.

Madelena gasps, clearly not expecting this. I shift my gaze to hers and watch her take it in, watch the play of emotions on her face. Confusion. Curiosity. Caution. Confusion again.

She draws away when I release her.

"I will come for you in one year's time. You will be my bride. Prepare yourself. Do whatever you need to do to wrap your brain around that. Because you are right. You will sleep in my bed. You will be mine in every way. And if you fight me, it won't be you I punish."

"What does that mean?"

"You love your brother very much, don't you?" It's a low blow, but there it is.

"Wh... What?"

"Just be ready, Madelena."

"How dare you—" she starts, but I stalk toward her, take hold of her, and spin her around so her back is against my chest and I have my hand over her mouth.

"Close your mouth. It's not your turn." She opens it again. "And if you fucking bite, so help me..."

She shuts her mouth. It's the first smart thing she's done tonight, yet her stubby fingernails don't stop digging into my forearm.

"You just make sure you keep yourself on my good side. Because being my wife will offer you some protections. But being my enemy?" I lean my mouth close to her ear so I'm sure she hears my words, feels them to her core. "That will only get you one thing. My wrath. And you do not want that, Madelena. You do not want to be my enemy." She shudders. Good. "Do you understand me?"

"Yes, I understand you, Santos. I've always understood you."

"Good." I release her, unsatisfied. "That doesn't come off," I say, pointing to the ring. "You eat with it, sleep with it, shower with it." I step toward her and, with a finger under her chin, tilt her face up to mine. "And when you use your little fingers to finish what I started tonight, you think of me as you press that diamond against your soft little pussy when you come."

"Get off me." She jerks her face away, but I see how red her cheeks are.

I grip her jaw and make her look at me. "It never comes off. Clear?"

"Crystal!"

I nod, take one more look around the room and cross it to the door.

"Why did you even come here tonight?" she asks.

I look over my shoulder.

She holds up her hand and I look at the oversized diamond on her small finger. She'll feel the weight of it every minute of every day. She'll think of me every time she looks at it.

"You didn't fly all the way here to give me this in the middle of the night."

With those words, with all that just happened, I feel more wretched than I did when I got here. I don't fucking know why the hell I came.

"I buried my father today," I say, feeling those words deep in my gut, feeling them devour me from the inside out. That beast I keep buried in that black hole that lives inside me, that is so much a part of me, throbs and comes alive. It wants to smother me, to swallow me whole.

But it's not that that does me in in the end. It's her. It's the look on her face, how her mouth opens into a surprised O. It's the way her eyes soften. It's the step she takes toward me.

It's those things that have me turning away and walking down the stairs and out of that building into the back of the waiting SUV. It's those things that have me telling the driver to take me to the nearest hole in the wall that's open all night and drinking myself into oblivion. Because even though as a rule I don't drink now, I used to. I know what men are capable of when they drink. I know what I'm capable of.

But some nights, it's not a choice.

And tonight is one of those nights.

11

MADELENA

1 Year Later
Present Day

The night I left Sacred Heart, a private jet flew me back to Avarice. I hoped I'd be taken to my house but knew chances were slim. I wasn't surprised to spend the night before my wedding in the same apartment and in the same bed as I had on my last night in town.

The club is beautifully decorated for Christmas, from what I glimpsed on my way in, just as it always is. Snow is falling, too. In Avarice, we always have a white Christmas, which means it's freezing, but so beautiful.

I sit in my wedding dress and watch as the women who did my hair and makeup pack the last of their things and leave. I have to admit, the dress is pretty; the pristine white gown of finest silk is simple, yet elegant with beautiful trumpet sleeves.

Once the women are gone, I get my makeup bag out of my duffel and go into the bathroom, where I rifle through it and find my worn-down eyeliner. I look at my reflection, remembering what the one said about Santos requesting minimal makeup. He did say he liked me better without it so he could see my face.

So, I enhance the line of my eyes with a more dramatic look than he'll appreciate, then wipe away the pink gloss and smear on my usual deep red. Satisfied, I return to the bedroom to watch the sky darken. Days are short this time of year, but I should have an hour before the wedding ceremony.

Back in the bedroom, I tuck the makeup bag into the bag I made sure to bring with me. This one has the things I can't live without. My notebooks, pencils, my photo of mom and Odin, and the one of us with Uncle Jax. Birth control pills—three months' worth, just in case.

And, tucked inside a pocket of the tote, is the ruined handkerchief from the night I first met Santos Augustine. It's darker now, the blood, as it's five years old. I still don't know why I took it out of the trash after Odin threw it away.

I slip it out of its pocket and feel the hardened silk between my fingers. I bring it to my nose, but the smell has long since faded. This is what I think about, what takes me back to the science lab at school the night of Junior Prom. When Santos Augustine had leaned close and inhaled my scent. His scent. It's unique. Custom made. I used the handkerchief to have it made for myself after much research. I wasn't sure if he'd noticed it back then, but a year ago, when he smelled it on me again, I knew he had known all along. He just hadn't said anything.

I tuck the handkerchief back in its place. Why haven't I thrown it away? Why had I had the scent made for myself? I'd even told the woman at the specialty shop that it was a gift for my boyfriend. My *boyfriend*. I cringe at how that sounds.

The first words he ever spoke to me replay in my mind. Without them, would there be anything between us apart from hate and obligation?

Forgive me.

Ever since he said them—before slicing my palm open—he's been like fucking Batman. It's like any time some shit is about to happen to me, a Bat-signal goes out, and there he is. Magically present, and ready to punish anyone who touches what is his.

My mind wanders to other things, more embarrassing things. He held himself back from touching me until I was eighteen. He has always been careful with me. Maybe it's just that no one apart from Odin or my Uncle Jax has ever been careful, has ever cared, that it gets to me. It does something to me.

Not that he cares, I remind myself. It's just that he's careful. There is a difference.

I can't fool myself. It's not me he wants. I'm not valuable. Not to him, nor to my own father. Hell, how valuable do I think I was to my mother if she could plan what she'd planned? Even if, in the end, she didn't go through with it?

The thought hurts, but I need it like I need the cuts sometimes. Pain helps. It keeps things manageable. Santos doesn't care about me. He cares that no one touches what is his. I am his, and I'm also a means to an end: a marriage to legitimize a criminal family once shunned by the elite of Avarice. That's all. I don't need to be an idiot about it. I don't need to have any feelings about it at all.

Besides, given the way we parted ways last year... Well, I'm not even sure where I stand now given that debacle.

I know when he'd come to the school, it hadn't been to give me that ring. That was an excuse. He'd been seeking comfort after his father's death. He'd been seeking it from me. I shake my head to clear that particular thought. Guilt nags at me about how I treated him that night, but I hadn't known.

My mind wanders to our kiss.

I've replayed it a million times, the feeling of his hands on my skin, and his fingers sliding into my panties. I still remember his words, too. That I be ready for him because tonight I will sleep in his bed.

I flush red. I'm so grateful I'll have the veil covering my face for the ceremony because I don't trust myself not to think about exactly this the instant I see him. As much as I hate the fact that I'm attracted to him, that I'm turned on by him, it's the truth. There is something that draws me to Santos Augustine. He may be a monster, but he makes my insides turn to fucking jelly and makes me want things I shouldn't want.

Someone knocks on the bedroom door, which immediately tells me it's not Santos. He wouldn't knock.

"Yes?" I call out. The door is opened by a woman in uniform.

She's carrying a box wrapped in pretty, white ribbon, and she stops to smile when she takes me in. "You look lovely," she tells me, then sets the box on the foot of the bed.

"Thank you," I tell her because she seems genuine. "What's that?"

She shrugs. "No card, but I assume it's a last-minute present from your fiancé."

Really? That surprises me.

Once she's gone, I perch on the edge of the bed and pull the ribbon off the box. Does he feel as anxious to see me as I do to see him after all this time? After how things ended that last night? Is this him easing his way into my good graces? Apologizing even?

I glance at my engagement ring, remembering his words when he slid it onto my finger —the warning in them, the humiliation. But I'd done what he wanted, what he'd told me to do. I never took the thing off. Not once.

But his warning about tonight, about my being ready or else... that *or else* had been spelled out. It won't be me who bears his punishment. It will be

Odin. Santos Augustine knows exactly how to make me bend the knee.

No, he's not easing his way into my good graces with this gift, whatever it is—if it's even from him. He doesn't have to. The threat to my brother will suffice.

I think of the last two years at Sacred Heart School of Art for Talented Young Ladies, rolling my eyes at the pretentiousness of the name. I was enrolled in a local school in Avarice until Santos decided I was no longer safe in my home and sent me away. Would things have been different for me if he hadn't seen the damage? If he'd let me go to the school I'd intended to attend, I'd still have had my brother in my life.

I absently touch the scar on the palm of my hand, shake my head, and let the ribbon fall away. The box is unmarked, so I don't know where it's from, but when I lift the lid off, I smell perfumed layers of white tissue paper. It's expensive.

Curious, I pull the paper apart and inside, I find a muff. I lift it out, searching for a card, but there isn't one.

Well, at least it's not real fur. It's as white as the falling snow, and I wonder if he sent it at the last minute given the weather? We'll drive to the cathedral, so I'll be outside for a few minutes at most. He's already arranged for a thick white cloak, which is hanging by the door. I won't freeze. But it's a nice touch, I guess.

I remember that I'd had something like this when I was a little girl. Uncle Jax had bought it for me one

Christmas to go with a matching coat and a pair of warm boots. Odin and I had been allowed to spend Christmas at our uncle's house. I'd been eight or nine years old. I still remember how happy I'd been when I'd seen the present.

I slip my hands into the muff now and feel the corner of what I assume is the card. I take it out, and am surprised to find it's not a card at all. It's a photograph. It's pretty grainy, and I have to peer close to see it.

It looks like a screenshot, the camera set high like a surveillance camera. There's a man in a black coat with dark hair, his head turned down. I can't see his face, but I swear I recognize the gate he's coming out of.

My heart races as I take in the date and time that are circled in red Sharpie. The digital timestamp in the corner. I know that date. I'll never forget it. It's the night my uncle died. We'd gotten the call the next morning when his housekeeper found him. The time is almost midnight.

Nausea has me setting one hand to my stomach. The gate is familiar because it's the one that leads to the back entrance of Uncle Jax's house. I think I know the set of those shoulders. And I recognize the stones of the bracelet peering out from under the cuff of the coat.

"Knock-knock," someone says, startling me as the door is opened.

I stumble to my feet, twisting my ankle in the high heel and dropping the muff to the floor. I shove my hand behind my back, hiding the photograph as I catch myself, wincing when I put weight on my right foot.

"Good lord, you're not that skittish, are you?" Evelyn Augustine asks me.

"I..." I open my mouth but only stutter because what the hell is this? What is this photograph? The security footage at my uncle's house had gone out at some point because of some sort of electrical issue. The investigators had confirmed that.

What was Santos doing at his house the night he died?

And who sent me this photograph?

"You look white as a ghost. This won't do."

"Excuse me," I say, unable to process, needing time to understand. I rush into the bathroom and slam the door, locking it. I grip the edge of the sink and try to level my breathing. I'm shaking when I finally sit on the edge of the tub and look at the photo again, really look, because there's no denying what this means—what someone has gone out of their way to tell me about the man who will be my husband in a matter of hours.

12

MADELENA

A full twenty minutes passes before I come out of the bathroom. I feign nerves. Wedding jitters. But it's not that. Of course, it's not that.

Evelyn is wearing black from head to toe. I wonder if it's to mourn her dead husband or my wedding to her son. She's irritated to have to wait for me but I barely hear her complaints. My mind is a blur of thoughts as I follow her obediently to the limousine waiting downstairs.

I think about the times I've seen Santos in person. First, the night of Uncle Jax's funeral when I was fifteen, when he'd said those two words, *forgive me*, that somehow drew me to him, bound me even before the blood oath did. Then nothing for two years until I had turned seventeen when he crashed the prom and most likely saved me from being attacked by the man I had thought was my fucking date.

Jason Cole. Christ. I'd thought he actually liked me.

Term was almost over by prom, with just a few weeks of school to go. Jason was a senior who had been repeating our science class and he'd passed his exams, thanks in part to me. But for the rest of that year and the senior year that had followed, no one called me Mad Elena again. No boy ever whistled or made lewd gestures when I walked by. The Janes and the Anas of the world slunk away when they saw me.

All I heard was the Augustine name. No one fucked with me again, not after they saw what happened to Jason. I'm guessing he still has a limp worse than Odin's. Did he deserve it? I don't think so. He deserved to be punished, yes, but Santos went too far.

Then came the night of the charity event hosted by the Augustines. He'd seen the bruises my father had left earlier that day and had come riding to my rescue to save me from the beast that was—and is—my father.

He's no white knight. Did I really think he was? Just for a minute, maybe? I'd hoped it. I can admit that, can't I? All these years, there's a part of me that has hoped exactly that.

What a fool I am.

I keep my gaze out the window and draw the veil down to cover my face, reaching underneath to wipe a tear. What was I thinking? That there could be something between us? That because he is protective of me that he's somehow good? I'm an idiot.

The limousine slows to a stop outside of St. Mark's

Cathedral. I can see how full the lot is from here. Everyone who is anyone in Avarice would be invited to this wedding. It's the event of the year. Of the fucking century. A De Léon will marry an Augustine. I wonder if anyone actually believes this is a love match and not what it truly is. I doubt it.

My door is opened but before I can step out, Evelyn sets her red-clawed hand on my arm.

"Don't forget the muff."

I look at it, look at her. "I don't need it," I say weakly, feeling sick to my stomach.

Did Santos do it? Did he hurt my uncle? Did he… kill him? Uncle Jax had drowned, but he'd been a champion swimmer. It had always sounded strange, had made no sense. They'd said drugs and alcohol were involved, but that also didn't fit. It just wasn't him.

"Maddy." The familiar voice draws me out of my reverie.

"Odin?" I am so surprised to see Odin standing in the falling snow, with no coat, holding out his hand for me, that I leap out of the car. I throw my arms around him so hard, he stumbles backward, laughing heartily when I want to sob.

Evelyn clucks her tongue as she walks past us, the driver holding an umbrella over her head to shield her from the snow. She can go fuck herself. I don't pay her any attention as she disappears into the church. I glance back at the car with its still-open door, and for one split second, I entertain the idea of running away, of getting into that car with my brother and driving. Just driving until we're far, far away and no one named Augustine can touch us.

But Santos's soldiers stand at attention, ready to drag me inside if I should refuse to walk in. There is no way I am getting out of this.

"What is it? Maddy, what's wrong?" Odin lifts my veil, brushes my tears with his thumbs.

"I need to talk to you," I tell him. "I... I can't do this."

His eyebrows furrow. "Maddy," he starts, glancing back at a guard. "I don't know how to get you out of it."

"We need to get inside," a man says, and I recognize him from the night of the charity event. It's Val.

"Just a minute," Odin tells him, eyes locked on me. "What happened?"

I look at him, think about all he's endured because of me—all to keep me safe from our father. If I don't walk in there, I'll be dragged in. If I don't speak the vows willingly, I'll be forced to say them. Santos has been very clear that when the time comes, he will hurt the one person I love more than life itself if I don't do as I'm told.

The image of the broad-shouldered man walking out of my uncle's house casually checking his watch after probably having committed murder tells me to tread carefully. His warning was not empty. He is a violent man. I know that. He would have no qualms about hurting Odin.

I'm starting to shake, although I'm pretty sure it's not because of the cold.

"What is it?" Odin asks me quietly.

I open my mouth to tell him what happened, but the cathedral door opens and Caius appears. I'm not sure if I'm more afraid or relieved that it's not Santos.

Caius takes one look at us and stalks down the stairs to take my arm. "Are you walking her in, or am I?" he asks Odin. "You get one shot."

Odin looks at me, and I turn from Caius to him. I steel myself. If I don't get my shit together right now, I will lose these precious moments with my brother, and I don't know if I'll be allowed more.

I stand straighter, squeezing my eyes shut and forcing back tears. All the while, my mind races. Did Santos kill my uncle? Why?

"Let's go, Maddy," Odin says, adjusting the veil back over my face, concern wrinkling his forehead. He hates this for me, but he's powerless to stop it. I know that.

Caius releases me but remains at my back as Odin takes my arm and walks me up the stairs. I see his limp, slight but permanent. My ankle burns with each step but mine is temporary.

"Wait," Caius calls out.

We turn to find him reaching into the car to take a bouquet of deepest, darkest purple calla lilies—my favorite, actually, wrapped with thick black ribbon. Santos had arranged for them. He'd sent a note with them to say he guessed I'd like them.

I take them from Caius's hand, shuddering when his fingers brush mine. I look into his blue eyes and think how deceptively beautiful they are. How duplicitous. I wonder about who sent the muff, who wanted me to see that photo today of all days when I can't do a damn thing about it.

Not that I could have done a thing if I'd received it a year ago. Two years ago. Nothing.

Caius's eyes burn into mine. He gives me a wide grin that feels colder than the air out here. Could it be him who sent it? He told me once he was loyal to Santos. Is that still the case? It's been two years since I last saw Caius Augustine. Things change. Maybe they've changed for the brothers.

Odin clears his throat and when I turn to him, his eyes are narrowed on Caius.

I let my brother take me into the church, where as soon as the doors are opened, the organist begins the wedding march. It's surreal, like it's not me walking down the aisle as people stand and peer back at me. I know nearly all the faces. I grew up among them. Even Ana is here, but I don't spare a thought for her. My mind is frantically working, trying to understand who would have sent the photo. Why.

I see Evelyn at her place in the front pew. Caius slips in beside her. My father sits across the aisle. I haven't seen him in two years, and I notice his right hand is gloved. More violence. A gift from Santos the night he saw what my father had done. Odin had finally told me.

I glance up to Odin, but he's looking straight ahead. I follow his gaze, too, and there, at the end of the aisle, is Santos Augustine. Santos looks more handsome than ever, but he's a devil in a suit. A killer.

When he asked me to forgive him before he slit the palm of my hand for our blood oath, it wasn't because he is good or in any way sorry for what he was about to do. He had conscience enough to know it was wrong, but he chose to carry through with it anyway. That's worse, isn't it? To know and to choose?

"Maddy," Odin whispers and I realize I've stopped walking, that I'm drawing back.

We're steps from the altar, and Santos sees it too. The mild smile on his face hardens. A moment later, it's not my brother's arm that mine is tucked into. It's not his familiar, soft warmth against my side. It's Santos's hard heat.

"Going somewhere, Little Kitty?" he asks in a whisper that sends a shiver down my spine. He tucks my arm tightly under his and holds onto my hand, and I swear he's measuring the difference in size between us—feeling how small I am compared to him, how powerless.

His words about having his protection, about not making an enemy of him, come back to me. Isn't that what I'm destined to do? Aren't we meant to hate one another forever? What else is there for a union like ours, one born of blood? I grip my flowers with my other hand, holding them so tightly I feel the crushing of their stems but knowing there is nothing I can do to stop this. There's nothing anyone can do.

Because just as Santos told me five years ago, I belong to him. Tonight, the contract will be fulfilled. There's no going back, because the bridge that led to my life before has burnt to ash and my future is in the palm of this vengeful monster's hand.

13

SANTOS

Madelena is white as a ghost, almost translucent. She looks like she's lost a few pounds that she honestly couldn't afford to lose. She's shaking, and her hand is icy.

Once we reach the altar and the priest instructs our guests to be seated, I draw her veil up to see her face. I told the woman doing her makeup that I wanted minimal. This is the opposite, but it's the look inside her honey-colored eyes that has me frowning.

"Are you all right?" I ask her in a low voice as we kneel before the priest at the altar. "Have you eaten?" She looks like she might pass out.

It's like she hears me only moments after I've spoken, and I watch her as her expression goes from sad and worried to one of disbelief.

Of bitterness.

I smooth out my forehead, remembering our last

meeting on the night I'd buried my father. How she'd welcomed me, how she comforted me—not.

Color me foolish for wanting something more than hate and rejection from her.

Without waiting for her response, I close my hand over the back of her neck. I don't need her permission. She's mine. To onlookers who do not know us, it may look like an endearment. To those who do know, they will understand what it truly is.

Madelena turns to the priest, and I'm not sure what I expect. She won't make a scene. She knows the consequence of disobedience. We suffer through the hour-long ceremony and come out on the other side of it. I keep hold of her hand, hers a fist inside mine, and lead her out to the waiting limousine. Our guests will go ahead to the club for an elaborate evening of excess, but I plan on sealing this union before I let my bride partake.

Once inside the limousine, I release her and notice her lean to rub her ankle. I see how it's red and a little swollen.

"What happened?" I ask.

She looks up at me, the calla lilies discarded on the floor of the car, one of the flowers crushed under her shoe. She searches my face, and I want to know what the fuck is going on in her head.

"Your ankle," I say.

She looks at it, as if that was the furthest thing from her mind. "I twisted it. It's fine."

"I'll have a look once we're at the club."

"It's fine. Don't pretend you care."

"What's the problem, Madelena?"

She snorts. "Seriously?"

"Yeah, seriously."

She looks like she has a hundred things to say, but she just shakes her head. The brief ride to the club is silent. Once we arrive, I take her hand and lead her out of the limousine. It's best to finish the conversation in private anyway. Snow is coming down harder now and I have to admit, as much as I hate the cold, it is fucking beautiful.

Several guests who arrived ahead of us stop us to offer their congratulations. I smile, nod my thanks, and take my bride to the penthouse.

Once we reach the door, the soldier standing guard opens it. I sweep Madelena up into my arms. Surprised, she resists, but I hold tight.

"Do you know why they do this?" I ask her as I carry her directly toward my bedroom.

"Put me down!"

I grip her tighter. "It's the sign of the cross." I push open my bedroom door. The room is twice the size of the one she slept in and has a view of the sea and the lighthouse on Avarice Point, or as I've heard it called, Suicide Rock. "Our bodies make the sign of the cross as we enter our marital home."

She shoves at my chest just as I set her on her feet, then give her a small nudge so she drops onto a seat at the foot of the bed.

I take off my jacket and toss it over the back of a

nearby chair. My eyes on her, I pull off my tie and undo the top buttons of my shirt. She doesn't move. Carefully, I unpin the veil from her hair and lift it off, setting it behind her on the bed.

She still doesn't move, doesn't fight me, and I'm reminded of her inexperience. She's only twenty years old, and she's led a very sheltered life. I've made sure of that.

I close my hands over her shoulders, squeezing once before I crouch down and slide my hands under the hem of her dress to slip off both her shoes at once.

"What are you doing?" she asks when I flip the soft silk of her skirt up and look at her ankle. It's a little reddish, but not too bad, and just slightly swollen. I squeeze gently.

"Does it hurt?" I ask, looking up.

She's watching me, expression confused, hurt, angry, all of it. She shakes her head once.

"We'll find you other shoes to wear to the reception," I tell her, straightening. I close my hands over her shoulders. "Are you hungry?" I ask. She shakes her head. "Thirsty?" Again, a shake of her head. "Good, then we can get to business. I asked you a question in the car. You didn't answer. So what's the problem, Madelena?"

"What's the problem? You just forced me to marry you," she spits, standing, wincing a little before shifting her weight to her uninjured foot. She's much smaller than me without the heels. I don't step back, so she has to crane her neck to look up at me. "That's the problem, Santos," she finishes with a poke of her finger to the middle of my chest.

"Did you have other prospects?" I ask, hands still on her shoulders, although I'm careful not to hurt her. It's taking effort not to shake her, though. Did she not hear anything I said the last time we were together? Has she not seen what I'll do to keep her safe?

"No, you made sure of that, didn't you?" She tries to slap my hands away, but I don't let her.

"I made sure you were safe. If I recall, all I've done is make sure you're safe."

She holds out her hand, palm up. "Right, this is you keeping me safe."

I look down at the scar I'd left. Something dark inside me stirs. It's a darkness that was born the night I avenged Alexia's murder. A thing I needed, one I called forth, nurtured all the nights that followed when I committed so many more. It morphed into something else over those years. A thing that grew powerful. That, if allowed, could overwhelm me. A beast I've learned to keep tight control of.

I take her hand in both of mine and trace the scar with my finger, then bring her palm to my mouth and kiss it.

"I realize you may never forgive me, but I am sorry for doing that to you. For hurting you when I know you're innocent."

She's taken aback, but the words are true.

"Why did he do it?" Sadness replaces the anger in her voice as her face contorts.

"Why did who do what?" I ask, confused.

"Why did my father give me away so easily? What do you have on him?"

Ah. This. It was only a matter of time before she asked.

"Why?" she repeats.

I release her, step backward, and walk to the window to watch the lighthouse's beacon shine its blurry light over the ocean.

"It doesn't matter, does it?" I ask, turning back to face her. "He doesn't matter."

"I'm not asking for him. I'm asking for me. I want to know why it was so easy to sell me, because that's what he did. He may hate me, but he hates you more. He wouldn't have given me to you unless he was backed into a corner. What do you have on him?"

"That's a long story, Madelena, one I'm not sure you want to hear."

"I want to hear the truth. Give me the abbreviated version."

I study her as she stands in her wedding dress on this, our wedding night. "Another time," I tell her, moving toward her.

"Tell me," she says, looking up at me.

"Tonight is to learn other secrets, Little Kitty." I reach behind her to pull the pin that holds her hair at the nape of her neck. Once freed, it spills over my hand and down her back in thick, dark waves. "I was wrong when I told you that you were pretty," I start, watching her eyes grow wider, more confused. "You're more. You're beautiful."

The compliment flusters her. I am reminded once more that she's not used to hearing them.

"Why do you call me that?" she finally asks. "Little Kitty."

"Because you need protecting, but you also have claws." I hold her gaze. She is fucking stunning, and she doesn't even know it. "And your eyes are like a cat's eyes. A tigress." I touch her chin and tilt her face up to mine. "And for reasons I can't quite explain, I like taking care of you."

"A tigress doesn't need taking care of."

"But you are just a baby tigress. Turn around, Little Kitty, so I can get this dress off and finally get a look at you." I start to turn her, but she sets both hands to the middle of my chest and stops me.

"I may be smaller than you, but I do have claws. So just watch out," she warns.

Her warning makes me chuckle. She does not know how cute she is. I touch a thumb to the dark liner at the corner of her eye and smudge it. "I told them not too much."

"Oh, they listened." She grins, wide and defiant, but at least I've distracted her from her question. "I just fixed it after they left."

"Maybe I should take you over my knee and spank you for your disobedience."

Her cheeks flush bright and I grin, remembering that this warning had the same effect the last time. My

Little Kitty may like what I'm suggesting. I make a mental note.

"If you lay a finger on me, I'll kill you," she says, wholly unconvincing as her eyes betray her arousal.

"Oh I plan on laying much more than a finger on you," I say. "And those claws…" I take her hands, kissing the knuckles of each. I lean in to inhale her scent. She's still wearing mine, and I find I like this oddity—like that she doesn't hide the fact that she wanted my scent on her, that she's been wearing it for years. "Those claws, Little Kitty," I whisper, kissing the curve of her neck before sliding the scruff of my jaw up to her ear and along the shell of it. "You can scratch them down my back when you come for me tonight."

She snarls, literally snarls. I can't help but laugh as she tries to shove me away, but I hold onto her wrists and walk her backward to the bed.

"I will never come for you," she tells me.

"Won't you?" I ask. "I accept the challenge." With a grin, I spin her to face away from me and keep her hands in one of mine at her stomach while I draw the hidden zipper down, the fine silk slipping away to expose her back. "Beautiful."

I brush my fingers over soft skin, pushing the dress off her shoulders, feeling her shudder as I do.

"Santos," she starts uncertainly as the dress slips off her arms and pools around her feet so she's left wearing a matching set of lace panties and bra in virginal white.

I take her in before I turn her to face me. My gaze

drops from her wide eyes to the pale, exposed skin, to the dark points of her nipples and, finally, the little triangle of hair barely hidden by the lace of her panties.

My dick responds. Ten years is a long time to only be intimate with one's hand.

Her throat works as she swallows, and when her anxious gaze moves down toward the erection pressing against my slacks, then back up to my face, her eyes are wide. The look inside them has me grinning.

"The question is how many times am I going to make you come," I say, grabbing her when she spins away, lifting her and laying her on the bed.

She gasps, gaze shifting once more to my erection before she scurries backward, but I catch her ankle easily and tug her toward me.

"Oh, I don't think so, Little Kitty. You and I are just getting started."

14

MADELENA

I'm trapped by his big hand. It's warm around my ankle, and I'm unsure where to look. His eyes have gone nearly black. He looks starved, more beast than man. I remember what he'd said, that he hadn't been with a woman in a decade.

Ten years.

How does a man do that? A man like him, at that? Don't they need to fuck every few days or weeks at least?

But I don't have time to think when he tugs me to the edge of the bed. I yelp, dropping backward onto my elbows as he crouches between my thighs, wrapping his arms around them, biceps straining his shirt. I watch him look at me, my open legs, my sex inches from his face, a scrap of lace the only thing between us.

When he presses his nose to me and breathes in deeply, I squeeze my eyes shut, embarrassed and aroused and unsure what to do.

"You're wet, Madelena," he says darkly. "And you smell like I can sink my teeth into you."

I cry out in surprise when he closes his mouth over the lace of my panties, his tongue hot and wet and soft, the lace rough. He growls—he fucking *growls*—and I see the effort it takes him to draw back.

I'm panting as he releases my thighs, dropping to his knees. He's breathing hard, too, as he slides the panties off me.

He pushes my legs apart, hands rough on my thighs as he shifts his gaze back to my pussy, taking his time to look his fill at me spread open before him, a feast to a starving beast.

"Fuck, Madelena," he says, the words more a vibration of his chest than sound before he buries his head between my legs.

My breath catches in my throat, and all I can do is grab hold of him, pulling his hair and I'm not sure if it's to push him off or grind against him as he sinks his teeth into me.

I've never felt anything like this. Nothing. And the sounds that I hear, it's me. It's me panting and whimpering as I grind against him. I fist handfuls of hair, my feet braced on his shoulders and when he closes his mouth around my clit and sucks, I am undone. I come like I've never come before. Never. I come so fucking hard, and my moan… it's his fucking *name*.

I'm whimpering, twisting onto my side, my fingers finally loosening as orgasm subsides. He watches me, his lips glistening as I shamelessly squeeze my thighs together to squeeze the last of this new, intense pleasure, still fucking moaning like some animal myself.

He watches, just watches, one hand disappearing where I can't see it. Is he fisting himself?

My breath trembles, my legs hanging limp over the foot of the bed.

Santos stands, his gaze imprisoning mine as he does. He watches me, wipes the back of his hand over his mouth and I see in his eyes that he's still hungry.

"What did you say about never coming for me?" he asks in a low voice.

It takes me a very long time to remember what I'd said. He grins, self-satisfied, and I force myself to sit up, glaring daggers at him.

"Remind me again?" he taunts, crossing the room to pour himself a glass of water from the chilled bottle. He turns back to me as he drinks it looking like the cat who swallowed the canary—and I'm the fucking canary.

He sets the glass down, then returns to me. I force my muscles to work, and climb up on my knees just as he reaches me.

"Remind me what it was you said about not coming for me," he says. Before I can do anything, he slips his hand into the front clasp of the lace bra and a moment later, it's gone, discarded along with the rest of my clothes.

I launch myself at him, using those claws he so enjoys mocking me about, raking my nails down his chest. He laughs, grabbing the back of my head to draw me to him, holding my face an inch from his, not kissing me though because he knows I'll fucking bite.

I tear at his shirt, feeling the strength of him, ripping it from him as his muscles bunch. I'm like an animal, wild and enraged. I hear myself as I attack, and I know I'm hurting him when he takes my arms, that grin finally gone as he tells me to stop—shakes me, any playfulness vanished.

"I said stop," he commands.

I manage to get a fistful of his dress shirt and rip it all the way down, buttons popping before he pulls me far enough to make me stop.

"Stop?" I ask, trying to get at him again. "Fuck you!"

An animal-like growl rumbles from inside his chest as he tosses me backward onto the bed then flips me onto my stomach. I yelp as he hauls my hips up and pushes my head down so I can't look back. He's got my arms criss-crossed behind me.

"You shouldn't have done that," he says with that rumble, like the warning rattle of a snake behind his words.

"What's the matter? You don't like it when the tables turn?" The bed dips as he climbs on and uses his knees to force mine to part. I fight him, but he's so much stronger than me. He holds onto my arms with one hand and brings the other to the back of my head to grip my hair and tug my head backward as he leans over me.

"No, Little Kitty. It's because some things are better

left unseen," he says, his voice different than moments ago, darker, more dangerous.

He straightens, and I'm not sure if it's the loss of his body heat or the words themselves that send a shiver through me.

I stop fighting and look back. His shirt is hanging off his shoulders, ripped apart. The glimpse of skin I get is strange. But when he shifts his attention from my face down to my ass, I'm hyper aware that right now, I am fully exposed to him. He can see every fucking inch of me, and he holds complete power over me.

He brings one hand between my legs, closes it over my sex and shifts his gaze to mine.

I suck in a breath as his fingers spread my lips and find my clit. He then draws those fingers through my folds and up to my ass.

"Santos," I start, embarrassed and aroused and I don't know what else. I don't know what the fuck just happened.

He looks at me for a long moment and I feel like he's warning me.

He finally draws his hand away and presses himself against me. I shudder, feeling the length of him through his slacks. And I admit, as much as I hate myself for it, I want him.

"Should I show you again how hard you'll come for me? This time with my cock stretching your cunt, because you're fucking dripping."

My face burns and I'm sure he sees it. "I fucking hate you, you know that?"

"I think you hate yourself more, sweetheart. Because you want this as much as I do. Remember, for years you've been wearing my scent on you of your own free will. You were begging to be mine. You want me to take you, to make you mine, as much as I want it. As much as I want you—and that's not how this is supposed to work."

I turn my face away because I can't look at him... because he's fucking right.

The minute I stop fighting him, he releases me, almost as if he's stopped fighting me, too. I flop down onto the bed, roll onto my back and watch as, keeping his eyes on me with his expression impassive, he gets off the bed and pulls the remnants of his shirt off his shoulders and lets it drop. The instant it does, I gasp, my hand coming up to cover my mouth.

He stands still and watches me as I sit up and look at him, unable to drag my gaze from his thickly muscled chest, which is covered in scars. Fucking *covered*. His upper arms are lined with old cuts that have turned into thick scar tissue, and so are his shoulders. I can see where he's had stitches on his sides, one clearly from a knife wound. The other a bullet?

"Uglier than you hoped for?" he asks.

I meet his eyes, shift my gaze down then up again to his. "It's the truth, isn't it? The ugliness?" I ask, not meaning it the way it sounds, the way it wounds, but knowing I'm doing it all the same.

He looks down over himself, then back at me.

"Remember, I tried to keep you from seeing it. Now turn around and get on your hands and knees."

I force myself to hold his gaze.

"I said turn around, Little Kitty, and get on your hands and knees."

"Why? Can't stand to look at me when you do it?"

I slip off the bed and go to him, standing so close that I can smell him. The cologne is subtly different when he wears it. It's the way his skin interacts with it. It's the thing I was missing all along—that scent of him beneath the cologne.

If he wants to fuck me tonight, he will look at me when he does it, and he will definitely get those claws down his back, exactly as he'd said.

"No," I say, looking up at his beautiful, cruel face. I think I must be a masochist because even as I reach out to touch one of the scars on his chest, I know all it will earn me is pain.

He catches my hand roughly. We stand still, both of us watching the other. He clearly didn't expect me to touch him. He was probably expecting me to cringe back at the mess that is his chest. He doesn't know me, though. No one does. What did he say about secrets? I have my own.

"I'm not afraid of a little truth, Santos." I need to show him that I'm not afraid of him, that I won't be cowed. I'm not weak.

He grins. "No?"

I shake my head. It's his turn to search my face now, to want answers from me that he won't get. He releases my hand and stands still as I trace the first scar, the deepest one. He shudders, muscle rippling beneath my fingers, almost as though he's not used to touch, and I remember what he said about being celibate for the last ten years.

"What is it?" I ask, curious, although I'm saving the most interesting ones for last.

"Hunting knife."

I look up at him, still surprised even though I kind of guessed. It's the violence of it.

"This one?" I ask, sliding my hand over hard muscle and soft skin toward the rougher tissue of another scar.

"Bullet."

"You're not easy to kill."

One corner of his mouth curves upward. "Are you going to try?"

I don't answer. He steals a kiss then, and I'm caught off guard. He swallows my gasp as I taste him, taste myself on him. This man... There's something about him, and there has been since day one. I need to be careful with him.

I shift my gaze to the lines. There must be two dozen in a row all along his arms, cuts deep enough to leave thick scars. Is this the thing about him that somehow connects us?

I reach to touch one, but he grips my wrist hard, harder than before.

"No," he says. "Not those."

I look at him, then again at them. "What are they?"

"You don't want to know, Little Kitty."

"Like I said, I'm not afraid of a little truth."

He studies me, a shadow creeping into his eyes, a dense darkness seeming to pour from his pores.

For the first time since I've known Santos Augustine, I realize I've never really been afraid of him, not like I am right now. Because whatever this is, it's dark, and it's alive It lives inside him, and it won't be careful with me.

I take a step backward.

"Not afraid of a little truth?" he asks, matching that step. "You sure about that? Take care, Little Kitty, before you get hurt."

I swallow. "Tell me."

He tilts his head to the side, studying me. I swear he sees me like no one ever has, not even Odin—and that might be the most terrifying thing of all.

"They're not like yours," he says.

I know what he's referring to and it shuts me up. He means my cuts. The ones he saw beneath the bruises of my father's belt.

My heart races as he walks me backward. He only stops when my back hits the wall. "Tell me something, Little Kitty." He reaches to touch the space on the underside of one arm, where my own scars, more delicate than his, line up like soldiers in neat rows. Like the ones on the insides of my thighs and in other hidden places no one could ever see. "Why do you cut?" he asks.

I stare up at him, my mouth dry, no words coming out.

He raises his eyebrows. "You don't want to tell me?" When I don't respond, he continues. "We all have secrets. Dark ones. I think it's best you learn now to let things be when I tell you to let them be. It's safest for you. Do you hear me, Little Kitty?"

I try to swallow, then nod.

"Good. But do you understand me? In here," he says, the flat of his hand coming to rest over my heart. Heat pulses between us—or maybe that's my heart's frantic beating. Can he feel it? He must.

"Santos, I—"

"Do you understand?"

"I... Yes."

"Good. Because I don't want to hurt you." I get caught on those words, and he must see it because he pauses as if giving me time to process before continuing. "There are two things we need to take care of, and then I'll make your excuses downstairs and you can sleep."

I nod, a tear sliding down my cheek that I don't understand. I wait, mute.

"You won't hurt yourself anymore."

My lip trembles and more tears fall, and I don't fucking understand them.

"Did you hear me?" he asks.

"Why do you care?"

"Because you belong to me. I am your master now. You no longer have the right. Am I clear?"

I nod, but I'm not sure why. Maybe it's that I'm not alone, and I don't have to carry the weight of it all myself. Or maybe I just want this over, want him to go—because no one knows this about me. No one, not even Odin.

"That's a good kitty."

"Don't call me that," I manage in barely a whisper.

He bends his knees and hoists me up, surprising me, holding me up against the wall and forcing me to wrap my legs around him.

"You don't like it? I think it fits." I realize what he's about to do when I hear the buckle of his belt, the zipper of his slacks.

It's the second thing that needs to happen.

He nods once as if to acknowledge my thoughts. "You understand. There's no way around this. You know that, don't you?" I feel him at my entrance and brace myself, my hands gripping his shoulders, eyes locked on eyes. "Use your nails, Little Kitty. Use your nails and let me feel how much you hate me," he says finally and pushes inside me.

It hurts. I cry out, burying my face in his shoulder to try to muffle the sound because it fucking hurts.

"Use your nails," he commands hoarsely, moving faster, driving deeper. "Hurt me."

I do. And as I bury my nails into his back and feel that breaking of skin, I feel a release. It's a strange, heavy letting go.

"Good. Good." He looks at me, eyes nearly black, and he shifts his grip to hold me closer, all the while burying himself inside me. The whole time, I can feel him trying to keep control of himself.

He thickens inside me, his moan anguished. He's trying to hold back. That's the sound of the effort it's taking. He's trying, and he's failing.

"Madelena."

The way he says my name, voice ragged, I don't know. It's like right now we're so close and everything is different with him. This secret he knows about me, it's more intimate than anything else. Some part of me is relieved that he knows it. It wants him to know.

He cups the back of my head pulling me close, kisses the corner of my mouth, then he drops his forehead into the curve of my neck and mutters a curse as his rhythm changes, growing more frantic.

I wrap my legs tight around him, pressing myself against him as he takes me and the sensation of pain is edged by something else. I press my mouth to his shoulder and cling tight to him.

"Come with me," he tells me, his hands on either side of my face lifting it, his body pressing mine to the wall. "Come, Madelena." His face is so close, his eyes dark and burning, and all I can think of is the tension building inside me. It's all I can *feel,* and I hear myself begin to moan.

His thrusts come harder, and in moments, I'm coming. My nails dug deep into his back, my face in his hands, our eyes locked, I am coming. The sounds I'm making are desperate gasps as he thrusts once more, twice, until, with a groan he buries his face in my neck and comes inside me, shuddering, saying my name, sinking his teeth into me. Literally.

When it's over and we're left panting, he draws backward, holding onto me as my legs slip from around his waist. Without once looking away, and without a word, he lifts me in his arms and carries me to the bed. He lays me down, looks me over, and I follow his gaze to the stain of blood and come on my thighs. When I look back up at him, he's watching me. Then, a moment later, he walks away into the bathroom.

I touch the place on the curve of my neck. Feel the imprint of his teeth.

He returns, his slacks buttoned up. He's holding a warm washcloth and when he touches my thigh, I draw away.

"Be still. I'm not going to hurt you."

I'm not going to hurt you. Why do I believe him? Why do I so desperately want to believe him?

I remain still, and he places the warm cloth between my legs. He presses gently and I wince, sore. If I concentrate, I can still feel him inside me—feel his thickness, his hardness. I watch him as he gently cleans me then disappears into the bathroom.

Chilled, I draw the blanket over myself, trembling a little. What just happened between us? What did I think it would be like? A taking. Only that.

But it wasn't only that.

Santos returns and looks at me. He has washed his

face, pushed wet hands through his hair. He comes to the bed and draws the blanket higher.

"Okay?" he asks.

I shrug because I can't really speak. I'm not sure what to say.

He nods once. Maybe he's not sure either, and I don't know what I want when he turns and walks toward the door. I don't know why I feel an ache in the very center of myself as I watch his back.

Because I think some part of me wanted to be held, wanted to press my face to his chest and listen to his heart beat and feel his arms around, strong and warm and safe.

I don't know. All I know is when that door closes behind him, I am alone. Again. Always.

15

SANTOS

"She stays inside," I tell Val. "No one goes in. No one."

Because I wouldn't be surprised if my mother decided to pay a visit to my wife to be sure our marriage was consummated. That everything is wrapped up tight.

To be honest, I'm glad to leave Madelena there because this is fucking hard, harder than I expected. Not that I thought she'd be any different. She has claws —she always has—and bite. I wonder if she realizes that.

But what happened just then, the way she responded, the way she looked at me, clung to me, the way she came? It wasn't what I expected or how I'd expected it to be. I took from her tonight, but she also gave to me, and I don't understand.

I strip off the rest of my clothes in the room she'd stayed in last night. This will be her bedroom for the nights she's not sleeping in mine. I walk into the bathroom and run the shower but turn to take in my reflection before stepping under the flow. She left rivulets of open skin down my back to match those on my chest. I don't think I'll ever forget her cry when I pushed into her. She'd tried to muffle the sound in my shoulder, but I heard it, felt it, and for one brief moment, it was her pain I felt.

But then the warmth of her took over, and everything else was background to that building of tension—of orgasm just there, just beyond. I gave myself over to the darkness because that is where all violence lies and sex is violence in its own way. A taking. But then her grip turned clinging. Her breathing shifted.

And when I looked into her eyes, I saw a darkness there. It's different from mine, though. Hers is desolate, alone, and something about that makes my chest tighten.

I shake my head, remembering the blood on her thighs. I should have been more careful with her. I should have tried harder to stave off the beast at least this first time. But it is too strong and always has been. Even though the Commander has been dead for five years—even though all that time has passed—it is ever present, and to think it ever sleeps is a mistake.

I step into the shower, turning the tap so the temperature is freezing cold. It's a small penance. I make myself look at the blood that washes off me. Her virgin blood. Why wasn't I more careful with her? Just as when I sliced her palm to make the blood oath, I think about how I do not deserve her—and how she certainly does not deserve me.

After my shower, when I can't stand the cold for another minute, I change into a different suit. I walk through the bedroom. Her things are here, mostly unpacked. Her tote is on the bed. I unzip it and look inside, finding her personal things, including her sketchbooks and the photos I remember from her room at the college. I leave it all alone.

She'll live here. I won't take her to the family house. I spend most nights here, too. I have for almost a year now. A few months after my father's will was read, I'd half moved out. It's not official, but it felt like the best thing to do.

What did my father hope to accomplish with that change? What did he think would happen when, apart from a stipend, he cut Caius off and left it all to me?

Then there was the sealed envelope. The executor had been instructed to unseal it before my brother, my mother, and myself. There was a single sheet of paper within, folded into a square, with one sentence written in my father's hand.

I know what you did, and this is your punishment.

I hadn't understood it. I looked at Caius, who appeared just as confused, then at my mother, but her face had been unreadable as ever.

"What does that mean?" I'd asked the executor, who was one of my father's oldest, most trusted attorneys—now one of mine.

He'd looked at the back of the page, then at me,

and shaken his head. He did not know any more than we did.

"Who is it addressed to?" Caius had asked.

"It's not."

I draw in a deep breath, preparing myself, and leave the apartment to head down to the ballroom. I am sure there will be speculation as to why the bride will not be attending her own wedding reception, but I couldn't give a fuck.

As the elevator doors slide open onto the lobby, I adjust my cuff, touching one of the stones of the bracelet Caius and I both wear before tucking it back into the sleeve. Conversation quiets once I appear, careful not to make eye contact but aware of every person in here.

"Forget something?" my brother asks casually. He disengages himself from the young woman around whose waist he had his arm. She's strangely familiar, although I can't place why. She's young, about Madelena's age, but that's not unusual for Caius. He has varied tastes and has never confined himself to one type. All those years when I refrained, when I wouldn't touch the women the Commander had sent me as a reward for work well done, Caius enjoyed the bounty while I was busy carving lines into my skin.

The Commander. Fuck. Why the hell am I thinking about him now? He's dead and rotting. Food for the fish.

"What?" I ask Caius, lost in thought.

"Your wife. Did you forget your wife?" he asks. "I think they'll expect to see her."

"Well, they'll be disappointed then," I say and walk past him toward the ballroom, the same one where I'd rescued Madelena from the idiots who'd cornered her two years ago.

Caius falls into step beside me. "Are you all right?" he asks as we stand at the entrance of the lavishly decorated space.

"Yeah. Fine. Just went differently than I expected." I wouldn't have undressed in front of her. I'd never considered that she'd see what was underneath the clothes. No one has seen my scars apart from my brother. Not even Dad had known what I did after the secret errands the Commander sent me on. Errands. As if people are just that.

"You got it done?" he asks, sounding uninterested, but I know him.

"The marriage can't be contested."

He turns to me and brushes something off my shoulder. He looks different since Dad's death, more serious. Older. But then his eyes meet mine, and he gives me a wink. "I have a feeling in this crowd, you'll get a few pats on the back for it."

"For what?" our mother asks, her heels clicking. "Where is your wife, darling?"

Dr. Cummings follows her, and I still don't like the look of him. He sets his hand on her lower back.

"She is indisposed, Mother," Caius says.

She looks at him then at me. "What do you mean? They'll expect to see her."

"Tell them she can't walk after a good, long fuc—"

"Hush your mouth," Mom snaps at Caius, who gives her an innocent *what did I say* look.

"It's fine," I say. "Excuse us," I tell Cummings and take my mother's elbow. "Shall we?" I gesture toward the head table. "We don't owe anyone an explanation." Once we reach it, I stand behind my seat as the room falls silent. I take the microphone one of the staff offers me. "Welcome, one and all. We're happy to have you with us to celebrate this precious day," I almost choke on the words. Caius snorts. "Sadly, my wife was… unable to join us this evening."

"Well done!" a man calls out from the back of the room and there's laughter. Idiots. The only one not laughing is Odin, whose eye I catch. He's at one of the front tables beside his father, who is possibly too drunk to follow what I'm saying.

"I invite you to eat and drink to your heart's content." I set the microphone aside and take my seat. Mom slides into Madelena's empty chair so I'm flanked by my family, the weight of responsibility heavy. Suffocating. I miss my dad at times like this.

"Well done, darling," she says and fills a champagne flute for me. I don't touch it. The three of us watch the people of Avarice return to their conversations as wine flows, and waiters serve lobster and steak. How I hate them all, these pretenders, with their pleasant conversation and their money and their status and their posturing.

The waiter places our plates in front of us. I tell him to send a tray up to the suite for Madelena. Caius picks up his knife and fork and slices into his bloody steak.

"Eat, Santos," Mom says. "They're watching even if they pretend they're not." She smiles at someone at a table across the way. "We're not there yet, remember."

"Give him a minute, Mom," Caius says. "He's done his duty."

"We don't have a minute," Mom snaps, and this close, I see through the brightness of her smile. "On to phase two, Santos," she says, expression never changing. Sometimes, I think she is more predatory than my father was, even though she may be subtler. He cared less about being accepted and more about having those around him know who he was—not that she cares what these people think. My mother's goals are different than my father's were. She wants a seat at the table. He wanted to own the damn table.

Phase two. I shake my head, tempted to ask for a whiskey. She talks like this is some top-secret mission. I guess to her, it is.

"We need to cement our place," she goes on.

"We are, Mother," I say. "Give it a rest for one night."

"She has birth control pills," she tells me as she pops a bite of steak into her mouth and chews as if we're discussing the weather. She uses her napkin to dab at the corner of her mouth.

"Did you go through her things?" I ask.

"Of course I did."

"Did you take them?"

She swallows, then smirks.

"Where are they?" I ask.

"In my purse."

"Hand them over."

"Why?" she asks.

"Because I think she might notice if her birth control pills are missing."

"That doesn't matter. She's ours. She does what we say."

"Let's be very clear on one thing. She's not *ours*. She *mine*."

My mother bristles, but I don't care about that. She wants power. I get it. I want the same. She wants status within the group of snobs who have always snubbed us. I get that too. Generations worth of Augustines have only ever served at their tables and scrubbed their toilets. We've never sat at the head of a gathering.

But I meant what I said to Madelena. I know what needs to happen, but I will protect her. She is mine. She is not theirs, and I won't see her hurt any more than she already will be. I won't fail her. I swear not to fail her.

"Yours. Ours. Tomato. Tomato," my brother says casually, digging for more lobster meat. "We all want the same thing. Let it go, Mom."

"Give me the pills," I tell her.

"Fine." She opens her clutch and pulls out three packets. Three months' worth.

I take them, shove them into my breast pocket, and look up to watch Odin approach our table. He's not smiling. I wouldn't be either if I were him.

"Where is my sister?" he asks without preamble.

Caius leans back in his seat and wipes his mouth. My mother watches Odin with disdain.

"I thought you'd be coming to offer your congratulations. To present a gift, perhaps," Mom says.

He doesn't bother with her, and I find I respect that. "Where is she? She was upset earlier. Why isn't she here?"

"She's fine. Just tired. You can see her in the morning."

"I want to see her now."

I pick up my knife and fork and slice off a piece of meat. I wonder if she's eating hers now. I place it into my mouth, seeing Marnix De Léon just beyond Odin's shoulder with this stupid gloved hand limp on the table as I address his son.

"You'll see her tomorrow or not at all. Take your seat, Odin. Unless you'd like to give a speech letting us all know how happy you are that our families have finally joined."

He grits his teeth. "If you hurt her—"

"I have no reason to hurt my own wife."

His eyes narrow. "If you hurt her, I'll kill you."

Grinning, I push my chair back and get to my feet. I

wipe my mouth before tossing my napkin onto my plate. "I've now heard that threat from two members of the De Léon family. I'm trembling." I signal to the orchestra to begin playing, then walk around the table to face Odin. I get just a little more in his space than I need to. "De Léons no longer give the orders. You take them. Now go sit like a good dog before I have to make you."

His hands fist at his sides, and his eyes narrow to slits.

"Go on," I tell him.

Caius gives a little bark from the table.

Odin ignores him. He draws a deep breath in, but he's not stupid. He exhales, then backs away a step. I nod, not bothering to wait for him to do as he's told. Instead, I walk out of the banquet hall and through the front room of the mansion, which resembles the lobby of a boutique hotel. I walk out the front doors of the building and around the cleared path toward the cliffs.

16

MADELENA

I hear the click of the lock turn, something that has become a common occurrence in my life over the last few years since Santos Augustine entered it.

A warm mixture of blood and come slides out of me when I sit up and push the blanket away. He cleaned me as best as he could, but even though the washcloth was soothing when he'd pressed it to me, I'm no less sore for it.

I force myself to move. I go into the bathroom and lock that door, although I don't think he's coming back. Not just yet. He'll go to the reception. One of us has to. It's humiliating that they'll all know what happened here. I can just hear the gossip, how I'm too weak to even carry on and get to my own wedding reception after being fucked by my husband. He'll probably get several pats on the back knowing the men of Avarice.

Ana will be at the reception. Does she still keep in

touch with all her friends from high school who lived to make my life hell? Will she report back my latest humiliation? I'm glad to say that I don't care much about that. She can't hurt me anymore. The worst she could have done is done.

I switch on the shower, turn it to the hottest possible temperature, and step under the flow. I close my eyes and just stand there, letting the night's events circle my mind. The photograph. My uncle's death. Those scars on Santos's body. The carved lines. The fact that he knew about my cuts. He'd seen them that night two years ago, but maybe he hadn't understood or maybe he'd just needed time to process that someone would do that to themselves.

Truth is, though, I haven't cut in a while. I used to. I'd started when I was thirteen. I can't remember the specifics of the event that triggered it, although it had to do with my father and my mother—the fact that I was alive and she was not. I hadn't realized it was a thing when I started. It was almost accidental. But in a moment of pain and rejection—why I kept thinking I could do something that would make my father hate me less was beyond me—I'd gone into my bathroom, where I'd seen the razor lying on the edge of the sink, and I'd carelessly cut my wrist.

I'm still not sure why I'd done it, or what I'd been seeking. It scares me to think about that moment.

But strangely, what I'd found was comfort. A different, wrong kind of comfort. No, maybe that's not the right word, but the pain of the cutting somehow managed to contain the rest of the pain. Like I could focus it. Concentrate it. Control it. It was how I could survive it.

I'd only done it sporadically because it still did hurt, and I used to be a wimp about pain. I'm better at taking it now.

When I turned fifteen, a momentous year for me apparently, I'd trusted Ana with this detail about my life. I'd told her about what I did, and why. About how it made me feel. It was after that that I started to do it regularly because it turned out I shouldn't have trusted her. I should have known better.

I still don't know if she did it to boost her social standing or to punish me for what my father had done to hers, but she used this secret—this deepest, darkest truth I'd told no one else—against me. Given my past, all those kids thought I was some freak anyway, and this just cemented it.

After Ana had betrayed me, I became more isolated than ever, and I cut and I cut and I cut.

But I'd stopped mostly by the time I was eighteen. There are moments where, like any addict, I think *just one more hit*. Just once more. The need can be overwhelming, but I know myself. I know there won't be a *one more time*, and there's always the fear that it won't be comfort I seek, but something else. Something darker. More terrifying.

When I think like this, I wonder if my mom's mental illness transferred to me while I was still in her womb, if I'm as sick as she was. But that thought is too terrible, and I shove it away, out of reach of my conscious mind.

Once the water starts to cool, I switch it off and reach for a towel. I dry off, being extra careful as I pat myself dry. I'm sore, but I'm not bleeding anymore. I slip on the too-big bathrobe and tie it.

When I return to the bedroom, I notice a tray of food has been brought up. My stomach growls when I smell steak, and I'm pleased to see a bottle of red wine. I can't imagine Santos sent the wine, but I guess he sent the food.

I go to the tray and pop the cork out of the bottle. It's been opened but recorked. I pour a generous glass for myself and drink a big swallow, then another. I take the lid off the plate of food and see the steak, lobster, potatoes, and steamed greens. I cover it again to take a look around first.

With the glass of wine in hand, I walk into his closet. It's huge. Santos certainly likes his bespoke suits. I almost laugh. But then I find myself reaching for the sleeve of one of his jackets and bringing it to my face. I close my eyes and inhale his familiar scent. It's all around me in here, and I just breathe it in.

I want to hate him. I do hate him, don't I?

Confused, I shake my head and look around.

I'm not sure what that was between us, how things have shifted. If he'd taken what he'd wanted and I'd felt nothing but pain, would this be easier to process?

I need to be smart about this. This is different than I expected—not necessarily worse, though. He's attracted to me, that's clear, and as much as I hate to admit it, I'm attracted to him. Sex with him felt good. Coming with him was different than it is when I make myself come. It's a whole other world I didn't know existed. From the way he looked at me, he felt it too. Or maybe it was his self-imposed celibacy—if I buy that.

That doesn't matter though, not now. What happened tonight changes things. Sex can be my weapon. Sex can be where I gain the upper hand, even if it is only for little bits of time.

I can do this. I can remember this and remind myself that we are enemies. Enemies with benefits.

With a smile, I sip my wine and look through his closet. It is so precisely organized. I'm not surprised. He's a control freak in every way. I look through all the drawers and find the usual things. I mess up some of the folded items just because and come up to one drawer with a locked metal box inside. It looks old and very different than anything else in here.

Lifting it out of the drawer, I take a close look at the lock. It can't be hard to pick but I'm not in the mood, not right now.

I finish my glass, drinking it like water as I return to the bedroom. I pour myself a second one and eat a bite of steak while watching the snow falling outside. There must be a foot on the ground already. Through the thick flakes, I can see the waves of the ocean every time the beacon of the lighthouse pans over the black water. I can't imagine how cold that water is. The thought makes me shudder.

I touch my fingertips to the glass of the window and look down. Odin thinks I'm afraid of heights, but he's not quite right. It's not the height that scares me. It's the cliffs. I'm afraid of dying on them.

Light pours from the windows of the ballroom below and I imagine all those people downstairs eating and drinking while I, the bride, am locked in this bedroom. Not that I want to be there, but it is strange how life just carries on.

I'm about to turn away when movement around the side of the building catches my eye and there, stalking rather than walking, I see Santos. No coat. I assume he's still wearing his dress shoes too. His head is cast down against the snow. I slink back a little. If he looks up, he'll see me. I watch him, wondering what he's thinking. Why he's not at the reception. Why he'd go outside on a night like this without a coat at the very least. Snow storms in Avarice are brutal, especially along this cliff's edge.

But then he turns onto the path that will lead to the lighthouse, and my heart stops for a minute. Why would he go out there? Does he know what happened there?

Another door opens, this one from the ballroom. I wonder if this is going to be a family reunion out in the middle of a snowstorm because it's Caius. He's pulling on a coat and carrying a second one. He stops, then turns back. Someone must have called after him. I can't see who it is from this angle, but he seems irritated, his body language abrupt, and a moment later, he follows in the direction of his brother.

Santos has almost disappeared from view by the time Caius goes after him, following the rapidly disappearing footprints in the snow. Caius catches up to him, and for a moment I think he's going to tell him to turn back, tell him that he'd be mad to go out to the lighthouse tonight. Maybe he does. Caius hands him the coat, and, after a brief conversation, Santos takes it. Wind here is no joke, and the lighthouse is a whole other kind of freezing. I know. They should turn back. It's a stupid night to go out there.

But to my dismay, they don't. Santos slips the coat on, and the pair of them continue along the path to the lighthouse and there's not a single thing I can do about it.

17

SANTOS

"I don't much feel like company, Caius," I tell my brother as I pull on the coat.

"That's too bad. You're in a state. What's going on?"

"Christ. Take a hint and leave me alone."

"I'm not leaving you alone. You literally walked out of your wedding reception into what is quickly turning into a blizzard without a coat and in fucking dress shoes."

I stop, look down at his feet, then up at him, eyebrows raised.

"Didn't have boots handy," he says, because he, too, is wearing dress shoes. "But I did bring the coats."

He makes a goofy face. It's the same one that has always let him get away with murder when it comes to Mom, and I get it, because I can't help but smile. Caius knows exactly when to be charming.

"Fine. Thank you for the coat."

"Welcome. Now can we go back inside where it's warm and it doesn't look like fucking Armageddon?"

"You go on. I want to see the lighthouse."

"You can see it tomorrow."

I don't answer. I just keep trudging through the snow. It has already penetrated my shoes, so my feet are wet and freezing.

He mutters a curse but follows. When we were little, it was like this too. Caius, my older half-brother, always has my back. I turn my collar up against the blowing wind and snow as we walk side-by-side over the narrowing neck of the land that will lead to the edge of the cliffs where the lighthouse stands.

Angry waves crash against the rocky coast, splashing drops of ice water at us at intervals. In contrast to the soft snowflakes, they're like little shards of glass. I shove my hands deep into my pockets.

As we approach, I see the graffiti that stains the walls.

"Thought we were having it cleaned up," I mention as I take the keys from my pocket.

"It'll be repainted this summer."

The graffiti is typical bullshit kids spray paint onto walls. It bothers me to no end when something as beautiful as a lighthouse over a century old is desecrated like this—and it is beautiful, even given its terrible history.

"Let's get it done next week, weather permitting," I tell him.

"I don't have my notepad with me, sir." I glance

back at Caius because his tone is off. "We're at your fucking wedding reception," he reminds me. "Can we take a break from work for one hot minute?"

"Fine. I'll take care of it." I put the key into the lock and turn it, but it must be broken because there's no resistance, no unlocking. Making a mental note to get it looked at, I pocket the key and push the door open. Caius enters first. He flips the switch, but nothing happens.

"Here." I hand him one of the flashlights standing on a shelf along the wall. "When it storms, it's not unusual for the lighthouse to lose power, apparently. Or so I'm told."

"Then how is the beacon working?"

"Generator?" I shrug and pan my flashlight around. Paraphernalia of parties litters the floor. Hence the broken lock.

"You know where it got the name Suicide Rock from, right?" Caius asks me.

I nod once. Oh, I know. "Don't tell me you're scared of ghosts," I say, trying to sound casual even though I feel anything but. I'd rather be alone right now, would rather see this on my own. It feels somehow intimate, this place that's gruesomely connected to Madelena.

"If ghosts exist, I'm guessing you're the one who should be worried, but you seem just fine."

"What does that mean?" I ask, although I know. I stop and turn to look at him. Caius knows the things I've done. All those years, I needed a confidante. Or a confessor.

"Nothing. That was in poor taste." He pats my back. "Let's go up, brother."

I drop it, not having the capacity to deal with more crap tonight. Truth is, my relationship with Caius has suffered since Dad died, since he changed the will the way he did. Caius has told me repeatedly that I'm imagining it, that nothing is different, but it is.

I tripled the stipend Dad left for him and have made him my equal as far as making decisions and running shit for the family, but ultimately, it's my name on the bottom line and we both know it. Dad also added a single damning clause that I've talked to the lawyer about undoing but so far, no luck. The Augustine fortune can only be handed down to my offspring. A male heir, ideally, but, if in a bind, a female will do. Dad was old-fashioned. But only my children can inherit. I've added my own clause to make sure my brother and his eventual family are taken care of. It doesn't make it any less shitty that Dad did it, though.

On top of that, I still have what happened between Madelena and me on my mind, how this night went. Not to mention Madelena asking what we have on her father. That's not going to go away. I'm going to have to figure out how to answer her eventually, because she can't ever discover the truth.

Once we get to the top, we stand at the large window that spans the circumference of the lighthouse and look out. Caius whistles.

"Holy hell. You can see the end of the world up here."

"Yeah." It's an inadequate response to the magnitude of what we're seeing. Given the storm, I can imagine it on a clear day. But it is exactly the storm that makes it so fucking incredible. The power of nature, the smallness of man, our impermanence. It's all right here, right in our fucking faces.

But that's not why I came.

Caius moves to the heavy metal door that leads out to the catwalk that circles the lighthouse. It's under construction that's been halted for weather. He tests the lock. It's secure though. Kids may have broken the lock below but down there is different than up here. Here, the past lingers.

He moves back to the windows and peers down onto the cliffs. "Fuck, I hate heights."

"You're indoors," I remind him, although I know he doesn't do well with heights.

"Still hate them. You think she felt herself falling? Crashing?"

It's a strange question, especially coming from him. Has he thought about what happened here?

"I hope not."

He glances at me, but I keep my gaze out over the water.

Madelena's mother committed suicide when Madelena was five years old. The story is that she'd brought Madelena with her, planning on taking her over the edge right along with herself, but for some reason, she hadn't. The note she'd left behind had been written before she'd changed her mind, which was how they'd known she'd meant to end her daughter's life along with her own.

It had taken them hours to find Madelena wandering around up here, freezing without a proper coat or shoes. I think she'd have been too small to see out of the windows, to see her mother's broken body below. But would she have seen her fall? The thought chills me through.

"This place gives me the creeps," Caius says as if feeling the same thing I am. "And it's fucking freezing. You've seen it. And I will agree that the view is something else, but can we go? Besides, I've got a sweet piece waiting for me," he says with a waggle of his eyebrows.

"The woman I saw you with. What's her name?" I ask, wanting to lighten the mood.

"Ana something. Don't much care," he says, and he starts to descend the stairs.

"You're an asshole, you know that?"

"Yep. And I'm okay with it." He stops when we get to the bottom and turns to me. "Don't worry about Mom. I'll keep her off your back. She's just anxious to get things finalized."

"Finalized. You make it sound like a business transaction. We're talking about a baby."

"And you have to keep thinking of it that way too, brother."

"Not to mention the woman who will have to carry the child of a man she hates."

"An heir," he says, making a point of using the

word. "An heir cements our place no matter what happens. Besides, she could have done worse. It could be me in your shoes, and I can tell you I wouldn't be half as considerate."

We stand like that in the aftermath of his words, each of us studying the other. I think how sometimes, it's as though I don't know Caius. There's a side of him he keeps from me. From everyone.

"Let's go back, brother," he says, turning from me to walk toward the stairs. I watch him go and think how little I like the idea of him in my shoes where Madelena is concerned.

18

MADELENA

By the time I hear the key in the lock, I'm not sure if I'm angry or just anxious.

I'm sitting cross-legged on the floor in front of the window, watching the snow fall. It's beautiful. I've always liked the snowstorms here, how they obliterate everything in their ferocity. Their sheer power.

The bottle of wine is empty at my side, and the thought of sex as a weapon is at the forefront of my mind. Can I do it? With him? He's so much more experienced than me in absolutely every way.

The brothers had returned over an hour ago, but I guess Santos went back to the reception. I get it, though. I'm sure it's more fun than being with me. I wish I could walk away from myself some days.

Santos pushes the door open as I finish the last of the wine in my glass. He stops when he sees me. He's in the middle of undoing his tie. I guess he's surprised

I'm not passed out after that fucking. He scans the room, which is a mess because the longer he was away and the more I drank, the more brazenly I went through everything.

But if he's going to lock me in his bedroom, he should expect no less. I'm not apologizing. We're enemies, whether or not we fuck. Because fucking is just fucking.

"Why aren't you asleep?" he asks me, stripping the tie over his head and tossing it onto the back of a chair. He drapes his jacket over that.

I expect him to be angry, to question me about the room and the mess I've made. But he just walks over, undoing his shirt buttons and reminding me of the map of horrors beneath.

"Not tired," I tell him when his gaze is back on mine. I tip the wine glass back again but barely get another drop.

He shakes his head, stopping when he reaches me. He bends to take the bottle and holds it up to the light.

"Where did you get this?"

I point to the dinner tray. "You sent it," I hiccup. My tongue feels numb.

"No, I didn't. Did you drink all of it?"

I decide to stand up. It takes me a few tries, and I am so wobbly that he has to grab my arm to steady me when I stumble backward.

"Who else?" I ask, tugging free and gesturing with my arm but realizing my comeback was too slow. I haven't had a single drink in two years. Not one. Sister

Catherine had made sure no one slipped me so much as a schnapps. So, this wine has definitely hit me hard.

"Christ, Madelena," he says, taking the empty glass from my hand and setting it and the bottle down on the tray. He then lifts the lid off the dish to see if I've eaten, and I get another shaking of his head. It seems I can only disappoint him. "You should have eaten."

I wonder for a minute if he's going to make me eat now, but the meat and lobster look kind of gross after so many hours.

"I drank," I say. "I figured the bottle was a wedding gift. Hey. Aren't you supposed to give me a wedding gift?" Either I'm swaying or the room is as I make my way to sit on the edge of the bed. It takes me two tries to plant my butt on it. "Pretty sure the muff wasn't from you."

I track his progress into the bathroom where I hear the medicine cabinet open and close before he returns to the bedroom. He tips two pills into his hand, then pours me a glass of water from the bottle on the tray. He hands it to me. "What muff?" he asks.

"I'm not thirsty," I say, getting back up to go to the window.

"Sit," he commands, hand on my shoulder helping me to do just that even though I resist.

"You should consider getting a dog."

"A dog? Why?"

"You like to give orders. You can teach a dog to obey them. Can't teach a wife that. Not this wife, at least." I hear how I sound, how my words are slurred. I'm apparently waving a finger at him, which is meant to be accusing, but my arm is too floppy. I give in and sit back down because the room is definitely spinning now.

He takes my hand, brings that finger to his lips, and kisses it, which catches me completely off guard and has me staring up at him, mute.

"I don't want a dog. I like little kitties better," he says, looking at me through his lashes, which I notice not for the first time are very thick, so thick I'm almost jealous. "One drunk Little Kitty, in particular. Here." He holds out the aspirin.

I look at the palm of his hand, then up at him. "I'm not drunk."

"No, of course you're not. Take these or you're going to have a monster of a headache tomorrow. Although maybe you deserve it."

I sigh, take the pills from him, and pop them into my mouth, then drink a sip of water. He seems satisfied and sets the cup aside.

"What muff?" he asks again.

I study him and think. He is really quite handsome with his olive skin and dark hair, which would curl if he'd let it grow. I get the feeling that like his closet, he likes to keep a tight rein on that, too. Even the five o'clock shadow is maintained to perfection, accentuating the sharp edge of his jaw just so. I reach out to touch the scruff of it, remembering how it felt between my legs.

The thought takes me a minute to process, and I

have to blink and force my eyes to focus. "What were we talking about?" I ask him and see the smile he's trying to suppress. "Are you laughing at me?"

"Now why would I do that?" he asks as I stand and reach out to grab hold of his arm to steady myself, very aware of how strong he is and how good that bicep feels. I bring my other hand to his other arm, study the expanse of his chest, then trail my fingers over the muscle there. He stands still, sucking in a breath as my fingers slide over hard abs, but when I hover them just over his slacks, he catches my hands.

He groans, and I see the press of his erection against his slacks. The sight of it makes my sex clench. I shouldn't want him—certainly not now. I'm still sore.

"Don't start something you can't finish," he says, tone dark.

I look up at him. "What makes you think I can't finish? Besides, I didn't get to see you."

His Adam's apple bobs as he swallows.

"I've been thinking—" I start.

"Have you?" he asks.

"Don't interrupt me." One corner of his mouth quirks, but he controls it and gestures for me to go ahead. "I've been thinking. We're enemies, you and me."

"Not necessarily."

"Yes. We have to be."

"Why?"

That throws me off. Why? Why do we have to be

enemies? "You're an Augustine, and I'm a De Léon. That makes us natural enemies."

He smiles, releases my wrists, and leans close to tilt my chin up with one finger. "You're an Augustine now, remember?" He pokes the tip of my nose. "And very cute when you're drunk, you know that?"

"I'm not..." I stop, take a deep breath in, and close my eyes for a minute so the spinning slows.

"Go on. What were you going to say?" he asks.

I nod, but when I open my mouth to speak, I hiccup again. He turns away, so I don't see him stifling his chuckle, but I can hear it. I grit my teeth and push one hand into his pants, grip his erection, and squeeze. That definitely gets his attention. And he's not laughing.

"Madelena," he starts, voice a growl. He takes hold of my wrist in a half-hearted attempt to pull me off. "You're drunk, sweetheart, and probably more than a little sore."

"Sweetheart?" I get caught on the term of endearment, losing the already fraying thread of my thoughts. I squeeze tighter and hear his sharp hiss of breath.

"I won't take you again tonight." He pulls my hand off him, but it's not without effort.

"We can be enemies with benefits," I say.

His forehead furrows as he considers and casually unties the belt of my robe so it falls open. He pushes it off one shoulder. His gaze sweeps over me and he runs his knuckles over my breast, my nipple tightening when touched.

"Enemies with benefits. Did the wine help you come up with that?" His gaze darkens. "Do you want to come again? Is that what this is about?"

"That's the benefit part."

"Is it now?" He grins a cocky grin. Santos Augustine has a playful side.

He walks me backward, and within a few steps, the backs of my knees hit the bed. He pushes my robe off then pulls his shirt over his head. I scan the chaos of scars that make up his chest, his shoulders, and his arms, wondering about his past.

"You want to see me, Little Kitty?" he asks, drawing me back into the present. He pushes his shoes and socks off, then his pants and briefs. He stands naked between my open legs. I look at him, my gaze hovering over his cock. I may not have seen him earlier, but I'd felt every inch of him—and he's not small.

I swallow because he's beautiful in that cruel way. When I reach for him, he shakes his head and gently lays me backward on the bed before opening my legs and looking down at me.

"Enemies with benefits," he says. "Turn over."

That's not what I expect him to say and he must see my confusion.

"Go on. Turn over on your stomach."

I do, looking back at him. He takes my hips, draws me toward the edge of the bed so the tips of my toes are on the floor and spreads my legs wider. I watch him watch me but when he kneels between my legs, I put my hands back to cover myself, alarmed.

"Stay," he commands, taking my wrists and pushing them away. "You want to come so I'm going to make you come. But first," he pauses, spreading my cheeks open. "I'm going to get a good, long look at you, Little Kitty."

"Santos!"

I don't get another word out. Instead, I suck in a breath as he licks me from behind, from my pussy to my ass and back. Within moments, I'm moaning as his tongue works, fingers coming to my clit as he licks me, not leaving any part of me untouched. I'm up on tip toe squeezing the muscles of my legs tight as he keeps me spread, seeing me, licking me, smelling me, tasting all of me, fucking me with his tongue. I'm gasping by the time I come, fisting handfuls of the thick duvet, burying my face in it to muffle my cry.

When it's over, and he softens his hold on me, I draw in a shuddering breath. This wasn't what I was expecting. It's not how I meant it to go. What happened to sex as a weapon? *My* weapon?

Santos lifts me up to lay me properly on the bed, climbing in behind me, his cock hard at my ass.

"I like how you look and I like how you feel and how you taste," he says, voice low. "And I especially like how you come."

"Aren't you..." I glance back at him thinking about how he just made me come, how he knows me so intimately. I feel my cheeks burn as I finish my question. "Don't you want to..."

"Oh, believe me, I want to. But if I fuck you again

tonight, I'll hurt you. So I won't. Go to sleep, sweetheart."

He switches out the light and I lay my head down, watching out the windows to see the beacon of the lighthouse scanning the sea.

I remember where he went. I think about what he knows about me. I think about what we just did. How he is with me, so careful not to hurt me.

Things are going sideways.

What happened earlier was supposed to be him taking. It had been, until I'd begun to participate. Until I'd come. Then this, now, me thinking that I might somehow get the upper hand, well, I'm a fool. An inexperienced, stupid, drunk fool.

He tugs me closer, as if sensing this shift in my mood.

"Why did you go to the lighthouse?" I ask, my voice quiet. I'm glad he can't see my face.

He doesn't answer for a minute. He must be surprised that I know. "I wanted to see it."

"Why?"

"Curious."

At that, I turn to face him, just able to make out his expression by the light coming in from the window. "Curious for the spectacle? Spoiler alert. There isn't one. It's just one sad life that ended violently and another that was destroyed in the process. What's there to be curious about?"

His eyes narrow, and he just watches me with an expression of exactly that: curiosity. There's an abundance of patience in that gaze. I remember his question from earlier, why we had to be enemies.

Because we do. That's all. That's the only way this can be.

"It's because of my mom they call it Suicide Rock. Did you know that?" I ask sharply. Because I don't want his patience. I don't want his gentleness. I don't want his goddamned kindness. I throw the blankets off, stand, and snatch the robe from the floor.

"Madelena," he starts, sitting up.

"What?" I snap, roughly pulling the robe on and tying it.

"Get back in bed."

"This isn't my bed."

"Christ. What is this about?"

"So, do you know the story? Or do you want me to tell it to you?" I ask, doubling the knot on the robe's belt. "I was there, after all."

"I'm not looking for gossip."

"Right."

"It's been a long night." He rubs his face, pushes his hands through his hair, and leans against the headboard. I can see on his face that the night has, indeed, been long. "I know your mother committed suicide there. I know the plan was to take you with her. I know you were found several hours later nearly having frozen to death. What is there to gossip about? It's tragic. But your life wasn't destroyed. You're alive. You survived."

I swallow hard. Can he see my face? Can he read

my eyes? I have my back to the window, so I don't think he can. Besides, all of that made the headlines for weeks. It doesn't mean anything that he knows those things. But it's not the facts themselves. It's the way he says that last part.

No one has ever mentioned that night with anything but morbid curiosity. Not one person. It's like they all want to get a look at the girl her crazy mother decided to spare at the last minute. Some have asked me why. I was fucking five, and she was fucking insane. She'd been diagnosed bipolar the year I was born and probably hadn't been very consistent with her meds. How the fuck would I know why she didn't throw me off before jumping herself? Who asks a child that?

"Madelena," Santos is saying. He's out of bed and pulling on his pants. When did he get out of bed? "I know everything there is to know about you. And I know what you've been through—"

"You know what I've been through?" I can't have this, can't have this kindness. "How the fuck do you know what I've been through?"

I walk toward the door, feeling exposed.

Santos is quick and catches my arm before I reach it. He spins me around to face him. "I am not your enemy."

"But you are. You have to be. Don't you get it?" I tug free of him and rub my face. Fuck. I'm tired, and that bottle of wine tastes stale on my tongue and makes my limbs feel heavy.

"Come back to bed, Madelena. Sleep it off."

"Do you mean *Mad Elena*?" I face him, those words still having so much fucking power over me. "Mad like my mom?" I'm going to cry soon. Fuck. I'm going to cry, and I really don't want to do that in front of him.

He just stands there watching me, and this time, I see fucking pity in his eyes. "Your mom was mentally ill. It's nothing to joke about or make fun of."

"Don't you wonder if I am?" I ask, barely hearing, not caring about that last part. Because this is where I always get caught, what I always come back to. Maybe those kids were right all along. Maybe they've known better than me just how fucked up and crazy I am.

"I know you do," Santos says. "It must be terrifying."

"Don't fucking patronize me!" I slap my hands against his chest and take two steps away. "Just leave me alone. You don't need to know anything about me. You don't get to. And you don't get to judge me."

"I'm not judging you," he says calmly, reclaiming the little bit of space I'd put between us.

I open the door, but stupid Val is standing right outside, so I just close it again.

"Let's go to bed. Get some sleep. This will all be much less dramatic in the morning."

"Dramatic?" I almost laugh. "I'm not being dramatic. Tell him to go."

"This is the alcohol talking. Back to bed. You'll sleep it off."

"Get away from me." I try to go around him, but he puts a hand on the door and blocks me. He grips my jaw, turning me to look at him. I feel a tear slide down my cheek. He watches it, eyes almost losing focus for a moment before his gaze settles on mine again.

"I think there's one thing you don't understand, Madelena. I know very well that you are innocent, that you are a pawn. And I meant what I said. I don't want to hurt you. But you can't fight me at every turn, and you don't have to be afraid of me knowing your secrets. I won't use them against you."

"I will fight you. I have to. Because no matter what you say, you will hurt me. You already have. You will use me to get what you want. Like you said, I'm a pawn."

"There was never an alternative for you. Not with a man like Marnix De Léon as your father."

"Wait a minute," I start, realizing something. "Have you convinced yourself that you've somehow saved me?" Again, I try to slip away. Again, I fail. "Do you really believe that? Because all that's happened is that you've taken me out of one prison and put me in another and at home, my doors weren't locked. You took any chance I had for a normal life away when I was fifteen. Fucking fifteen, Santos. Don't think you're some white knight riding in to rescue me from the monster in my life—"

"You don't know what your father is capable of. I'm not sure you'd have survived this long if I hadn't taken you out of that house."

"Because you are just as much a monster," I finish, completely ignoring his words.

His eyes narrow.

"I'm not telling you anything you don't already know, Santos. I mean, look at you." I motion to his chest. "Who looks like that unless they've lived their lives committing horrific acts!"

His hands clench. What I'm saying is getting to him. So, I push.

"You're a violent man who has lived a violent life. Here is more proof." I hold up my hand, palm toward him.

His jaw tenses. He's on the verge of losing control. He clenches his teeth, one corner of his mouth curling upward. "What's really bothering you?" he asks, and I know I've won. I've pushed him far enough to fight me. "What's really the matter, *Maddy*?"

"Don't you dare call me Maddy!" Only Odin calls me Maddy. He told me once Mom used to call me that too. I don't remember though.

"Is it the fact that I don't quite turn your stomach?" he taunts, cocking his head as he presses a hand to the middle of my belly and pins me to the door. "The fact that you want me? That you have wanted me all these years? Dreamt about me? About me fucking you?" he whispers that last part. "You can't hide from that truth. I know you."

"You don't know me. Fuck off."

"I don't think so, sweetheart. You want to fight? Fine. I'll give you a fight. But I want you fully present for it. Fully accountable." He shifts his hand from my stomach to my arm and reaches around me to open the door. Val stands there awkwardly. I'm sure he's heard everything. "We can't have this conversation after you've drunk an entire bottle of wine. If you want to sleep in your own bed, fine by me. Just make sure you do sleep. We leave bright and early tomorrow morning." Then to Val, he says, "Take her to her room."

"What?" I ask. "Where are you taking me tomorrow?"

Santos smiles, takes hold of my jaw and plants a quick kiss on my mouth, too fast for me to bite. "Our honeymoon, sweetheart. You didn't think I wouldn't give you a honeymoon, did you?"

I open my mouth but before I can answer, he hands me off to Val and gestures for him to take me away, turning his back and closing the door before I've even taken a step.

19

SANTOS

I don't get much sleep after that and morning comes too soon, bringing with it a headache of my own. I clean up the mess she made of my room, irritated that the kitchen staff had sent up the bottle of wine when I'd only ordered the meal but let it go. I'll just be sure to be more specific next time.

I noticed when getting dressed this morning that she'd also been through the closet. I double check that the locked box I keep in a drawer hasn't been disturbed. Taking the key out of its hiding place in one of the cabinets, I unlock the drawer and open it. The bundle of Madelena's sketches from her time in college are on top, including the one I took from her wall. I wonder if she ever noticed it was gone.

Beneath them are Alexia's letters, and at the bottom of that stack is the little folder. My smile fades as I pick it up and open it. Inside is a photograph of Alexia and me. We had just left the doctor's office, and she'd wanted to snap the selfie. It's the last photo of her alive. On the opposite side, tucked into the little flap, is a sonogram image. The baby was almost eight weeks old. Our baby.

There were a series of images as the technician took various measurements. I shouldn't have let her take them home. If I hadn't let her take them, her father wouldn't have found them. But she'd insisted, although she'd promised she'd wait to tell him when I was with her. I knew how he could get, especially if he'd had a few drinks in him. But he must have found them and confronted her.

I was at home when she was killed. I'd told Caius about the surprise pregnancy, about our intention to get married. He'd been supportive, if cautious. I'd been naïve. Stupid, actually. Neither her father nor mine would have let us marry. Hers for who I was; mine for who she wasn't. I think my father's plans for me were cemented years before I heard the first whisper about them.

I'd gone up to bed after my talk with Caius, after deciding to go to her the next day. But the next day was too late for Alexia and our baby. She'd been killed long before I got there.

I force a deep breath in then out. Putting everything back into the box, I lock it and set it back into the drawer. Now isn't the time to think about Alexia, about the accidental baby that never had a chance to live. Because that story leads to an even darker one—to the reason my body is carved up the way it is.

Because irony of ironies, what I did after Alexia's murder was what led to the years I spent doing the Commander's bidding, and those were the very same events that eventually led us Augustines climb to the top of the food chain.

I need to focus on the next few days now. The next few days with my wife.

Last night's storm has passed, and the sun is breaking the horizon. I go to the window to watch it rise. It is magnificent.

After a shower, I go into the kitchen, where coffee has already been made and breakfast has been set up on the bar, buffet style. I don't know what she likes just yet, so I've arranged to have some of everything.

I pour two mugs of coffee and head to her bedroom. Val has been relieved by another soldier, whom I recognize although I can't remember his name.

"Morning," I say in greeting, to which he nods and opens the door. Madelena is already up and fresh from a shower. She has a towel wrapped around herself, and her hair is twisted into a bun at the top of her head. She's standing at the unmade bed where the contents of her bag have been dumped and she's searching inside it. She's so focused on her task that she barely spares me a glance. I have a feeling I know exactly what she's looking for.

I set her coffee mug down on the dresser and reach into my pocket.

"I'm guessing you're looking for this?" I ask, taking

out one of the three containers of birth control pills my mother had confiscated.

She looks at the little plastic blue compact then up at me. Her mouth opens, but before saying anything, she closes the space between us and tries to grab them out of my hand.

"Give those to me!" she demands.

"Patience. I didn't come here for a fight."

"Where are the others? I had three months' worth. How dare you go through my things?"

"Sit."

"Get a dog."

"Don't you remember? I prefer little kitties."

"This isn't funny." She bites her lip, eyeing the pills. She looks more worried than angry. I get it. "Give those back, *please*."

"Better." I hold out the pills.

She snatches them. "The rest?"

"You get one month."

"What?" she asks, panicked.

I decide I'm not having this conversation now. "I don't know the doctor who prescribed those. Once you finish this cycle, we'll arrange for the next one." It's not quite a lie.

She studies me, opens the little compact, and inspects it before popping the next pill in the rotation into her mouth and swallowing it dry.

"Why do you have them anyway?" I ask. She'd been a virgin.

"So I won't get pregnant."

Smartass. "You'd already been taking them when you were at the college." Sister Catherine had mentioned it, but I'd told her to let it be.

"I get bad periods. They help manage the pain," she says quickly, averting her gaze. She's lying.

A knock on the door interrupts the moment.

"Yes," I say.

The door opens and the housekeeper glances at us and smiles a good morning. "Mr. De León is here to see his sister."

"Odin!" Madelena starts for the door, but I catch her around her middle.

"Have him wait in the living room. My wife will be right out."

The woman nods and leaves, and the soldier closes the door. I turn to Madelena. "Get dressed first, then you can see him. We leave for the airport in an hour. Clothes will be arranged for you, but if there are any essentials, pack those. We'll be gone for a few days."

"I get an hour? I haven't seen him in two years."

"He walked you down the aisle."

"You know what I mean."

"We're on a tight schedule. But if you're good, when we're back, he can visit again."

"You're going to dangle that like a carrot to get me to do what you want, aren't you?"

"I'm not your enemy, Madelena." She snorts at that. "You just need to get used to me. Go get dressed. We leave in just under an hour. How much of that time you spend with your brother is up to you."

"You're a jerk."

I grin, check my watch, and turn to walk away.

"I'm not having a baby," she blurts just as I get to the door. It's so unexpected that I stop and turn. "Not with you, not with anyone. Ever. If that's what you're thinking." I expect to see defiance on her face, and I do, but there's something else too. Fear. True fear. "I'm not that stupid," she adds more quietly.

I consider what she said, the way she said it, but I decide to shelf it. Now is not the time for psychoanalysis. "Tick tock, Little Kitty."

20

MADELENA

I'm not sure why I said that, but the words were out before I could stop them. I'm not having a baby. Not now, not ever, not with anyone.

With a sigh, I turn to get dressed, the *tick tock, Little Kitty* playing in my mind. I hate that he calls me that.

Tucking the photograph into my pocket, I hurry to see Odin, grateful Santos doesn't stick around. The guard is there though, hovering along the edges of the room. Ignoring him, I hug my brother. He hugs me back, then holds me at arm's length and looks me over.

"How are you?" he asks, very aware of the soldier.

"I'm okay," I answer. "We need to talk though."

He glances at the soldier, casually signaling it's probably not a good moment.

"How was the reception?" I ask, wanting to sound natural for the soldier's sake.

"A wedding reception without the bride present? How do you think?"

"Well, I'm glad I was missed." I smile, glance at the guard, then look at the buffet. "I'll make you a plate."

Odin never eats breakfast. Just coffee. He knows I know that, so he nods and accompanies me to the bar, where I take a plate. "I hope you're hungry," I say, sliding a hand into my pocket to slip the folded photo out then switching my grip so the plate hides the it.

I hand it to him, and he looks at me with a questioning expression but subtly slips it into his pocket. We fill our plates and sit down at the table.

"Someone dropped off a last-minute gift. With a surprise inside," I say as quietly as I can.

His forehead is furrowed.

"Maybe you can look into it." I'm confusing him even more because he has no idea what I'm talking about, but he will once he sees what it is he has in his pocket. "Anyway, it sounds like we're going away for a few days, but maybe when I'm back we can discuss it further."

"How long?" he asks, and we carry on with casual conversation until it's time for Odin to go. It feels good to be near my brother again. He's the one person I can trust. The one man I can count on not to hurt me and to have my back no matter what.

Santos and I fly to Miami, where I learn pretty quickly that it's not a honeymoon at all—not that I expected it to be—but part of his agenda to insert himself into our business. Does his contract with my father go this far? Tonight is the first of three political fund-raisers that De Léon Enterprises has always attended.

More than attended, really. De Léon Enterprises is a generous donor to each of these politicians. Favors are always good things to have. I still remember when I overheard my father and uncle discussing it. My father had always attended these, even before my uncle's death. His role has just grown since.

I've never been, and I wonder what Santos is planning. But if he sticks to the schedule, we'll be at meetings in Miami, Philadelphia, then back home in Avarice.

Once we're at the hotel, Santos promptly deposits me in our suite and leaves for some meeting or other. We hardly talked during the flight since he's been busy on calls, and I'm glad for it.

I don't want to discuss last night. I'm not ready for that, and my mind is on the birth control pills. I have three weeks' worth in the current cycle. If he denies me birth control after that, I'm not sure what I'll do apart from banning him from my bed… although I'm not sure that's up to me.

I can't have a baby with him, or with anyone. Because what if I'm capable of doing what my mother did but going a little further? I look exactly like her. Everyone says so. I'm sure I have inherited her traits—definitely more of hers than my father's. I'm probably sick like her, and it's just a matter of time before the illness manifests.

Shoving those thoughts aside, I spend the afternoon in the lavish presidential suite overlooking South Beach. It's hard to believe the waters I see here are part of the same ocean I see in Avarice. Here, it's turquoise, warmth, and happiness. At home, it's wild, gray, and cold. Angry even.

I am drawn to the ocean, even though I'm terrified of it and the cliffs in Avarice with their constantly churning waves. I sometimes wonder if Mom intended to drown. She hit rock, though, not water. Maybe that was better. Faster.

Sadly, Santos had the telephone removed from the room upon our arrival, not even bothering to make up an excuse. It's early evening by the time he's back and in the meantime, I get dressed, hair and makeup done for the event.

As soon as I hear him, I walk out into the living room but stop when I see he's not alone. Caius is beside him.

Their conversation pauses when I walk into the room and Santos's gaze sweeps over me. I'm wearing a form-fitting, floor length deep crimson gown with a black lace overlay. It is a color I love. My hair is twisted elegantly, and I insisted on heavy eye makeup. The woman had accommodated me when I'd threatened to add my own if she wouldn't. It's still less liner than I'd do, but it looks good.

My stomach flutters stupidly when I watch Santos

look me over. His eyes darken and in them, I see want. I hate that some part of me is satisfied to see it. Maybe I was even waiting for that look, because it's his stamp of approval.

Caius, on the other hand, looks like he usually does. Sneaky, like a snake.

"Sis," he says, walking toward me. I stiffen but hold my ground when he kisses my cheeks, the scruff of his jaw scratching my skin. "Don't you look lovely."

I don't bother with him. I don't trust him, and I don't like seeing him with Santos.

"Don't you think so, brother?" Caius asks, pouring himself a whiskey as he watches Santos watch me.

Santos nods.

Caius keeps his gaze on us as he swallows his drink. "I'll go get dressed. See you downstairs?"

"Yeah."

Caius sets his empty glass down and leaves.

"Why is your brother here?" I ask.

"Business. He and I are partners, and tonight we'll not only be meeting some of the advertisers who are used to doing business with your father, but also the candidates for political office who have had relationships with him."

I consider this, trying to hear what he's not saying. "I don't trust Caius." The words are out before I can think better of it.

"Does that mean you trust me?"

I hope my narrowed eyes give him the answer he

seeks. "I don't have anything to do with the company. I'm not sure why I'm here."

De Léon Enterprises was formerly Donovan Media, a media giant for more than three generations. It's the company my uncle was CEO of. My uncle was the last Donovan to run it. My father actually met my mother when he was in talks about a merger between De Léon Enterprises and Donovan Media.

Things had been headed in that direction for years, although it was only in the last six months of Uncle Jax's life that they'd reached an agreement, but I also know Uncle Jax was under pressure from Dad. I still remember some of the conversations I overheard between him and my father.

Uncle Jax didn't trust him. My grandfather had thought he was using our mother to make headway into the company. I think ultimately my mother's family blamed him for what happened to her which, even though I know my father, I don't think is quite fair. But in the final months of Uncle Jax's life, Donovan Media and De Léon Enterprises did merge, the name Donovan Media being kept, a concession from my dad that he never appreciated having to make. I overheard those conversations too. It only became De Léon Enterprises a full year after my uncle's death due to a clause in the bylaws Uncle Jax had added. I never liked that Dad did that, erasing the Donovan name like it had never been.

"What am I doing here?" I ask instead of answering. "Neither Odin nor I have anything to do with the business. That's all my father." My brother is as much a disappointment to my father as I am. In many ways, Odin's had it worse than me. I think our mother may have been a disappointment to Dad too.

"I want the world to see me with my beautiful wife. Is that wrong?"

"You want my father's associates to see me on your arm."

"Your father's and your uncle's. He was better liked than your father if I recall."

"Will my father be there?" I ask, not liking the feeling of my stomach tensing. It's easier to tell myself he doesn't scare me when he's not around. But the reality isn't quite that and I don't like it. It makes me feel weak.

"No, not tonight or tomorrow night." I must look relieved because he continues, "You don't have to be afraid of him anymore, Madelena. He won't come near you."

"I know what you did to him," I say after a long minute.

He studies me but doesn't add anything.

"Why did you do it?" I ask.

"Because he hurt you and he needed to be punished."

"Because he touched what's yours?"

His forehead creases momentarily, but he smiles a small smile. "Because he hurt you. Period."

I don't know how to respond.

"I need to get changed," he says.

I stop him, finally registering what he'd said a minute ago. "How did you know my uncle was better liked than my father?"

He waits a beat. "It's not hard to be better liked than Marnix De León. There's a difference between being tolerated and liked."

"But how did you know? You'd have to be involved in their lives to know such a detail."

I'm not sure if I imagine it or if his jaw tenses. "History between the Augustines and the De Léons goes back many years. I know details about your family you probably never will."

"What does that mean?"

"Nothing. Drop it." He checks his watch.

It takes all I have to keep my face neutral, to not ask him what he was doing at my uncle's house on the night he died. But I can't do that. Not yet. Not until I know more.

I wonder again who sent me that photo, who wanted me to know that he was there, at the scene of the crime. Santos has enemies, I know that he must, but this is my family we're talking about.

"I should warn you that you may know Caius's date," he says.

"Why would I care about Caius's date? Answer my question, Santos." I assume he's trying to change the subject.

"It's Ana Hollis," he says, watching my reaction.

"Ana?" Hearing her name catches me completely off guard.

He nods.

"Why? How does he even know Ana?"

He shrugs a shoulder. "Met at the club probably."

Why would Caius be with Ana? Why would he bring her here? I can imagine the stories she's told him about me, the things he'll tell Santos.

And just like that, it's like I'm back in high school again.

"I'll change and we'll go. Just wanted you to be prepared," Santos says. He's already told me he knows everything about me, and I'm starting to believe him.

Santos changes into a more formal dark suit than the one he wore during the day, and we ride down on the elevator with two men. Once we get to the banquet hall, the soldiers enter and stand near the double doors. I can pick them out around the room, too. They're dressed like guests, but they look off. No one would notice at a quick glance, but once you see that subtle difference, it's hard to unsee it.

"Why do you always have soldiers around?" I ask Santos as we enter, his hand warm and possessive on my lower back.

"When you're in the business we're in, you need bodyguards." He nods a greeting to someone across the room as he says it.

"When you're a criminal, you mean?" I ask with a smile painted on my face, recognizing one of my uncle's business associates, Joseph Lowe. I get the feeling he was waiting for me, as he disentangles himself and his wife from the couple he's talking to and makes his way toward us.

"Exactly," Santos says, trailing his hand up my bare back, his touch leaving goosebumps in its wake. "Just like your father." He turns to me. "When you're as powerful as we are, your hands are never all that clean." He leans in to kiss my cheek. "Be good," he warns.

"Madelena," Mrs. Lowe says, the couple coming to stand before us. I vaguely remember them from parties my uncle held at the house, a few of which took place when Odin and I were spending weekends with him, especially those at Christmas. "How are you, dear? It's been so long," she says, leaning to touch her cheeks to mine.

"Since the funeral," I say, making her immediately uncomfortable even though that's not my intent. It's just the truth. We had no reason to see each other. I'd been fifteen when my uncle died.

"Congratulations to you both, Mr. Augustine," Mr. Lowe says quickly, smiling to Santos. He extends his hand.

Santos takes it. This is why we're here, after all. From conversations I've overheard, Mr. and Mrs. Lowe's money funds a chunk of the company. "Thank you," Santos says. "And call me Santos, please."

"Santos. I hear you'll be joining the board of De Léon Enterprises."

I glance at Santos. I'm not surprised, am I?

"News travels fast," he says as I watch him. He's

relaxed and casual. "I'll be offering my guidance and direction."

"Is it true the De León name will be erased altogether to become Augustine Media?" he asks, with a pointed look in my direction.

I turn to Santos. This is the first I've heard of it.

"Nothing is set in stone just yet. As an investor, you'll be among the first to know. If you'll excuse us," Santos says as Caius approaches with a woman. I do a double take. If I didn't already know it was Ana, I wouldn't have guessed it from a casual glance because she's changed. A lot.

"You're removing my family's name?" I ask Santos.

He scans the room with a keen eye before meeting my gaze. "Your name is now Augustine, remember?"

"But—" I start, but before I can finish, Caius and Ana reach us. I hate that my heart races when I see her.

Caius's expression is set in stone, different from the usual casual asshole vibe he gives off, but I don't dwell. I need to process Ana's presence, and it's going to take all my energy.

Ana takes Santos in with big doe eyes, and I find myself leaning a little closer to him. Has Caius noticed? Has Santos? She is pretty, always has been, although now it's with hair dyed almost as dark as mine. Naturally it's a light brown. I wonder why she dyed it. She was prettier with her natural color. She must have extensions in too because it was never that thick or that long. Her makeup is heavier than I remember her wearing, and her lipstick is a familiar red. It's applied so thickly it's already cracking. My gaze falls to her chest because her boobs are out there for all the world to see. She's had some work done.

I'm glad to see Santos only spares her a glance, barely acknowledging her presence while she's staring up at him like a puppy. I remember his comment about being celibate. Is he oblivious to her adoring gaze? Is Caius? Isn't he pissed?

"Caius, Ana," Santos says in greeting.

"Santos, it's so nice to see you again," she says demurely, smiling.

Caius remains stoic and turns his brother away to say something too quietly for me to hear. I'm wondering what it is when both brothers' gazes follow a family of four who have just entered the reception hall, two men and two women. One of the men looks to be a little older than Santos. The other must be in his mid-twenties, similar to the younger of the two women. I wonder if maybe the older woman is their mother because she's much older. There is a clear resemblance between them all, especially the younger man and woman.

But it's not those things that stand out. It's that they also seem to travel with soldiers who are less subtle than the Augustine bunch. As I watch their progress, the younger woman turns her attention in our direction, her gaze passing completely over Ana, pausing on me, then turning fully to Santos. That's when she smiles a wide, gleaming smile, one that sets my teeth on edge.

The younger man sets his hand on her arm. He leans close to her as she speaks and he, too, turns toward us. They look so much alike I wonder if they're twins. But it's not that that makes my mouth go dry and the hair on the back of my neck stand on end. It's when his gaze lands squarely on me—and he isn't smiling.

Santos's entire body goes rigid. His hands fist at his sides. Caius's eyes narrow as he takes in the family, who stop to pick up drinks from a waiter's tray. Only then does the younger woman look away from Santos; only then do his hands unclench. I think that's when he realizes the man with her is still staring at me, and I feel like a deer caught in the crosshairs.

Santos wraps his hand around the nape of my neck and draws me close. My heart races. We stand like that for a moment, not saying anything. Not a word. But the act itself denotes possession and weirdly, I'm grateful for it. I feel safer for it, although I have questions. They clearly know Santos and they may know me, but I don't know anything about them at all.

"Madelena," Ana says as the family moves away.

Santos's grip relaxes and, exhaling, I turn to her. At least she doesn't use the *Mad Elena* they used to call me at school. The nickname she started. She had a way of saying it subtly enough that at first, I wasn't quite sure she did it on purpose, but she had. Every single time.

"Ana." I don't bother to smile. If she thinks I've forgotten or forgiven, she's wrong. I'm not so generous.

Santos signals to Val, who must have arrived after

us. He comes over. "Take my wife and my brother's date to our table."

"Yes, sir," Val says, and I see Ana smile like she feels so very important. I want to scream at her that Val is a fucking soldier.

Santos sweeps his fingertips along my spine, sending a shiver through me. He leans in like he's kissing my cheek. "Don't stray," he whispers, the lips brushing my ear sending a thrill through me. He lingers, and I wonder if he feels it too, the strange connection between us.

"Who are they?" I ask in a whisper, knowing this is important.

His gaze darkens. "No one who matters," he says, calm tone forced, and I know without a doubt that they do matter. They matter very much because I've never seen Santos Augustine have such a visceral reaction to anyone. I've never seen his hate personified in every cell, tensed in every muscle of his body.

"Santos?" I ask, reaching out for his hand when he steps away, catching the tips of his fingers.

He looks back at me, at the brief contact of our hands before I draw back. What am I doing?

Caius finishes doing whatever he's doing on his phone and tucks it into his pocket. He all but ignores Ana when he nods in silent communication to Santos, and the two walk purposefully away.

"I wonder what that's about," Ana says, taking a flute of champagne off a passing waiter's tray. I notice the family is leaving the room through a different door.

I cut my gaze to her. Does she think we're going to be friends?

"Ladies," Val says, gesturing for us to walk ahead of him toward the room where dinner will be served and speeches will be given. The tables are filling up, and Val finds ours at the front. If I recall, this is a ten-thousand-dollar-a-plate event.

Once we're seated and Val retreats, Ana turns to me. "They're cute, the brothers. I always thought you'd land him after what he did to Jason Cole." She looks me over, then sips her drink. "He's really into you for some reason, isn't he?"

Was she always so good at the barely veiled insults? She pushes dark hair over her shoulder, and I realize what's off with the new look. The hair, the makeup. She looks like me. No, that can't be right. I still remember the Morticia Addams joke from years ago. "Watch yourself with Caius. You're out of his league."

She snorts.

I mean it as a warning to her, but of course she takes it the wrong way. "He's dangerous, Ana."

"Are you jealous?" she asks, arching a perfectly sculpted eyebrow. "You always were jealous."

I open my mouth to respond but decide it's not worth it. She's not worth it. So I close it again.

"Who's that family?" she asks after a minute. I follow her gaze to find the family from earlier being led to a table at the very front, to the tables that are reserved for the most generous donors. I'm grateful we're at opposite ends of the room. Once they reach the table, the younger two of the four are seated while the older man and woman excuse themselves. The two left at the table turn their attention directly to me.

"Do you know them? They seem to know you." Ana is still talking.

"Excuse me," I say, standing, turning to find a bathroom to disappear into. But Val is at my side in an instant.

"Mrs. Augustine?" he asks, so respectfully. I should remind him how he handled me last night when he deposited me in my bedroom and locked the door.

"I need to use the ladies' room," I tell him, trying to shoulder past him. I don't manage to, of course. But Ana stands and takes my wrist in a too tight grip.

"I'll go with you. I know where it is," she says, and Val follows us as she hurries toward an exit I hadn't noticed. We reach a door marked *Ladies*, and she turns to Val. "Sorry, women only," she tells him as she pushes the door open, and we slip inside.

She makes a motion like she's wiping sweat off her forehead, her smile revealing the dimples on her cheeks. I wonder if she needed to throw me under the bus to get in with the it crowd in school. She always had the looks but lacked the confidence, always had an inferiority complex.

"He really does keep you under lock and key, doesn't he? There's something so sexy about such a possessive man."

"Not really," I start, but she shrugs.

"I need to wee," she says, using the term we used

when we were kids. She walks down the corridor toward another door. There are several. It's not just a bathroom but a full lounge with separate rooms with sofas, private stalls, and a nursing mother's room.

Hiding out in a toilet stall takes me back to high school prom, and I promised myself a long time ago I wasn't doing that anymore. I walk into the next room, where there's an empty attendant's table with a sign on top that says she'll return shortly. On the counter are various perfumes and other toiletries. I walk to the farthest end, setting my clutch down and taking my lipstick out just to have something to do. I wonder where Santos and Caius went, if their departure had to do with that family.

I need to talk to Santos about his plans to remove the De Léon name from the company. How is he able to do that? What does he have on my father that he has so much power?

I dab on lipstick then tuck the tube into my purse and choose one of the bottles of perfume. I spray it into the air and sniff and am about to test another when the clicking of shoes signals someone walking in behind me. I assume it's Ana, so I don't bother turning or even looking at the reflection in the mirror, so I'm startled a moment later when the woman steps up to the counter beside me.

"This one's my favorite," she says, picking up one of the bottles and holding it out to me.

I look up to find the younger woman from that family standing closer than necessary. I'm caught off guard and find myself staring for a long, awkward minute. I could see from across the room that she was beautiful, but close up, she's stunning.

"He'll like this one." She smiles, although it's not a real one. She's studying me, taking in every detail of my face. She's about an inch taller than me with palest blond hair pulled into a chignon at the nape of her neck. She's so close I can see the pins that are holding it in place, and I wonder if it hurts.

I register what she just said but don't really know how to respond. She puts the bottle down and takes a lip gloss out of her clutch. I watch her in profile as she turns her attention to her reflection to reapply. I get the feeling she's giving me time to look at her, to see her.

Each of her features is perfect independent of each other, and it makes for an almost unreal, inhuman beauty, the kind that hurts to look at. Once she's satisfied with the gloss, she drops the tube back into her clutch and turns her cornflower blue eyes to me. I'm still staring. Her skin is the palest, smoothest ivory. Her eyelashes are thick and dark with mascara and it makes the pale of her skin and the blue of her eyes that much more striking.

Her pink glossed lips stretch into a wide smile. She's used to people staring. I can tell, and it somehow takes away from her power. I clear my throat as she steps slightly back to look me over fully, taking her time. I don't know if she doesn't realize how awkward it is or if she just doesn't care.

"So, you're the girl Santos married. Madelena,

right?" she asks, tone soft and sweet like you'd expect someone who looks like her to sound. But I know there's nothing soft or sweet about her. She's dangerous.

I nod. I'm not easily flustered. I know how to deal with women who don't like me. But this is different than that. "And you are?"

"Camilla," she says, extending her hand toward me —not to shake it, but the way a royal might hold out her hand to be kissed. I don't. "Camilla Avery. Maybe you've heard the name?"

I don't like her. I wouldn't trust her with a kitten. "Can't say I have."

"Oh, that's surprising." She makes a face like she truly is surprised, but I already know that everything this woman does is calculated. "Santos and I go way back. I thought for sure he'd have mentioned me." I shake my head again. Her face falls. "Well, my father did have a greater influence in his life, of course. Commander Avery? Alistair Avery. Ring any bells in there?" I almost expect her to tap the side of my head.

"No, sorry to disappoint you," I say, irritated and not sure what she wants with me. I just want to leave.

"Well, Santos knew him as the Commander, of course, so maybe…" she trails off, shrugging.

Ana enters the room, halting when she sees Camilla. It takes her a moment to recover. "There you are," she says cheerily, again acting as if we are friends, except that this time I'm glad to see her.

Camilla spares her the briefest of glances as if Ana

isn't quite worth the trouble, before returning her attention to me.

"You should ask him about the Commander. I'm sure he'll want to tell you all about him. My father was a sort of mentor to Santos for a good five years. The defining years, he used to say. He was only eighteen when he came to live with us, you know." She says it almost wistfully.

"I'll be sure to do that. Excuse me," I say, wanting to get away from her. I manage to take a step, but just as I do, another door opens near the empty attendant's table. A man enters. My heart races and adrenaline rushes through me, the warning to flee blaring like a siren in my head. But I remain still, rooted to the spot because I'm not sure I'll be able to get past these two.

"Sister," the man says. She smiles at him but keeps her eyes locked on me, just like she had earlier. His looks match hers except they're masculine. Harder. The false veneer of soft sweetness is too thin to hide the cruelty beneath.

Ana giggles nervously. She always used to do that. "We'd better get back. I don't think Caius likes me gone too long." I don't look at her. No one does.

"I wondered where you'd gone off to," he says, coming to stand beside Camilla. He smiles down at her. "Mother would have had me sending a search party soon."

Camilla slips her hand into his and they turn matching eyes to me. The force of it, of them, has me taking an unconscious step back right into a stool I didn't know was there. I gasp, falling backward, until the man lunges forward to catch me.

"Careful, Madelena," he says, voice low, his hands big and hard on my arms as he steadies me. How does he know my name? How did she?

"Let me go," I say, trying to wriggle free. He only squeezes harder, and the way he tilts his head just a little and grins is almost inhuman.

"Santos didn't tell her about us, brother," Camilla says, stepping closer. The two of them have me trapped, and I'm not sure it's their physical proximity or just their presence that makes it feel like they're standing too close. "You'd think he would have, considering. I'm a little hurt, to be honest."

"Don't be hurt. You know Santos isn't very open about that part of his life. Understandably." The man looks me over, his gaze searching my face, my mouth, hovering over the exposed swell of my breasts above the necklines of the dress. "I'm Liam, by the way."

"Madelena, but you knew that."

"I did. We all do. Madelena De Léon. Augustine now." He looks me over again, that smile vanishing. "Promised to Santos at the tender age of fifteen."

I gasp, surprised when he takes my hand and turns it over. It's the one with the scar. He traces it. I shudder, unable to pull free as he meets my eyes.

"Blood oath," he says, sending an icy chill down my spine. How does he know this? "Brutality comes naturally to the Augustines, doesn't it?"

My mouth goes dry, or maybe it was already dry

and I'm just noticing as I stare up into his eyes. They may be that pretty blue, but there's nothing pretty in the way he's looking at me. It's not quite hate I see in them, though, and although I'm struggling to put words to the emotion, the animosity they convey is unmistakable.

He leans close to me, and I swear he inhales like he's taking in my scent. It's the most unsettling thing. "You take good care with that husband of yours, little Madelena De Léon," he whispers. "He's been known to crush bigger creatures than you."

"Get your fucking hands off my wife!"

I startle at the roar of the command, my breath a tremble, and a wash of relief flooding my system. Ana actually yelps and jumps backward as Santos's big hand closes over Liam's shoulder. Caius is behind his brother, with Val behind him, and soldiers stand at the entrance of both doors. Two are ours.

Ours. When did they become ours, not his?

But those questions don't matter now. Not when those soldiers reach into their jackets to draw their weapons.

21

MADELENA

"I said, get your motherfucking hands off my wife!" Santos physically pulls Liam off.

"Not to nit-pick, but you didn't use *mother*fucking. Had I known you'd be so upset—" Liam says with a casual, relaxed grin until Santos cuts him off by fisting a handful of his shirt and jerking him toward himself. He has a predator's confidence, Liam, and they're well matched although Santos's anger is somehow more. He has a bigger stake in this.

Standing nose to nose, Liam looks every bit as amused as Santos does furious. This only irritates Santos, who shoves Liam hard against the wall, forcing his breath out of his lungs. But Liam still stupidly manages a chuckle.

"You ever so much as lay a finger on my wife again, and I will rip your arms from your body. Do you fucking hear me?" Santos asks in a tone so low, so menacing, that I believe him.

"That wasn't your specialty, if I recall, although I don't doubt you'd do it."

Santos jerks him forward then slams him against the wall again, this time making Liam's head bounce off it.

"What the hell is going on in here?"

We all turn to the man who has just entered—at least, everyone except Santos and Liam, the latter of whom is no longer amused but ugly. Vengeful. Hateful.

"We were just introducing ourselves to Santos's new wife," Camilla says in that soft, almost child-like way she has. She's all big blue eyes and innocence. Not. "I mean, if we're going to be neighbors, we should be neighborly. It's what Daddy always taught us."

Neighbors? What does that mean?

Santos's body goes rigid, and a weighty silence descends like a shadow.

Caius puts a hand on Santos's shoulder. A long moment later, Santos's grip eases on Liam. He breathes in a tight breath as he takes a step backward, then turns to the man who just entered and shoves Liam in his direction.

"Keep control of your family," Santos says through gritted teeth.

The man, who is bigger and clearly older than Liam, catches him, looks him over and straightens his shirt before releasing him. His eyes cut to me, and his expression doesn't change as he takes my measure. I'm not sure which out of the three is the most dangerous. This one, with a scar that marks his throat from ear to ear may look the most violent, but the others are just as terrifying.

"Thiago," Camilla starts, going to him, head tilted to the side, lips in a pout. "We really were just being nice."

He shifts his gaze to her. "I told you both to stay put."

"I had to pee." She shrugs her shoulders, somehow making her big eyes even bigger.

He exhales loudly, gestures with a nod of his head to one of his soldiers, who steps forward. "My brother and sister will be returning home."

Camilla stomps a foot. She literally stomps her foot like a two-year old. "We just got here!"

Thiago steps toward her. I expect her to back away, but she stands her ground.

"You act like a fucking child, and you will be treated like a fucking child," Thiago says.

She glares, then gets control of herself. A moment passes where that innocent, pretty face is replaced by something other, something ugly, but it's gone in the blink of an eye. She grins, glances at me, and gives me that blinding smile again. "See you soon, Madelena. It was really lovely to meet you. Come on, Liam. Let's go. This is boring anyway."

Liam, like a little puppy, follows her out, tugging his arm free of the soldier who tries to take hold of him.

Thiago faces Santos. They're the same height, and

of similar build, two dangerous men in a space too small to contain them both.

"He comes near my wife again, and he won't walk away. I don't care who he is to you, Thiago."

Thiago's jaw is so tense I can imagine how hard he's gritting his teeth. I hold my breath as I wait for his response, but he forces a breath in and his entire demeanor changes. His eyes move to me, over me, and his mouth morphs into a smile. He looks more like his brother and sister now. A little more. He'll never be quite as pretty as them. He was once, I can see that, but no more.

One corner of his mouth curves up into a grin and he shifts his gaze back to Santos. "Family is important to men like us, isn't it? The things we care about, we'll do anything to protect. Which makes them a weakness." That last part is a threat. Even I hear that.

Santos's hands clench into fists at his sides. I get the feeling he's about to get in Thiago's face when Caius steps between them, stopping him. He puts a hand onto Thiago's shoulder. I can't see Caius's face; his back is to me. But I watch Thiago's, as does Santos. Thiago's eyes move to Caius's hand. He sucks in a slow, tight breath, every muscle tensing like he wants to pounce.

Caius says something too quietly for me to hear.

"Never. Touch. Me," Thiago says.

Caius doesn't remove his hand for what feels like a full minute, then chuckles and steps backward, arms at his sides.

"Just trying to help you, buddy."

Thiago's gaze moves to Santos, and his expression is different as he looks at the brothers. He hates them both, I think. But it's different, and I can't put my finger on how. I get the feeling that he's swallowing a bitter pill when he turns to go. But he leaves, and his soldiers follow after him.

Caius turns to Santos.

"What did you say to him?" Santos asks.

Caius tucks his hand into his pocket and cocks his head, looking relaxed. "Asked him if he thought a shootout was a good idea, considering."

Santos studies his brother while I take them both in, trying to understand through their body language and facial expressions. But Santos turns to me, deciding to drop it, I guess.

"Did he hurt you?" he asks me, closing his hands over my arms. Caius is standing behind Santos. He watches us just like I watched them. Maybe he's trying to figure out the dynamic between us, too.

I shake my head. Santos's grip alternately tightens and softens, like he's still clenching and unclenching his fists.

"She tripped. He caught her. That's all," Ana offers, setting a hand on Santos's arm.

Santos lets out a deep, animalistic growl and drags his gaze from me to where she's touching him. Without a word, he manages to communicate to her to get the fuck off him, and she quickly retreats.

"I'll stay," Caius says, coming up to Santos. "You

take a fucking breath. Get it together, brother. We've come too far to blow it now."

Santos looks over at him. "Fuck them."

Caius shakes his head, glances at me, then looks back at his brother. "Take her. Get out of here. Do whatever the fuck you need to do to get your head on straight again. We have another one of these to get through tomorrow night and another one the night after that. You can't lose your shit."

Santos's jaw tightens.

"He's an asshole, I get it," Caius says. "Go. Take care of your wife. I'll take care of things down here."

"Fine," Santos says with a sigh.

"Let's go," Caius says to Ana, taking her by the arm and marching her out without another word.

22

SANTOS

"Who are they?" Madelena asks when we're finally back in the penthouse. I only half hear her because my mind is still on what took place downstairs. Camilla's comment about being neighbors—what the fuck was that?

But it's Caius I'm thinking about now. He lied to me. Caius has a tell when he lies. I have observed it in him time and time again. He tucks one hand into his pocket and cocks his head in the opposite direction, his stance that of a fully relaxed man. Except that the hand in his pocket is a fist.

But why would he lie to me?

Two guards stand outside in the hallway while Val and another are inside. There's no reason for anyone to come up here unless they are guests of the penthouse, which takes up the entire floor. To even access this level, you need a special key to the elevator—which is great but also may not be my smartest move. If we are attacked, we're backed into a corner and I don't trust Thiago or his family not to attack.

I tell Val to arrange another hotel and car and tell him we'll be ready within half an hour. Because there's one thing I need to take care of now before we go.

"What's happening? What are you doing? You're hurting me!" Madelena tries to shrug free of me, but I only release her once we're through the bedroom and standing in the large bathroom.

"Get undressed, Madelena," I tell her, removing my jacket and setting it aside before rolling up my sleeve and switching on the taps in the large, freestanding bath in the middle of the bathroom. Once the water is to temperature, maybe a degree or two hotter than comfortable, I plug it and dry my hand on the towel.

"Why? What the hell, Santos?"

Steam rises from the tub, and I turn to find her standing with her back against the vanity, watching me. "I'm not doing anything or going anywhere until you tell me who they are."

I spin her around to unzip the dress.

"Wait. Stop! What are you doing?"

I push the dress down over her shoulders, past her hips, and listen to the whoosh of the layers as it slips to the floor. I look her over, not sure what I'm expecting. Camilla and Liam wouldn't be stupid enough to hurt her. But they did touch her, and I need to get their filth off her.

"Santos! Talk to me!"

She keeps her hands on the counter as I strip off

her panties so she's standing just in her high heels. I meet her gaze in the reflection of the mirror, her body bared to me.

A weakness.

The things we care about, we'll do anything to protect.

I shake my head. We're too vulnerable here. "I need to get their stain off you."

"What?"

I point to the tub. "I can't have their touch on you. You don't know them."

"You're being crazy."

"Get in the bath, Madelena," I say hoarsely because she doesn't know the Avery family. If she did, she'd be scrubbing her skin raw.

I'm not sure what she sees in my eyes but after another moment, she slips off her shoes and steps in. I take hold of her arm to steady her as she hisses at the heat.

"It's too hot."

"It's fine. You just need to get used to it."

"Santos—"

"Get in. I mean it," I tell her, hand heavy on her shoulder.

She sinks down onto her knees. The water is only a few inches deep and I look at her there, with her hands on her thighs, nipples tight, toes curled under, and her hips just resting on her heels.

I swallow, walk around the tub, taking her in. Seeing her like this, naked and kneeling, stirs something inside me.

Her gaze follows me, and I feel every bit the predator she must sense. I roll my other sleeve up as I complete the circle, then settle on the wide edge of the tub at her back. The only sound is that of the water as I tear the bar of soap out of its packaging, smear some on the loofah, and begin to scrub the Avery twins off her.

"You're hurting me."

How could I have let them get so fucking close to her? How? I grip her arm to hold her steady as I scrub.

"I'll do it. Jesus, stop! You're going to take my skin off."

She wrestles the loofah and soap from me. I see how red the skin I scrubbed is and watch as she washes herself. By the time the water has filled about half the tub, I can't stand the noise anymore and switch it off.

"Who are they?" she asks.

I shake my head, lost in thought. "Harder. More soap. It's not enough." Their particular evil is vapor. It seeps into your pores, gets inside you. It turns any good inside you to ash and leaves darkness where light once was.

"You're being crazy," she repeats more quietly, and I know I must appear insane to her. I get it. I close my eyes. They only had a few minutes. "Satisfied? Can I get out now?"

Her skin is flushed red. The water is hot. I get a towel, and when she stands, I wrap her in it and lift her out of the tub. I set her down, dry her front, then turn her to dry her back. All the while, she stares at me in the mirror, her forehead furrowed. But she remains still when I drop the towel and look her over.

"You're mine. Not theirs. Do you understand?"

I run my fingers up along her back, then hold onto her shoulders and bend her over. I slide my feet between hers, urging her knees apart.

"Mine, Madelena. Not theirs."

"Santos..."

I drag my hands to her ass and spread her open. She gasps but remains bent over, her knuckles turning white as she grips the edges of the counter. I can still see her face in the reflection, see her watching me. I undo my belt and slacks, take myself out.

"Mine. Say it."

Pushing her knees wider, I look at her.

"I don't under—"

I spank her ass once, and she yelps. "I said, say it!"

"I'm yours!" I push into her as she says the words.

"Say it again." I draw out, thrust again.

"Yours," she says, the word a breath forced from her.

"Again," I whisper roughly.

"You're scaring me," she gasps.

It makes me stop momentarily. I lean over her. "I'm not the one to fear," I growl. "Say it. Say it again."

"Yours."

"Good." I grind against her, then draw back to swat her ass until both cheeks quiver, demanding she repeat one word and one word only again and again until she is trembling from the effort. "Mine," I add, punishing her with each thrust. "Say it." Because she needs to know it.

"Yours."

Mine. Not theirs. Not anyone else's.

I pour my rage into her with each thrust until that rage morphs into an all-consuming desire to protect her, to keep her safe as she repeats that one word over and over and over—a mantra. *Only mine, not theirs*, I repeat in time with her until I come, my hands kneading the flesh of her ass as I empty inside her because she's fucking mine. Mine. Only mine. If anyone tries to take her from me, I swear I will do what I warned Liam I'd do. I will tear them limb from limb with my bare hands. I will rip them to shreds. I will bring all that the Commander taught me to rain down on my enemies.

23

MADELENA

We change hotels, going across town. What happened in the bathroom was strange. It was a little frightening, if I'm being honest. In the time I've known Santos, and granted it hasn't been long, but there's one thing he's always exerted. Control. When he began to lose it, he made sure I wasn't around to bear witness.

But tonight was different. Tonight, I became the object of his attention—not simply the thing he lost control over, but the outlet, too. I became the object to bear the brunt of his aggression, because that fucking was him making an outlet of me. It had been him somehow proving to himself that he had control when he did not.

Because I think finding me with the Avery twins scared him.

Thiago's words echo in my mind, what he said

about family being a weakness... about the things we care about being a weakness.

Except that he was wrong. I'm neither of those things to Santos. I am not his family; I am simply his.

I watch Santos because he's not himself. This hotel is not as lavish as the last one. It's much more out of the way and nondescript. He sends me into the bedroom. Through the cracked door, I hear him talking to Val in the living room, making sure we're near an exit, making sure those exits are guarded.

There's a second bedroom for Caius across from our room. I assume he'll bring Ana with him, and I wonder what the hell he's doing with her. Why would he be with her of all the women in the world? From the moments I saw them together, he's not interested in her, and the way she looked at Santos was off. Weird.

I scramble away from the door when they finish talking, but I'm pretty sure it's obvious I was listening when Santos enters the bedroom.

"Why aren't you ready for bed?" he asks, looking me over. He'd instructed me to get to bed before he'd left to talk to Val.

"Because I'm not a child who needs to be put to bed."

He sighs heavily.

"I have questions," I say, folding my arms across my chest.

"Not tonight. I need to go." He crosses the room to where one of our suitcases is sitting on top of a luggage rack and opens it. I have no idea what's in them since I didn't pack anything. Rifling through, he finds what he wants and turns to me. It's a lace nightie. "Put this on," he says, tossing it onto the bed and walking into the bathroom. He doesn't close the door, and I hear the water run. He returns a moment later, wiping his face on a towel. He looks unsettled, like what happened and those people got to him.

"Where are you going?" I ask, not having moved.

"Meeting."

"With the Commander?"

At that, Santos's jaw tightens, his entire body tensing.

He's been known to crush bigger creatures than you.

Santos fists the towel, eyes on me, and I see the effort it's taking him to draw in a slow breath. I wonder if he's counting to ten. He sets the towel on a nearby table and comes toward me.

"You need to get some rest." He reaches for me, but I back away.

"Stop. Tell me who the Commander is. Who that family is. Because they know me, Santos. They know about this." I hold up my hand, palm to him. "And from how it sounded, they know you pretty well. So, who are they?"

"You don't have to worry about them. They won't come near you again."

"That doesn't answer my question."

"They have nothing to do with you. Get changed. Get to bed. I'll take care of it." He steps toward me, ready to force me into submission, but I won't let him have his way without a fight.

"What was that scar on Thiago's neck?"

"For fuck's sake, just do as I say." This time, he takes me by the arms and marches me to the bed.

I struggle, but we both know he's stronger than me. "Okay, how about this. How about telling me what the fuck that was in the bathroom? Or is that just how it's going to be from now on? You scrub my skin raw then bend me over and fuck me?" I ask when the backs of my knees hit the bed. "Have me tell you I'm yours until you come? You're not that insecure, are you, husband?"

His hands tighten around my arms, and he growls with frustration.

"Because that was fucking weird," I add.

"It's not about insecurity. You don't understand."

"Then explain it."

Nothing.

"If we're running in the same circles with these people, I should be prepared, don't you think?"

"You won't be seeing them again."

"I doubt that. They seemed pretty determined to corner me."

He checks his watch, jaw tight. "The Averys... They're a poison, Madelena. They destroy anything they touch. I won't let them touch you."

"They said they knew you. Really well, actually. Were you with Camilla or something?" I find myself sounding defensive when I ask the question, not really sure why I'd ask that.

"Camilla?" There's a burst of unhinged laughter. "She's a fucking psychopath. Exactly like her father."

"Her father, the Commander?"

His eyes narrow, but he nods once. That's something. "I lived with them for a time. Not by choice. And they don't like how I left. Satisfied?"

"How long?"

"Does it matter?"

"It does to me. Tell me. And don't lie about it."

"I have never lied to you."

"Withholding is lying," I say.

"It's a mercy."

"I don't want your mercy. Why do they hate you?"

"Madelena—"

"Just tell me."

He studies me, and a moment later, he must make some decision or maybe see some way out because his posture relaxes a little. "Their father disappeared around the time I left," he says grimly.

"Disappeared?" A chill makes the hair on the back of my neck stand on end.

Santos nods. "Don't feel sorry for him. He was an evil man. Inhuman."

"Was?"

This, he doesn't answer with words but with a long, heavy silence. He then releases me and steps backward, taking a moment to look out of the window onto the quiet, dark street below. "Thiago's scar? The Commander gave it to him—a lesson in obedience."

I feel nauseated. How fathers can hurt their own

flesh and blood is something I'll never be able to wrap my brain around. Mothers too.

"His wife, Bea, is no better. All they left were scars," Santos adds, sounding distracted and, strangely, sad. Hopeless.

"Did he leave the marks on you?" I ask, my mouth going dry. "Those lines?"

It's so long before he speaks that I'm not sure he's going to answer me. Finally, he turns to me, studies me, and his answer when he does respond is more unsettling than I imagined it could be. "No, sweetheart," he says, his tone defeated. "The scars he left me with run much deeper."

I'm confused, trying to process, to figure out how to respond. His gaze moves over my face and hovers at my mouth.

"I need to be inside you again," he says.

"What?"

He steps toward me, a hand snaking up my back and fingers weaving into my hair. He tugs my head backward and kisses my mouth hard, then moves to my neck.

"Besides, you didn't come," he says as he slides a hand up along the inside of my thigh, pushing my panties aside to close his fingers over my sex.

I gasp.

"And I like watching you come," he says, his fingers working expertly, like he has always known exactly how to play me.

My hands move to his shoulders, holding onto him

as he circles my clit. His other arm wraps around me, and he lifts me up, walking me backward to the wall.

A knock on the door startles me, but Santos isn't bothered. He just draws my attention by turning my face back to his.

"Car's ready," Val calls out.

"Be right down," Santos says to the closed door. "I don't have time to fuck you properly, but I'll make you come, Little Kitty. And then I expect you to do as you're told and go to bed, do you understand?" he asks, hoisting me up. I hear the zipper of his slacks as he tugs the crotch of my panties aside, not even bothering to take them off.

I swallow. "Where are you going?"

"Do you understand?" he repeats, flicking his fingers over my clit, making me forget what I'm asking.

I nod.

"Good Little Kitty," he says and with one hard thrust, he pushes into me, forcing a grunt from me as he grips my ass cheeks with his hands. I cling to him, wrapping my legs around him.

The sound of men moving in the other room distracts me. Is the door locked? Would one of them walk in? Santos is clearly unbothered.

"Eyes on me, sweetheart." He shifts his grip to bring his thumb to my clit, and I let out a deep moan, writhing against his hand. "That's a good Kitty." He grins and kisses me, still massaging my clit. I'm sure I'll come apart if he continues much longer. "You're so fucking tight and wet." He kisses my open mouth and whispers. "I want to hear my name on your lips when you come." His fingers work over my clit as the tension before orgasm builds, winding my body tighter and tighter.

I find myself kissing him back, tongue on tongue, him tasting me, me tasting him, and I do just as he says. I come for him, and I'm sure they hear me in the next room when I call out his name. I hold tight to him, every muscle tensed as he watches me. His hard cock is still inside me when my legs go limp, and he bears my weight as he draws out of me, leaving me confused when he adjusts my panties and tucks himself back into his slacks.

Santos carries me to the bed, draws the blanket back, and sits me on the edge of it. I'm like a ragdoll while he pulls my dress off over my head then lays me down. He draws the blanket up to my chest and smiles, brushing hair that's sticking to my forehead away before adjusting his erection.

"What about you?" I ask, because he's still hard.

"When I'm back," he says, caressing my cheek. "In the meantime, I want you to remember one thing. Remember that you belong to me. Only me. Understand?"

I nod, not really understanding why he's asking that. Not sure why the thought has butterflies fluttering their wings in my stomach.

"Get some sleep." He bends to touch his lips to my forehead, and it's a strangely tender thing to do, so opposite the Santos he shows the world.

"You never answered about Camilla," I say when he reaches the door.

The words stop him. His back tenses, and I prop myself on my elbows. What we just did was him distracting me, and I admit, it felt good. Amazing, even. But it doesn't change anything. Making me come is something. The tenderness he handles me with is at times confusing.

But I'm not that easy to manipulate or distract.

"You want to know if I fucked her?" he asks, turning to face me.

His eyes have changed. They've grown cold and empty. They've lost their shine. I don't like it. It's like the darkness I sensed within him before has seeped to the surface. It's this thing inside him that's frightening. Not his violence, not his rage, but this—this deadness, that truly scares me.

"I wouldn't touch that snake with a ten-foot pole," he says, with disgust and loathing in his voice. It doesn't leave me feeling relieved, but instead questioning what happened with him and that family that the mention of them draws this visceral of a response.

24

SANTOS

I take the stairs down to the garage where Val has the SUV waiting for me. The man sitting in the driver's seat gets out and opens the back door.

"Not necessary. I'll go alone."

He's confused. "Sir—"

"Keys inside?" I glance over his shoulder to see them still in the ignition.

"Yes sir."

"Tell Val I'll be back ASAP."

"But you'll be on your own."

I pat his shoulder to nudge him out of the way. "I can handle myself." He has no idea just how capable I am. I have the Commander to thank for that.

Climbing into the SUV, I take the gun out of my shoulder holster and set it in the glove compartment. It's late, and where we are it's quiet, but I head toward a seedier part of town.

The Avery family has a home here in Miami—not

where I'm going, but where the wealthy, upstanding citizens live. They also have one in Todt Hill in New Jersey. I lived in both with them during my years of service.

I let my mind wander to that time, to the circumstances that got me there. Blackmail, essentially. I'd been days away from my eighteenth birthday when I'd committed my first murder. I'd have been tried as an adult, especially given the gruesomeness of the act. Never mind that Alexia's father deserved worse. Never mind that he himself was a violent man, a murderer who beat his own daughter to death and killed his unborn grandchild.

Those details have me gripping the steering wheel harder, and I shove the thoughts back into their box and lock it. Those particular memories will weaken me. Thiago was right. Family and those you care about become a weakness. We both learned that lesson years ago.

So, I think instead of what happened after—of the arrest, of the Commander's visit to my father at home while I sat in a dark, dirty cell in an abandoned building.

At that time, the Augustine family was a known crime family. Not powerful, and nowhere near the top of the food chain, but we had a reputation. My father's hands were dirty. Caius's hands were dirty. And all it took was that one murder to soak mine in blood.

The Commander offered my father an out. A reprieve. He could make the charges go away. Vanish.

He could make it so that Alexia's father had never been. The alternative was a lifetime behind bars because he could arrange for that, too. He made certain my father understood his power.

So, a deal had been struck. I'd left my home to live with the Avery family, and I became the Commander's most powerful weapon. I slowly destroyed whole families, exerting as much pain as each situation allowed and then some—all to the specifications of the Commander, while he attended this party or other, always being seen in public as the do-gooder he liked to project himself to be.

I had no issues with the men who deserved to die. It was the other side of things that got to me, the part where the Commander felt he needed more. Felt he was *due* more, or just wanted to send a broader, unmistakable message to his enemies. Fuck with me and this is the consequence. It worked. It kept the Avery family firmly in power.

It's the collateral damage that steals my sleep. The innocents I left in my wake. They make up that vast chasm of darkness inside me as if their souls linger there still. My beast is made up of their pain. They're suffering at my hands. They haunt my nightmares and I deserve nothing less.

But there was one thing the Commander didn't see. Didn't anticipate. We Augustines are an ambitious bunch, and damn, are we vengeful. An eye for an eye, every single time. That's the part the Commander didn't count on—that, and the fact that every single time I went home after a job well done, I reported back to my father.

Together, we built a database. Because for the Commander I killed, but for my father I stole. I stole information. I stole evidence. That's why we're at the top of the food chain now. That knowledge has made the Augustine family invincible.

Wiping the Commander from the face of the earth? That was my due.

I navigate the SUV through narrower, dirtier streets of Miami. Up ahead, I see the flashing lights of the strip club. It's a seedy place, but it's one that offers privacy. It's where we used to come after some of the particularly bad nights. Where Thiago and I could get away from under the Commander's ever-watchful eye.

This is where he'll be if he's anywhere at all.

I park at the end of the street under a busted-out streetlamp. Val would tell me to take the pistol, but I know the no guns rule. Besides, I don't need a weapon. Men have a way of clearing a path when I approach. Instinctively, they sense the danger. Subconsciously, they move away from the plague I carry as if to avoid the devastation that follows me.

The flashing sign of the woman taking a turn on the stripper pole shines red over my face as I approach the doors. The security guards outside rise from their stools. One looks me over, then glances at his partner. I'm dressed a little differently than the usual clientele in my formal suit that costs more than they'll earn this month.

"No guns," he says.

I open my jacket. "No guns."

He pats me down anyway, then gestures for me to enter. I pull the wooden door open, and the familiar stench of the place washes over me: sweat, sex, and greed. I'd forgotten it, but damn how a scent can carry you back.

It takes me a moment, but I stand in the entrance and force myself to breathe it in.

To remember.

I look around the large space, which is lit dimly but for the spotlights shining on the strippers on stage. A bar I know is sticky to the touch stretches the length of one wall. Tables and booths dot the space, leaving just enough room for the women to work lap dances. Through the curtain at the back are the private rooms. Nothing is off limits there as long as you pay. Two men as big as the ones at the front doors guard that curtained entrance.

I'm not interested in that, though. I never was. The Commander would send me *gifts* after a particularly well-executed job. Women. A lot of women. I'd preferred the reprieve of a night in my own home, my own bed. Caius would often meet me, though, when the reward was women. Why waste a night, he'd say. I'd let him have them and walk away.

I didn't care. Fucking was the last thing I wanted to do after those nights. Contrary to what the Commander may have believed, killing, especially killing innocents, didn't make my dick hard. It made me sick. So instead, I'd done what I always had. I carved the marks into my skin. I felt their pain. I remembered their names... and the name of the man who held my life in his hands.

An older woman with an empty tray at her side approaches. I smile when I see her. It takes her a minute, but as soon as she recognizes me, her face breaks out into a wide smile.

"Well, I don't believe my eyes! Two in one night! Santos Augustine, what the hell are you doing back in this shithole?" We hug, and it's somehow more comforting than I imagined it would be.

"Addy, how are you doing, sweetheart?" Addy used to dance here, but that was before my time. She's in her late forties and has become a sort of mother hen to the younger women over the years. With a loan from myself and Thiago that she repays at a rate of a single dollar a month, she now owns fifty-one percent of the club.

"Doing all right. Let me get a look at you." She stands back, looks me over, then frowns. "How are you doing?"

"I'm fine. You know I always land on my feet." She has seen me when I was at my lowest and has helped bring me back from the brink on more than one occasion.

"You do," she says, although she's scrutinizing me. "He looks worse," she says, gesturing to a booth at the back corner.

So he's here. Good.

I nod because there's not much to say about that. Someone calls her, and she tells them she'll be right there.

"It's good to see you, Santos."

"Same."

I walk toward the back booth. It's our usual, though it's been more than five years. But there in that last booth with its high-backed benches that offer privacy sits Thiago Avery, a bottle of whiskey in front of him. In his hand is a glass he tips in greeting before he swallows the contents. I slide into the opposite seat.

He pushes the second glass toward me. It's what we used to do. Down a bottle—two, some nights, when they'd been especially bad.

I go to lift the glass to set it aside. It sticks.

"Nothing has changed here," Thiago says with an attempt at a smile.

"Part of its charm," I say, the comment out of place.

Thiago snorts.

There's nothing to laugh at here though. We're not friends, he and I. We could never be that. But we have an old and ugly history. We both belonged to the Commander. Me for a time, him for most of his life.

But that's the past, and the future is why I'm here.

I face the Commander's first-born son. His successor. My enemy.

"It's time we talked."

25

MADELENA

I get out of bed when Santos is gone and slip on the shirt he'd discarded earlier when he'd changed into his more formal suit. It smells like him. Why do I feel so attached to that smell? Why does its familiarity feel so warm?

I button up the shirt and roll the sleeves up before walking to the door and, after a quick listen, opening it. The living room is empty. I assume Val or the other guards are outside in the hallway. I go to the window, but I'm not sure what I'm looking for. It's not like I'm going to follow Santos. How and why would I do that?

Camilla's name comes to mind, and I am very aware of what that feeling in my gut is called. *Jealousy*. I don't like it. He hates her, though. I heard that much in his words, but more importantly, I saw it in his eyes, in the way they'd emptied. Deadened.

What happened to him? What did they do to him? He lived with them for a time and at the end, the

Commander, their father, went missing. I gather that Santos was responsible for that. What did the Commander do that was so evil?

The image of Thiago's scar is followed by Santos's words. His father did that to him as a lesson in obedience. If he could do that to his own son, what did he do to Santos?

I shudder and turn to go into the bedroom when I hear the sound of the key card being used to unlock the suite door. Before I can make it to the bedroom, it opens and Ana enters with Caius right behind her. She stops as soon as she sees me. Caius is talking to Val, but as soon as he notices me, he, too, stops. He takes me in, and I remember I'm naked but for Santos's dress shirt. I wrap my arms around myself instinctively because his gaze has that effect on me. It makes me feel cold. Exposed. Vulnerable.

"Sis," he says, nudging Ana farther into the room.

Val meets my gaze, but he's shut out when Caius closes the door. I wonder if Caius were to threaten me, would Val defend me if Santos wasn't around?

"Should we have a drink?" Ana says, setting her clutch down and moving to the wet bar as if they're just getting back after a nice night out. Maybe they are. What do I know?

Caius drags his gaze from me and turns to her. "Go to the bedroom. Wait for me there." She glances at me, opens her mouth, but Caius shuts her up with a single command. "Get out."

I watch her in my periphery because I'm keeping

my eyes locked on Caius. Ana is a prop. Nothing more. He's using her for something. Maybe it's just sex, but I don't think so. It's too coincidental. Her family is established in Avarice, though. Maybe he's going to do with her what Santos is doing with me, a marriage of convenience?

"Where's my brother?" Caius asks after eyeing what I'm wearing again.

"I don't know." I shrug and turn to walk into my bedroom, wanting to be away from him.

Caius is on my heels though, and before I can get too far, he captures my arm and stops me.

"What do you mean, you don't know?"

"I mean he didn't tell me. In case you haven't noticed, I'm not his confidante."

His gaze moves to the shirt I'm wearing. "But you two are getting cozy."

I raise my eyebrows. "Let go of my arm. I want to go to bed."

"Warming the bed for my brother? Is that what he instructed you to do?"

"Is that any of your business?"

"No, I guess not. You're adults. You can fuck without my permission. And I hope you are, come to think of it." He releases my arm and walks over to the wet bar to pour himself a whiskey.

"What does that mean?"

He studies me as he sips his drink. "Nothing. Just that it's the only way to get pregnant."

"What?"

"He didn't mention it?"

Did I believe Santos when he told me he'd have me visit a doctor he trusts to refill my birth control prescription? I'm not sure what I thought. I have three weeks though, and there were more pressing things to get through, like my honeymoon.

"Oops," he says. "Cat's out of the bag, I guess."

Dickhead.

"But tell me, you are getting cozy. I mean, you're wearing his shirt. I'd think you'd want anything that reminded you of him far, far away, considering he forced you into his bed. Unless, of course, he didn't have to force you."

I study him. This is bothering him. "Would it upset you to know we were getting close, Caius?"

His jaw tenses. He doesn't like the idea. I get it, don't I? I'm the enemy. Caius wants to make sure his brother is firmly on the right side of things. His.

"So, you and Ana were besties once?" he casually asks.

"Until she betrayed me. You'd do well to watch yourself with her," I warn him, wanting to give him something to worry about too, although I know he has his own agenda with her.

"She told me how you were bullied."

My stomach tenses, and I get that sick feeling like I used to when I was in high school and the kids were getting started.

"Sounds pretty shitty what she did to you, honestly."

I'm confused, and I don't understand his motives.

"Anyway," he shakes his head. "Just weird past stuff. Speaking of, Santos and Camilla were supposed to tie the knot at one point."

"What?" I ask, surprised at that.

"Yeah. Santos and Camilla. An item. Personally, I think she's a bitch, but she's not bad looking." He makes a point of letting his gaze move over me like he's silently comparing us and I'm coming up way short. "They went pretty hard for a while, but she is a fucking ice queen. I get it why he'd choose you. Girls like you run pretty hot in bed."

"Girls like me?"

"Yeah, you know, a little off. A little weird."

"Fuck you."

He chuckles, turns to pour himself another drink. "Kidding. Seriously though, do you know where he went?" he asks, turning around. "If he went to a bar, I need to go get him."

"He doesn't drink."

He almost spits his whiskey out. "Is that what he told you?"

I find myself wrapping my arms around myself again. Did he lie about that? Would that mean he lied about Camilla? And what does that mean for my future? Does he really intend to get me pregnant? No. He wouldn't. He can't.

Caius closes the space between us and it takes all I have to stand my ground. "Where did he go, Madelena?"

"I don't know, Caius."

"Did he tell you to tell me that?"

"No."

"Because it is partially true, I guess, that he doesn't drink. He tries not to. You don't want to see him drunk. And you definitely don't want to be alone with him when he is," Caius says.

"Why?"

"He loses control."

"What does that mean?'

"He gets violent. Just watch yourself. Okay? Be careful around him when he drinks. That scar on Thiago's neck? That was Santos drunk out of his mind."

My mouth goes dry.

"Between you and me, the Commander was an asshole to him. To them both. They bonded over that, as weird as that sounds, and the Commander needed to teach them obedience. So he did what works best. Turned them against each other."

"Santos did that to Thiago?" He nods. "How?"

"I don't know the details. Rope, I guess. Almost killed him, from what I heard. Listen, don't tell him you know that. It'll mess with him. I know he's not proud of what he did those years he lived with that family. They're no good, the whole lot of them. And them showing up tonight is not a good sign."

I remember Camilla's strange comment about being neighborly. What did that mean? I'm struck silent by all of this. It's information I thought I wanted. But maybe Santos was right. Withholding is a mercy.

The bedroom door opens, and we both turn to find Ana standing there with her hair down and wearing a short baby-doll negligee that must be made of rice paper because I can see right through it.

She catches my eye, making sure I get a good look, before she turns her gaze to Caius and gives him a provocative smile.

"If you keep me waiting much longer, I'll have to start without you," she taunts.

Caius swallows his drink, greedy eyes eating her up. She looks good, I have to say.

"That's not a bad idea. Go get started. Leave the door open. I'll be right in."

She blinks her eyes demurely.

Caius turns to me, and I see Ana behind him climbing onto the bed, spreading her legs and slipping her fingers between them. Her eyes hold mine as she begins to caress herself.

Caius is grinning when I turn my gaze to him. "I'd invite you to join, but I have a feeling my brother won't appreciate it. You can watch if you want, though. No harm in that."

I have no idea how to respond. Caius must see that because he laughs outright, sets his glass down on the coffee table, and moves toward his bedroom, stripping off his shirt as he goes. I watch his back, no scars there, just skin and muscle rippling beneath. Nothing like his brother. He takes hold of Ana's ankles, making her yelp when he tugs her to the end of the bed and bends his head between her legs. I turn and run into our bedroom then, but not before hearing Ana's deep, guttural moan of pleasure before I slam the door shut and lock it.

26

SANTOS

I sip my club soda and study Thiago. He's about my age, with just a couple of months between us, but hell if he doesn't look a decade older. His dark blond hair has grayed at the temples, and along his jaw is a patch of skin where hair doesn't grow anymore.

I remember when that happened. Between that, the other scars on his face and forearms, and the thick line where the rope bit into his neck as he hanged strangling while we watched, he looks like what he is: a killer, a machine trained and programmed to kill.

In some ways, I feel sorry for him. He shares the Commander's blood. What he and I did is different for me. The Commander was my tormentor, my enemy. Nothing more. For Thiago, the baggage came with a whole lot of other baggage.

"The years haven't been too hard on you," Thiago says in his thick, gravelly voice.

"Harder on you, I think."

A ghost of a smile widens his lips, and he tips the glass in my direction. "Here's to the truth." He swallows the contents and pours another. The bottle is nearly empty, and I'm guessing that's all him. "Don't drink anymore?"

I shake my head. "Can't. Not if I want my head on straight."

He nods because he knows me. In fact, Thiago Avery may know me better than anyone else in the whole world, even Caius, if I'm honest with myself. He's seen me in my darkest hours.

"You climbed high on the social ladder, Santos. Let me see your hands." Confused, I hold them over the table and turn them over. "Just as I thought. Can't quite wash the blood off."

I study this man who was once a friend because I think it was that friendship that destroyed him, that turned the Commander so wholly against his own flesh and blood, and that made Thiago's punishments a hundred times worse than mine.

"Are you doing okay, Thiago?"

"Loaded question." He drinks. "As okay as anyone who is guilty of what I am guilty of can be. You?"

I take a breath in. "Your father lost any power over me when he disappeared. It was a choice I made. A conscious choice. You should do the same."

"Are you a philosopher now? Have you found Jesus?"

I grit my jaw, take the bottle of whiskey, and pour myself two fingers.

Thiago smiles, then touches his glass to mine, and we drink.

"What did your sister mean about being neighbors?"

He shrugs. "Real estate is a solid investment. You must know that, given your holdings."

"What did you do?"

"Avarice was too small for my father, but turns out my family wants to try the small-town experience after all. I did what any good son and brother would do. I bought them a house."

My heart thuds a slow, heavy beat and I wait.

"Although if I know my kid sister, there was nothing neighborly in her intent with your wife." He grins and takes a swallow. I can understand him. He's torn, like he always was, between what is right and what is duty. "Between you and me, she's still a little heartsick over your rejection," he says, leaning in for effect.

"You'd have to have a heart for it to be sick."

Again, he shrugs. "Just keep a close eye on your wife. Wouldn't want her to get hurt."

"What do you want, Thiago?"

"Me? Nothing. There is nothing on this earth that I could ever want. My family, though? They want. They grasp. They are greedy for more. Always more." His lip curls in disgust. "And vengeance runs thick in our blood. Dad's special gift. They want revenge."

"Revenge against me?"

"Who else?"

"For what, exactly? I was your father's puppet. I should be the one seeking revenge."

"Come on, Santos. This is me. I know what you did. What *we* did."

I take a moment. "Do they know your involvement?"

He looks down into his glass, swirling it, studying it as if there could be an answer there. He shakes his head. "I don't think so."

"I won't tell them."

He looks up at me. "I'm not afraid of them, and I don't need you to do me any favors."

"It's not a favor."

"No? In exchange for keeping my secret, you probably want me to nix the move to Avarice. Right?"

"Like you said, you and I will do anything for our families. For those we care about."

"Do you care about her then?"

The question catches me off guard. "What?"

One corner of his mouth turns upward. "Santos, Santos, Santos." He clucks his tongue and shakes his head. "Take good care to make sure Camilla never knows that."

"She's one of the innocents. You remember those?"

At that he smiles fully, all teeth. "Oh, do I ever. I wish I could forget them for one fucking minute." He pours the last of the whiskey into his glass, filling it all the way, and drinks it like it's water.

I understand him because I can hear them too. I can feel their screams locked in each line that marks my arms and shoulders. They burn like fire, as if I were cutting into myself even now. But that was the point, wasn't it?

He reaches into his breast pocket and takes out his wallet. From inside he draws two hundred-dollar bills and drops them onto the table before sliding to the edge of the booth. "Watch yourself, Santos."

"You're full of warnings tonight, old friend."

"Old friend." He considers this. "We were friends once, weren't we? And I still owe you. I haven't forgotten. I won't forget. I'll make things even-Steven when the time comes. Just remember one thing. No one is to be trusted. No one. Not our brothers, not our mothers, not my sister. You and I are truly alone." He pauses for a full minute, and I have a strange sense of déjà vu. My father had said something almost exactly like this on his deathbed. "Don't forget it," Thiago finishes before walking away.

I watch him go, seeing how his shoulders hunch a little more deeply than they used to. I pick the whiskey bottle up, tip the last drops into my cup, and signal to the passing waitress for another.

27

MADELENA

Santos doesn't return that night.

He doesn't return the next day.

By evening, I'm worried, but I'm not sure why. Is it for him? Did he drink? Is Caius telling the truth that he gets violent when he drinks? Did something happen? If so, what does it mean for me?

My mother-in-law is here, though. She flew in for the event. I'm not sure if it was scheduled or she is here because Santos has gone missing. I have my ear to the door and can hear her arguing with Caius in the living room. I don't hear Ana, so I'm not sure if she's been banished to her bedroom. I chose to stay in mine. I don't want to be anywhere near the snakes inside.

"Go get changed. I'll see to Madelena," Evelyn says and I back away from the door just as she knocks and opens it simultaneously, not waiting to be invited in.

She stops in the doorway and looks around the bedroom. It's nothing special, although it's the best the hotel had to offer. Her eyes settle on me. I'm wearing a pair of jeans and a simple black T-shirt. My hair is braided on either side of my head and I'm not wearing makeup, which is unusual for me. I had too much on my mind to bother.

"How old are you again?" she asks me, approaching.

"Twenty."

She takes my face in her hands, turns it this way and that, blood-red fingernails digging into soft flesh. "You look like a child without makeup." She lets go and looks around. "Where's your dress?"

"Where's Santos?"

"God knows. Caius will escort you tonight. I'll be there to smooth the way."

"Caius? I don't want to go with Caius."

"Well, that's too bad, isn't it? Where's the dress?"

"Closet."

She walks over to the large, walk-in closet and returns with the dress still in its garment bag. She unzips it, then hooks the hanger onto the back of the closet door to look it over. It's the first time I'm seeing it. It's a shimmering black gown, and it's beautiful, maybe more beautiful than the last. It's fitted from bust to hips with a draped neckline and a sheer chiffon cape, and the skirt has a dramatic side slit.

Evelyn makes a face at the cape, but I know why Santos chose it. My arms will be exposed, but between the cape and the draping neckline the scars from old cuts won't be visible.

The thought that he chose this for me, that he did it with that in mind, is strangely comforting.

Evelyn sighs. "I suppose it's too late to have this thing removed. Can't leave dress choices to the men, can we?" she asks, but she's not really asking me. She checks her watch. "You need to get dressed. Hair and makeup will be here in twenty minutes. We leave in an hour. I don't like being late." She walks to the door.

"What about Ana?"

She stops, turns to me. "Ana?" she asks like she's confused, but then she remembers. "She'll sit this one out. It's more important our family is seen with you." She looks me over at that, sending me a very clear message how she feels about it.

"And Santos? Is someone looking for him?"

Her lips pull tight into a smile that shows her displeasure. "Santos isn't my concern right now. Not when he's chosen to go on one of his binges at the worst possible time. Get dressed. If you delay us, you'll be punished."

I raise my eyebrows at that because what the fuck does that mean?

She leaves, and I can breathe again. Honestly, that woman is scary.

With a sigh, I change into the dress, not wanting to test her. It'll be better if I'm out among people rather than locked in here with them. I'm still holding out hope that Santos will show up. That hope, however, vanishes when Caius enters as the women are putting the finishing touches on my makeup and hair. Our eyes meet in the mirror. He's wearing a tuxedo and has shaved his face clean. He's handsome in a very different way than Santos.

Caius whistles appreciatively, and I roll my eyes, embarrassed at this overdone attention I don't want from him. He dismisses the women. I make sure to thank them before they leave, then sit on the edge of the bed to take my shoes out of their box.

"Christ. How much did you spend on these clothes and shoes?" I ask, studying the pair of Jimmy Choo sandals with shimmering stones dangling along the ankle strap. "Not exactly my style." I hold one up and study the pinpoint heel.

"Chunky boots aren't my style." He's referring to my Dr. Martens. He checks his watch. "Put them on. We need to go."

"Mommy doesn't like to be kept waiting. Tell me something. What did she mean exactly with punishing me if I'm late? Would I miss dinner?" I raise my eyebrows but focus on slipping the sandals on and adjusting the straps around my ankles. "Perhaps be sent to bed early?"

He crosses the room and crouches to help with one of the shoes. I try to pull away, but he grips my leg, his big hand rough. He doesn't let go. "Stay."

"Don't touch me. I belong to your brother, not you." Wow. Did I just really say that out loud?

He closes the strap, and I can see at this angle that he's grinning. He mutters something under his breath, and I swear it sounds like he says *for now*.

"For now? What does that mean?" I ask once he stands. He towers over me, so I stand too, but even with the heels—just as with Santos—the top of my head barely comes to his chin.

"Nothing, sis. You misheard." He threads my arm through his and tugs me close. Standing like this, I can smell his aftershave and feel the heat coming off him.

I try to pull free, but he tightens his grip.

"Relax. It's all for show. Happy family and all."

"Let me go. You don't have to touch me."

"Be good or I'll let Mommy do what she's itching to do anyway just because you're who you are."

"And what's that?"

"Strap your ass."

My mouth falls open.

He chuckles. "Relax. She won't touch you. You have Santos's protection. He's made that clear."

He has? "Santos isn't here," I point out.

"Don't remind her," he says, face serious. "I know you don't like me or trust me, and I get it. But do as I say tonight. Understand, Madelena?"

"Why would I do that?"

"Because you have more enemies than you know." Silence falls heavy between us until he shifts his gaze to adjust the cape of the dress, draping the material over the tops of my arms. His fingertips graze my skin, and I look down to see he's touching one of the scars there.

My mouth goes dry and when I look at him, he's watching me.

"Your secret's safe with me," he says.

His words send a chill through me, making me shudder noticeably. Santos told him?

"We need to go."

"Do you know where he is?" I ask, stopping Caius before we walk out of my bedroom.

His cocky expression gives way to one of worry, and he shakes his head. "He'll turn up."

Before I can ask anything else, we're out in the living room. Ana is leaning against the door of her bedroom, arms folded across her chest and staring daggers at me.

"Don't pout, Ana. It's not becoming on you," Evelyn says, dismissing her as she gives Caius and me a once-over, nods her approval, and leads the way out.

My head is spinning with information I'm trying to make sense of. I don't speak during the ride, but the two of them keep up a quiet conversation. I barely listen.

Once we're in the hall, Caius hands me a glass of champagne. I'm grateful for it. We stand at the entrance of the grand room, and I watch Evelyn Augustine take it all in. She scans faces, and I get the feeling she's cataloging them. When she pauses and her expression shifts infinitesimally, I follow the line of her sight and almost gasp when I see she's looking at Bea Avery. Bea is looking back at her, too. And I swear I see a crack in Evelyn's ice-queen armor.

Evelyn clears her throat and turns to us. "Let's mingle, shall we?" she says, and pastes a smile on her face. I glance at Bea as I'm led into the room and find her eyes locked on Evelyn's back. There's history here. I doubt it's pretty.

Evelyn is charming as we work the room. She and Caius do most of the talking. I am an arm piece… and a key. Everyone here knows me—well, knows the De Léon name. I am welcome and in turn, so are they.

When they ask where my husband is, Evelyn tells them he wasn't feeling well. She makes a point of mentioning how Caius stepped up to accompany his sister-in-law, whom he already is very close with. I barely get a few words in as Evelyn and Caius talk and laugh easily. I wonder what will happen to me once they're accepted into the circles they want so badly to be a part of because I will have worn out my usefulness.

That thought brings me to the comment Caius made last night about a baby. Is that what Santos wants me for? I know this is a marriage of convenience. But a baby? That's a step too far. He doesn't need to do that. With me, a De Léon, on his arm, all the doors will be opened to him. And quite frankly, with all the money and power the Augustines have now, I'm not sure how much they really need me anyway.

But then I remember what Odin had told me about the history between our families. I need to find out what exactly happened between Santos's aunt and my father because that part is personal. The rest, like the marriage, is Santos climbing the social ladder.

At least this will be over tomorrow. We have one

more event, but that will be held in Avarice. Odin will be there. I'll see my brother, and I'll be on home turf.

The night drags on, and when Caius announces it's time for me to go back to the hotel, I'm grateful that I'll be going alone while he and his mother stay. I'm also grateful that apart from Bea Avery, the rest of the Avery family was absent.

Could Santos be with them? Was Caius telling the truth about him and Camilla?

Caius walks me out to our waiting limo and opens the door. I turn to him, trying to figure out his angle. What he wants. He's gone behind Santos's back to tell me things. Is that to manipulate me? How much of what he's said is true? Because from what I've seen, Santos trusts him.

"Sleep tight, sis. Don't forget to lock your door." he says and before I can get away, he plants a kiss on my cheek. "Check in on Ana, will you?"

I won't.

I settle into the back of the limo and reach to close the door myself when he just keeps standing there but he stops me and leans in. "Let her know to get started without me and I'll finish her off when I get there," he whispers.

"You're disgusting," I say, tugging at the door.

"Offer stands if you want to watch."

I flip him off and he laughs, then closes the door, and I'm finally free.

28

MADELENA

There is a part of me that hopes Santos will be back at the hotel when I arrive. I tell myself it's because he's the devil I know a tiny bit more than the others, the lesser of all the evils. I'm not sure that's the truth, though. Because I'm feeling something new with him—something akin to hope.

Regardless, that hope is short-lived because the only person to greet me apart from a soldier I don't recognize is Ana. She's sitting in the middle of the couch with much the same expression as she wore earlier, her arms still folded across her chest. The only difference is she's holding a glass of wine in her hand. She swallows the contents when she sees me. I get the feeling she's been sitting here seething all this time.

"Had fun?" she asks with a smile so fake she's not even trying to mask her true feelings.

"No, actually, I didn't. Thanks for asking." A glance at the bottle tells me it's almost empty. I'm going to assume she drank it all. I walk past her to my bedroom only to find the door open. I'm pretty sure I closed it before I left. I peer inside but don't see anything amiss. There are no drawers overturned. The bed isn't tossed apart. But when I turn back to Ana, the smug expression on her face tells me she has been inside. "Did you look through my things?"

"Why would I do that?" she asks demurely.

I almost start to argue with her, but what's the point? I open my mouth but close it again and just shake my head. She's not worth it. I walk into the bedroom. I plan on closing the door and locking it behind me, but she's there before I can with her foot jammed between the door and the frame.

"What? What were you going to say?" Ana asks.

"Nothing. Get out, Ana."

"He's mine."

"Who? Caius? Yes, he's all yours. Congratulations. You really snagged a winner in Caius Augustine. Get. Out."

"He's the older brother. He should have what Santos has."

"What?" I shake my head. "You're drunk. Go to bed."

"Yes, Your Royal Highness. All high and mighty just like you used to be. You'd think you'd have learned your lesson, *Mad Elena*."

I look at her, and maybe I'm too angry to be hurt, or maybe I've just gotten better at putting fury first because that's the predominant emotion right now.

Hearing her call me that again makes me angry. "This isn't high school anymore. Your friends are gone. It's just you all alone, just like I was all those years. And you're fucking pathetic. Grow up."

"Me? I'm pathetic?"

I take a deep breath in and remind myself it's not worth it. She wants a fight. I'm not going to give it to her. I turn and cross the room to the bathroom. If she wants to follow me in, fine. But then I stop because there, tossed over the back of a chair, is a jacket I recognize. With a gasp, I rush to pick it up. It's his. I have no doubt. When I bring it to my nose, I can smell his scent on it. But I smell more, too.

"Is he here?" I ask, spinning to face Ana.

She grins. "He was. But he had to rush out. I guess his wife isn't that important to him."

"What the hell is wrong with you?" I try to push past her, but she stands squarely in front of me, blocking my path.

"Let me tell you something about the Augustines, Mad Elena. You may be valuable now, but that won't last. They'll get what they need from you sooner rather than later and then you're gone."

"And what? You'll take my place? Is that why you colored your hair to match mine? Is that why your makeup looks just like mine? The lipstick, car-crash red, right?"

Her face flushes, and I know it's true. The thought of it just makes me feel sorry for her, though, because she is pathetic and it's sad.

"You know what? I don't want any of this. I never did. I don't deserve it, and believe it or not, neither do you and I mean that in the best way," I say.

Before she can answer, I walk into the bathroom and lock the door. I switch on the tap and take a few minutes to level my breathing and my heartbeat. I look at myself. With the back of my hand, I wipe away the deep red of my lipstick. Car-crash red. It smears along my cheek, and I think how apt the name is. I look like a car crash.

My eyes grow moist because what happened with Ana and I all those years ago didn't have to happen. Even though I understood why she turned on me, it was something completely out of my control. But when her father lost a chunk of money to mine, she punished me. It didn't have to be the way it was. We could just have been friends. I wanted that. I want it now. Not with her. She can never be that. But I want a friend. I don't think I've ever had one, not really.

But I stop myself there. I've had enough pity parties for myself over the years, and I'm done with those. I wipe away the tears that fall, not caring that I'm smearing eyeliner because none of that is worth thinking about. You can't change the past, and I'm fine without friends.

I have Odin and he has me, and we're all each of us needs. I look again at the jacket in my hands, bring it to my nose. His cologne, the one I know intimately, is layered with cigarette smoke and alcohol and something else. Perfume?

Just then, I hear the deep rumble of his voice and I don't want to think about what feels like hope swelling in my chest when I do. I pull the door open just in time to see Santos stalking into the bedroom, Val on his heels.

"Santos!"

He stops when he sees me, looking confused as he takes in my dress. Had he forgotten what tonight was? I lift my gaze to Val's, and he looks worried. I realize why that is when Santos stalks toward me.

He's drunk. He is completely out of his head drunk.

29

SANTOS

It takes me a minute to focus my eyes on Madelena. She is stunning in the shimmering black gown. I chose it especially for her, but I missed seeing her in it tonight.

The high heels emphasize her long, slender legs, and one thigh is exposed by the dramatic slit of the dress. I don't know if it's the years of self-imposed celibacy or what that have me so drawn to this woman. I want her. But it's not only physical. I have a responsibility to her—but again, it's not that simple.

I drag my gaze to her face. Her hair is coming apart, and her makeup is smudged, with remnants of deep red lipstick across her cheek. Her eyeliner is smeared, the whites of her eyes pink.

She hugs my jacket to herself. I'm not sure she's aware of how tightly she's holding it, and on the back of one hand I see the same red as on her cheek. It's the hand she used to wipe it away.

"Where were you?" she asks quietly, her gaze cautious, a line creasing the space between her eyebrows. That relief I thought I saw moments ago has vanished. Was it there at all? Does it make sense that she'd be relieved to see me?

The whiskey I've drunk over the last day and half churns in my gut. I stopped drinking a few hours ago, but it's going to take longer than that to burn off the effects of this quantity of alcohol.

I glance at Val. "Leave. Make sure no one interrupts us."

He looks at Madelena, hesitating.

"I said, go."

He goes. I turn my attention back to my wife and my strange conversation with Thiago echoes in my mind.

"Do you care about her then?"

"What?"

"Santos, Santos, Santos. Take good care to make sure Camilla never knows that."

I clear my throat, then close the space between us. I touch her cheek, brushing my thumb over the smear of eyeliner. I do care about her, but it's not what he thinks. I am responsible for her. I have been since the moment I slit the palm of her hand and made my oath. Hers was forced. Mine, well, I held the knife. She can't navigate my world and all the people in it who will do her harm, who will take what they need from her and discard her... if she's lucky.

No one is to be trusted. No one. Not our brothers, not our mothers, not my sister. You and I are truly alone.

"Madelena. Were you crying?" My voice is hoarse. Raw. I take my jacket from her and toss it aside, but when my fingers graze the curve of her neck, she shrugs me off and takes a step backward.

"You disappeared."

"I had to take care of something."

"You were gone overnight. A full day and night."

"I'm back. I'm not leaving again." I reach for her once more, but she puts more distance between us.

"Did you tell your brother?"

I raise my eyebrows, assuming she's not done yet because I don't have a clue what she's talking about.

"The cuts. He knew."

Now I'm confused. "No. Of course not."

"Then who..." she trails off, shakes her head. "You're drunk. You told me you don't drink, yet you stink of a distillery. You lied to me. How many times have you lied to me?"

I close the space between us, then wrap an arm around her shoulders to weave my fingers into her hair. She won't be walking away from me again.

"What else are you lying about?" she asks. I want to ask what she's talking about, but she continues before I can. "You left me here alone with them," she says and for a moment, she's that girl from five years ago. She was alone then, too, with only her brother to protect her—a brother too young and ill-equipped against men like the Augustines.

I realize as the whiskey-induced fog in my mind clears that she was scared.

"No one would hurt you," I say, running the backs of my fingers over her cheekbone where her tears have left streaks. "They know they can't touch you. I've made it clear."

She laughs a short, ugly laugh. "You don't know them." She turns, but I catch her arm before she can walk away.

"Madelena?"

She shakes her head. "Let me go, Santos."

I don't. "Are you hurt? Is that why you were crying?"

"I'm not crying." Her eyes dart away like she's embarrassed.

"If they hurt you, touched you..."

She searches my face before her gaze moves down to my open collar. I'm sure I look like shit. A bender will do that to you, and I should shower, get out of these clothes, and eat something. But the look on her face has my gut tightening. Something happened.

I take hold of both her arms. "What is it?"

"If you were so concerned for me, why did you just leave me here with them?"

"They know they are not to touch you."

"The rules aren't the same when you're gone."

I look her over, seeing the dress anew. The hair and makeup. She would have attended tonight's dinner. My mother would have given her no choice... and she wouldn't have let her show up alone. I lean in and sniff her neck then bring her wrists to my nose and inhale.

No one is to be trusted. No one. Not our brothers, not our mothers, not my sister. You and I are truly alone.

"Why do I smell my brother on you?"

"I don't think you get to interrogate me. It should be the other way around, don't you think?"

"Why, Madelena?"

"Let me go."

"Tell me."

"You're hurting me," she says, twisting a little, and I realize how hard I'm squeezing her wrists.

I loosen my grip, look her over. Shifting both of her wrists into one hand, I grip the draped neckline of her dress and tug.

She gasps but I keep hold of her as I tear the dress away. She won't be wearing it again anyway. It's not violent or rushed or angry. I just want her naked. I need to have her naked. To know for myself.

"What the hell are you doing?"

Once the dress is gone and she's standing in panties, a strapless bra and high-heeled shoes, I look her over.

"He touched you?" I ask, using my free hand to unhook the bra and let it slip away.

Her expression hardens, jaw setting. "Of course he did," she says, her tone goading. "You weren't here, remember? Tell me something, Santos."

I let my gaze move over her bare chest, her breasts. I can see the beginnings of the scars that line the undersides of her arms. What state of mind is one in to do that? To self-mutilate?

That dark presence inside me laughs out loud at that because I should talk. But my scars, they're different. They're punishments I deserved. I can't imagine she deserved that mutilation, the self-harm.

"Are you even listening to me?" she asks.

I blink, forcing my eyes to focus on hers because she was talking, and I was so lost in thought I didn't hear.

"Tell me something," she starts again. "Am I yours?"

"What kind of question is that?"

"Like that jacket is yours. Am I yours?" She points to the jacket I'd tossed aside. I'm not sure where she's going with this. "Because you discarded that easily enough. Am I like all your possessions? Easily discarded?"

"Christ, Madelena," I say, the beginnings of a headache throbbing against my temples. I shake my head, lift her. She yelps when I do, but I carry her to the bed and sit her on the edge of it, standing close enough so she can't run away. I undo more buttons of my shirt, hearing it tear as I tug it off.

She sets her hands on my stomach, gaze moving over me momentarily and her eyes widening as she takes in the map of a violent past. She tries to push me backward to stand, so I let her, holding her close, skin to skin. She is still for a moment, and I take in the warmth of her, lean in to kiss her neck. But what I smell is another man's scent on her. Brother or not, I don't like it.

I meet her eyes, wrap my hand around the back of her neck, and weave my fingers into her hair to tug her head backward and sniff like I'm a fucking dog. I draw back, and she stares up at me.

"Why do I smell my brother on you?"

"Because you weren't here, remember?"

"What did he do?"

"Do you care?"

"What. Did. He. Do?"

Her gaze falters. I hear how I sound, and I know how I must look because she looks wary of me. "He took me to the dinner."

I grip her jaw, see that smear of lipstick. I touch it, wondering suddenly if it was her who wiped it away or if it's smeared from kissing because Thiago's damning words keep going around and around in my head.

Caius wouldn't touch what's mine. Would he?

"Did he see you?"

"See me?"

"Like this." I draw back, sweeping my gaze over her. Her nipples pebble, and her arms are dotted with goosebumps. "Did he see you undressed?"

"Would you care if he did?"

"Damn it! Did he see you?"

"Would you care if he did?" she asks again, dropping into a seat, no longer fighting. Just quiet. Just sad.

It's that sadness that makes me pause. "You are my wife, Madelena. You belong to me. Only me."

"I'm your possession."

I study her. And I see her. Beneath that sadness, I see her—and I see hurt.

I draw her up to stand, pull her to me, because I realize something as I look into those honey-colored depths and see the stain of tears. I know it as I caress her hair, my touch gentle. Careful. It's a thing I've always known about her on some level. And I know it now in the twisting of my gut.

"Are you so unaccustomed to being wanted?" I hear myself ask, and it's those words that make her go perfectly still, that have tears streaming from the corners of her beautiful eyes. Those words that have her resisting, fighting, but also giving in, hands coming to my shoulders not to push me away but to hold onto me.

She looks at me through that veil of sadness, touches my face, pushes my hair back. And then she kisses me. Eyes open, she kisses me. It's the first time she's done that, the first time I haven't taken the kiss. And that kiss, it moves something in my gut. My chest.

That kiss, it's everything.

My exhale is her name as I lay her on the bed, stripping away her panties and pushing into her. She clings to me, arching her back with an audible exhale as I watch.

I've only fucked one other woman apart from her. I've never wanted anyone else, not even for simple release. What I want with her now, it's not sex. It's not to come. It's more, so much more. I need to be inside her, to be close to her. It's raw and full and I can't get close enough to this woman.

What we're doing, me moving inside her, her clinging to me, it's love making. Deep and soft and hard at once. And needy. So fucking needy. I can't fucking stop kissing her, looking at her. I can't stop breathing in her breath, and I can't fucking look away from her eyes, from the brokenness, the openness. The vulnerability inside them. She's giving it to me like a gift.

That thought and the damage I can do is more terrifying than any game the Commander could play, any sadistic punishment he could think up.

Because in my arms, beneath me, is my redemption.

But it's a double-edged sword because I know I can break her.

Madelena sucks in a ragged breath and her teeth find my lower lip. When the walls of her pussy throb around my cock, I feel the pain of this knowledge. The only relief is the fact that just as I can break her, so can she break me.

I know it as I draw back to look at her soft face in the aftermath of our love making.

She and I have always been destined to be together. For better or worse. Even before our blood oath. We can each be the other's savior. Or the other's destruction. This is our destiny. Until death do us part.

30

SANTOS

"Val does not leave. Am I clear, Mother?"

My mother sits in one of the armchairs in what used to be Dad's study, sipping her vodka martini. It would have been mine, but since I moved out to Augustine's, she took it over. I don't really care. I need the space apart from them, honestly, especially now with Madelena in the picture. Truth is, there wasn't anything new in Thiago's warning. It just gave more weight to my father's own warning, to the words that have echoed subtly in my mind for years.

After getting back to Avarice, I left Madelena to rest before tonight's event and took the opportunity to see Caius and my mother. We need to get some things straight between us.

Caius is quiet, his eyes on us.

"I don't see why you're so upset. A soldier is a soldier."

I step in front of her so she has to look at me. "Am I

clear?" I don't like that she's sent Val away and replaced him with someone I don't know.

She shrugs. Sips. "Fine. Besides, we have a more pressing issue." She sets her drink aside and gets up to walk around her desk. I glance at Caius, who's been strangely silent, but turn back to my mother as, from inside the drawer, she retrieves a familiar little blue plastic compact and tosses it to me. I catch it. "Care to explain?"

"This again? Where did you get it?" It's the compact of birth control pills I'd given back to Madelena.

"Ana found them among your wife's things."

"What the fuck was Ana doing going through her things?"

"She had time on her hands when your brother was forced to escort Madelena to an event you should have been in attendance for! But you disappeared. For fuck's sake, Santos. What the hell were you thinking? This is important!"

I tuck the pills into my jacket pocket and sigh.

"What is she doing with those pills?" she continues, pointing an accusing finger at me. "You know what has to happen. Why is she still taking those things?"

"I'm handling it."

"You're not handling it."

"We will do this on my terms."

She walks around the desk and comes right up to me. "No, Santos, not your terms. *Our* terms. We had a plan in place. We've had a plan in place since before your father died. We Augustines have the same end goal in our minds and hearts—"

"Unless that's changed," Caius cuts her off. He speaks the words quietly but they stop everything.

I turn to him, eyes narrowed, and take a step in his direction.

He simply raises his eyebrows and casually sips from his glass.

"Has it changed?" my mother asks, drawing my attention back from my brother.

"For fuck's sake! No, of course not. We are on track. Nothing has changed. But we will be doing this my way. On. My. Terms."

The finality in my voice has my mother backing off. She picks up her drink and returns to her seat in front of the fire but keeps her eyes on me.

"We have another issue," I say, wanting to change this subject.

"What's that?" she asks.

"The Averys have purchased a property in Avarice."

My mother's gaze moves from me to my brother.

Caius finishes his drink and sets his glass down loudly, muttering a curse. "Not an issue," he says finally.

"No?" Mom asks. "How is that? They're here to make trouble."

"What can they do?" Caius asks. "Truly, what can they do?"

"Apart from accusing your brother of killing the

Commander, you mean?" she asks. "Poking their noses where they don't belong and stirring up the past?"

Caius and I lock gazes. "Lucky for us, Santos has never given a single fuck when it comes to rumors."

"I assume they'll be in attendance tonight?" Mom asks.

I nod. "Saw them on the guest list."

"And we can't bar them from Augustine's? I mean, we do own the club."

"It's not a good idea. It would just give them ammunition," I say.

Caius pours himself another drink. "You know you could just accuse Thiago of offing his father to take over—"

"What the fuck does that mean?" I cut him off.

He puts his hands up, palms toward me in mock surrender. "Just a thought. Relax."

"Mother, can you excuse us?" I say without taking my eyes off my brother.

She checks her watch. "Fine. I have to get ready anyway. Don't fight. You're on the same side." With those words, she leaves.

"What did you say to Madelena the other night?"

"I don't know. What?"

"The cuts. You inferred you knew."

"Ah. Well, I do know."

"Ana," I say. Of course it was Ana.

He nods.

"Is that why you're with her? So she can feed you information?"

"She's a piece of ass."

"Don't fucking bring up the cutting with Madelena or anyone else again, do you hear me?"

"Touchy."

"I mean it, brother. Don't. It's not a subject to be discussed with anyone."

He raises both arms in mock surrender, clearly amused.

I shake my head, grit my teeth. Caius has a way of getting under my skin like no one else can.

"Fine. No problem," he finally says.

"Good. Now tell me one other thing. Did you touch her?"

"Excuse me? Touch her? What did she tell you I did, exactly? Because I had to step up when you went on your bender and escort her to the event you should have been present at. So the way I see it, you should be thanking me, not accusing me of touching my brother's wife. Get your head out of your ass. You're fucking her, I get it. Just take care you don't get lost in her cunt."

Before I can think, I have his collar in the fist of my hand and am pressing him up against the wall. "Be. Fucking. Careful."

Caius shoves me away. "You be fucking careful, brother. Because you're fucking this up, and you seem to have forgotten what you're supposed to be doing. We're on the same side, remember? You trust me, remember? Isn't that what you've been telling me for years?"

I push a hand into my hair, turn to the fire and take a deep breath in.

"Did you meet with Thiago?" Caius asks.

I turn back to him, but don't answer.

"Addy mentioned you were back at the strip club."

"When did you talk to Addy?"

"I was looking for you, so I made some calls. After what happened with Camilla and her freak brother, Thiago disappeared too so I put two and two together. Look," he says, stepping toward me, putting a hand on my shoulder that I shove away. He just puts it there again. "You two went through some shit together. What the Commander did to you, I know he did twice fold to his own son. You told me that yourself. Back when you considered me a friend."

"Caius—"

"No, it's true. Something's changed with us. Ever since Madelena, something's different. You don't trust me."

"It changed when Dad's will was read."

"Back to that?"

"He cut you out for something you have no control over. For not being his by blood."

"Yeah, I know. And do you think I don't know that that was him and had nothing to do with you?"

"It's still done. Same end result."

"Ah, little brother. You're a fucking idiot some days, you know that?" He shakes his head, picks up his glass to pour himself another whiskey, then drinks before continuing, "I think seeing Thiago and the whole fucking family fucked with you. Did he say something to you? That why you disappeared?"

"He told me not to trust anyone. Not you, not Mom, not him. No one."

"And you listened to him because...?" He pats my back, pulls me close. "Come on, man. This is me."

I look at him. He's right. Why am I letting all this stuff fuck with me? The comment about the cuts, Ana told him. Him bringing it up to Madelena was him messing with her. I wonder if he's jealous of her.

"Dad's note. *I know what you did, and this is your punishment.* What did it mean?" I ask.

"I don't fucking know. We're never going to know. Don't let it divide us. Don't let any of this shit divide us. Because Mom's got her agenda. The Averys have theirs. You've got your wife. And me? I don't want to lose my brother. Believe it or not, I do have your back. I will always have your back. Me sending men to keep an eye on you is me having your back. Me escorting your wife to an event is me having your back. It's me keeping an eye on her when she's on her own. Would you rather I left her at the mercy of our mother?"

"Christ. No."

"You trusted me once. I haven't done anything to deserve anything less than your trust now."

I put my hands up. "All right. Enough. I'm getting a fucking headache."

He knocks on my forehead. "It's a sign I'm getting through that thick skull. We need to get ready. One more night. Then we can relax."

"I want you to talk to Ana. Make sure she doesn't go near Madelena. Understand?"

"Fine. She's jealous of her. That's all that is."

"Why did you choose her? Of all the women available to you? You know they have history."

He shrugs. "Like I said, she's a piece of ass. She's up for anything, available, and happens to be part of Avarice's high society. Even if her family is broke, thanks to Marnix De Léon. Win. Win. Win. That's all."

I take a deep breath in. "I'm sorry, Caius."

"For being a dick?"

"Fuck you."

He ruffles my hair. "It's okay, little brother. I have always known you were a dick."

31

MADELENA

"*Are you so unaccustomed to being wanted?*"

Shame burns inside me, and I am grateful to be alone. Santos sees me. He sees me like no one has ever seen me. It undoes me. I don't know what to make of last night, of the strange moment we shared. When we made love. All I wanted was for him to see me, to want me, and to make me feel safe like only he can. But at the same time, I'm so angry.

Angry at him for making me feel so vulnerable. Angry at myself for allowing it.

I push off the chair and stare out of the window at the shadow the lighthouse always seems to cast. We flew back to Avarice earlier, and in a way, I am glad to be back. Familiarity, I suppose. Not home. This isn't home, this luxurious apartment. I'm not sure the house I grew up in is home either, though.

Being away at school for those two years was in a

way a blessing. Santos had no idea, of course, but not having the lighthouse hulking in the backdrop of my life provided a relief. Room to breathe. Yes, I missed Odin, but that space made it bearable.

The sun is setting. It will be time to go downstairs soon. Santos went to see his family. I'm dressed in another beautiful gown, this one a purple so deep it looks black. My hair is curled and flowing loose down my back. I didn't want to have it up tonight. I was getting a headache from all the pins. At least, that's what I told the hairdresser. The headache was from something else, though.

There's a knock on my door.

"Come in."

Val enters, carrying my suitcase. "Where should I put it?"

I point to the bed. "Here's fine. Thanks."

He sets it down and leaves. I open it immediately. I hurried to pack but didn't have too many things. The dresses and shoes I wore to the events had been sent ahead and would be sent back separately.

I unpack the personal things I'd brought and carry my makeup bag into the bathroom. I open it, because I need to take my pill. That's another thing. I feel like after last night, I trust him to keep his promise to give me the other two months' worth.

But a quick search through the makeup bag where I know I'd left the little plastic compact has me coming up short.

"Madelena?" Santos calls from the bedroom.

I look through the bag again, taking things out. I know I put it in here. I have always kept it in here.

There's a knock on the bathroom door, and Santos calls my name again.

"Just a second."

It's not here. Had Ana taken them when she'd gone through my things? Why would she, though? The last time I took it was the night before last. Maybe it's in the suitcase.

Santos's knuckles rap against the door and despite my best efforts, I feel a pull in my chest, the racing of my heart in anticipation. I open the door, and just as he seems taken aback by the sight of me, so am I with him. He's dressed in a designer suit, the barely contained muscles of his arms and shoulders making my stomach flutter. His hair is casually slicked back, permanent five o'clock shadow trimmed to accentuate the steel cut of his jaw.

Time slows. I find myself biting my lower lip on a smile, feeling like a teenager with a crush. No. It's so much more than that. I'm drawn to this man with an intensity that goes far beyond simple physical attraction.

"Are you so unaccustomed to being wanted?"

He wants me.

His eyes widen, then darken, as his gaze skims over me. "You look beautiful," he says, holding out his hand.

"Did you take anything out of my bag?" I ask.

His gaze shifts away momentarily. "Why?"

"I'm missing my pills."

"They're probably in the suitcase. Come with me. We should talk for a minute before we go down."

"I'm sure I left them in my makeup bag."

"I'll help you look for them later." He smiles. "Come, sit with me for a minute. Don't worry. I'll help you."

I nod, but the look on his face is serious, and it has me even more worried. "What is it?"

"The Avery family will likely be here tonight."

The room seems to tilt. "Why?"

"I found out from Thiago that they have bought some property in Avarice."

"Here?"

"It doesn't matter. They don't matter. I just wanted you to be prepared."

"Can I ask you something? About Camilla?"

He nods.

"Were you together once?"

His eyebrows furrow. "Why?"

"Caius mentioned—"

"Caius?"

"He said you two were supposed to get married."

Santos's face shuts down, eyes losing that sheen of moments ago and the line of his mouth tightening. "Did he?"

"Is it true?"

"You have no reason to be jealous."

"I'm not. I just want to know the truth."

He studies me. "There was a moment in time that Camilla may have thought she wanted that, but I can assure you I did not, and she was far too young to make that sort of decision."

"So were you engaged?" I push because I want a straight answer.

"No. Absolutely not."

"Have you slept with her?"

"Fuck no." He pauses, seeming to consider something. "I've only slept with one other woman in my life, and it wasn't Camilla Avery," he says, a sadness lingering along the edges of his words that makes me want to ask him about this woman. "Listen, Madelena, my brother has been known to stir the pot. The cuts," he says, pausing.

I look away. I can't hold his gaze.

"I didn't tell him about those. As far as I'm concerned, it's no one's business but ours. Ana told him, and he was fucking with you. With us. That's all."

At that last part, I look up at him. I'd guessed it was Ana when Santos told me he hadn't mentioned it. But the word us? That catches me off guard.

Santos smiles, lines forming around his eyes that have me smiling a small smile too. He wraps one big hand around the back of my head and pulls me toward him.

"You have to learn to trust me, okay? I won't lie to you. I may leave things out when there is nothing but hurt that can come from my words, but I won't lie to you. Understand?"

I bite the inside of my cheek, feeling my eyes warm. I nod. I do understand, and there's a part of me that wants it to be real, that wants him to be honest.

That wants him to want me.

Because he's right. I am utterly unaccustomed to being wanted. And when you know something like that, when you know it in your bones, it's hard to un-know.

"Good." He tilts my head up. "No tears. Not tonight."

I nod again, still biting my lip, not sure I'll be able to give him that. He takes my hands in his, does that thing where he weaves his fingers with mine, and God, it feels good. It feels safe and warm and good. Can I trust him? Can I trust this man who entered my life with the words *forgive me* on his lips just before slitting my palm open?

"Come. Sooner we make an appearance, the sooner we'll be able to leave."

32

MADELENA

The ballroom is decorated elegantly, the floor shining like a mirror and the chandeliers sparkling with brilliant golden light. I enter on Santos's arm. His mother, Caius, and Ana follow us in. I can feel Ana's gaze boring into the back of my head, but I don't focus on it. She can't hurt me. She can't touch me unless I allow her to.

Unless I give her power.

She may know my past, all my ugly secrets. She may share them with Caius. Hell, she already has. But she can't hurt me unless I allow her to.

Tonight's event is probably the most important of the three. Local lawmakers are present as well as those from the tri-state area. Since De Léon Enterprises is headquartered here, it is the most important for the business.

The Avery family is here. Most of them, at least. Camilla, Liam, and their mother are seated a few tables away, and Camilla's voice can be heard over the crowd as she charms every man and woman at their table. I don't understand it. Don't people see beyond the physical? She's lovely to look at and listen to, but she's rotten on the inside. I felt that from the first instant I saw her.

Ana and Caius are seated at their table, probably to keep an eye on them. There is one empty chair there. I know Santos noticed because I saw how his jaw tensed when he did.

Thiago Avery is missing tonight.

My father is here. He is seated at the table farthest from ours, banished to the shadowy corners when once he sat at the head of every table. He doesn't smile or acknowledge me in any way, but he does glare at my husband.

I see how he picks up his usual drink with his left hand. Whiskey with dinner. Whiskey with breakfast. Not to mention lunch. The right one is gloved and rests uselessly on the table beside his untouched plate. I shudder at the thought of why that is and glance to my husband, who is laughing at a joke someone makes. How many sides are there to this man? His violence is at his core. It's etched out in his skin. If these people saw that, saw him bared, would they smile so easily? Would they want his approval? His feigned friendship?

Then there's the other side. This one. Genial. Relaxed. Socially acceptable among Avarice's high society. This one doesn't matter because it's not real. It's put on for people who don't matter.

The way he is with me is another side. As I think it, he wraps his hand around the back of my neck under my hair. He gives a gentle, warm squeeze. I catch his mother's glance when he does it, and I see how her eyes narrow infinitesimally. I won't let her get to me tonight, either, because this is the side of my husband I like best. This is the side that makes my heart skip a beat and has me wishing I was alone with him. Wishing I had his weight on me and the strength of his arms circling me.

Waiters come to clear our plates, and in the midst of it, Odin appears at the back of my chair, setting a hand on my shoulder.

"Maddy," he says. There are drops of rain on the shoulders of his jacket, and his hair is damp.

"Odin." I take his hand, feel how cold it is.

"Santos," he greets my husband with a nod.

Santos pushes his chair back and stands. "Odin." He extends his hand to shake, but it takes Odin a moment. He does, although his smile is forced.

"Were you outside?" I ask.

"Just getting a breath of fresh air."

"In this weather?" Santos asks.

"I've lived in Avarice all my life. It doesn't bother me. If you don't mind, I'll take my sister for a dance." The orchestra is playing a waltz, and several couples are already on the dance floor.

I watch my brother. Something is up. He sounds strange, his body too stiff, and I have a sinking feeling it might be about the image I passed on to him—the one of Santos at Uncle Jax's house the night Uncle Jax died.

Santos's expression shifts. I think he's going to say no, but Odin doesn't wait for a response. He shifts his full attention to me and holds out his hand, palm up.

I take it and stand, worry settling like a brick in my stomach.

"Of course," Santos says because what else can he say with all these people watching?

Odin keeps my hand in his as we walk solemnly toward the dance floor. We weave through dancing couples to take a spot at their center, and I'm very aware we're putting plenty of space between us and the Augustines. We begin to dance.

"What is it?" I ask when Odin doesn't speak right away but only looks at me, worry etching his face.

"I watched you with him throughout dinner. You seemed not unhappy."

I shrug, trying to appear casual although I feel guilty. "I was just glad not to have to be near Caius and Ana. Not to mention his mother. She is a witch. It's confirmed." He gives me a pitying smile. "What is it, Odin? Tell me."

"How has he been with you?"

"Fine," I say, not wanting to go into it. Because I'm not unhappy, not right at this moment, and I should be. I should hate him. "He's not unkind to me. Mostly. You're scaring me. Tell me what you found out."

Odin smiles at a couple whose arms brush ours as they spin. That smile remains on his face as he turns back to me. It's not real though—not remotely so as he says, "There's more security footage."

My heart drops.

"I thought... The electrical issue..." The investigators had told us there had been an outage and there was no usable footage.

"It's not good, Maddy," he continues as if I haven't spoken.

My throat goes dry, my chest tightening. "Tell me."

"He was there for over an hour. I saw when he entered. Saw him out on the back terrace at one point." There are cameras all over the exterior of the house. Our uncle was obsessed with security. I wouldn't be surprised if there were cameras planted inside. "Time of death was consistent with when Santos was in the house."

I stop dancing momentarily, the room blurring around me, the floor tilting beneath my feet. Odin gives me a nudge to keep me moving.

"No," I say, shaking my head as I try to make sense of it. "No. He drowned."

"He was an accomplished swimmer who did the same laps in the same pool for over twenty years. You and I have always known he didn't drown."

"But..." I don't want this to be true.

"And there's more."

My hands feel clammy against Odin's suit jacket, and the meal I ate sits heavy in my stomach.

"When Santos was a few weeks shy of eighteen, he killed a man."

"What?"

"I don't know the full story. Had to do something with the man's daughter. He was arrested."

I know his past is violent. He's made no secret of it.

"But then the whole thing went away. Like no crime had been committed. And Santos went MIA for five years. The Augustine family didn't have the kind of power to make that happen. Not then. They were low level criminals. Thugs."

"Is that when he lived with the Avery family?"

He nods, looks over my shoulder. "You know about the Commander then? He told you?"

"A little."

"The Commander headed up a secret police force that operated out of Miami, but there was more. His power reached much farther. And this force, I get the feeling a lot of people turned a blind eye. The end justifying the means sort of thing."

I think about what Santos said about Thiago's scar. But then Caius's different version comes to mind.

"This Commander had private dealings in the northeast," Odin continues. "Holdings and investments up and down the coast, actually. From what I gathered, he used Santos as well as his own son, Thiago Avery, as his enforcers."

"God."

"They did some bad shit, Maddy. Really bad."

"May I cut in?"

Odin stiffens.

I startle at Santos's sudden appearance. When did

he get so close without us noticing? And what did he hear?

Odin turns to face him, but Santos doesn't take his eyes from me, and I can't drag mine from his. Odin hands me off because Santos wasn't asking, and I shudder when Santos's big hands touch me, one wrapping around my waist to span my lower back, the other holding my now limp hand.

I watch him, my husband. I knew what he was the night I met him, didn't I? What man does what he did to me when I was only fifteen years old? The Augustine family is a mafia family. No matter how far they've come, their hands are dirty, and they've probably climbed that social ladder on the backs of the corpses they've left in their wake.

But my uncle? Was my uncle one of those corpses?

"You look like you've seen a ghost."

I shake my head, force myself to breathe. "It's hot in here. I need some air." I slip out of his grasp before he can stop me, and honestly, if I don't, I might just throw up right here on the dance floor.

He follows as I weave through the room, hurrying to one of the exits. The closest one happens to be at the back of the building.

As if on cue or some strange sign from above, lightning crashes overhead as soon as I step outside. I jump, shuddering with the sudden cold. Sea water slams loud and violent against the cliffs beyond, the eerie beacon of the lighthouse ever present over the wild sea. I run from the building, the music, the light inside, and all those happy people.

"Madelena!" Santos is behind me, but I don't stop. Water pelts my bare arms, my hair, my face. It's ice cold but nowhere near the snowstorm of a few nights ago, the remnants of which have turned to slush. "Madelena, stop!"

He catches me, his hand closing over my arm and tugging me into his chest. Momentum has me bouncing backward, but he keeps me from falling. Santos's forehead creases with worry. I shiver, my teeth chattering, and within a moment, he's slipped off his jacket and has wrapped it around my shoulders. It's warm and smells like him, like the cologne I had made for myself years ago. I want to hug it to myself.

The thought leaves me with a longing so deep, it hurts.

Because I realize something, and the knowledge of it has me stumbling backward out of his grasp and doubling over.

"Madelena?" Santos asks.

How long has it been? How long have I been falling in love with this man?

Are you so unaccustomed to being wanted?

Because as I straighten to look up at him, I know that's what it is. I have been falling in love with him in small increments over the years. From the first words he spoke to me, and every time he appeared as if by magic to rescue me from one evil or another, I have been falling in love with Santos Augustine. I have been wanting to be wanted by him. And this new truth, his betrayal, it hurts so much.

"Did you kill him?" I blurt out, wind howling, stealing my words, carrying them away.

"What?" he asks, walking us farther from the glass walls of the building to take shelter around the corner, out of the wind.

"Did you do it?"

"What are you talking about?"

"My uncle. Was it you?"

He stops, and for the first time in all the time I've known him, he is at a loss. Shocked even.

And I have my answer.

I try to pull free, but he only tugs me closer. "He drowned," he says, voice different. Controlled. Low and dangerous.

"There was camera footage, Santos," I tell him, because it doesn't matter anymore, does it?

He waits, forehead furrowing.

"The gift someone sent, that muff? I thought it was you at first, but it wasn't. And the muff wasn't the gift. It was to hide a message someone wanted to send. A warning, maybe." I'm not sure if I'm explaining it to him or trying to understand it myself.

"What are you talking about?"

"There was a photograph tucked inside it."

"What?"

"It was a photo of you." My voice breaks on a sob and it takes me a minute to continue. "A still captured on the security cameras my uncle had all around his house. It was you. You were there the night he died."

His grip tightens on my arms as his jaw clenches with barely controlled emotion. He clearly never thought I'd find out, never thought anyone would.

"It's not what you think," he says.

"When you said you might leave things out, is this what you meant?" When I try to pull free, he tugs me to himself. "Let me go. Don't touch me."

"We need to get you inside. It's too cold."

I shake my head, but it doesn't matter what I want. It's never mattered what I wanted. Not when it comes to Santos Augustine.

Within moments, I'm half-walking, half being carried toward a staff entrance. Warmth immediately envelops me as the sound of dishes clattering and orders being called out overwhelms me. Santos keeps me close, my face buried against his side as we make our way to an elevator reserved for staff. As soon as the doors close and we're alone, he pulls me back to look at me.

"Christ," he mutters.

"What else have you lied about?"

"It's not what you think. Give me a minute."

The elevator doors slide open and we're on our floor. There's no guard at the door. He's probably on break since no one's up here.

Santos marches us to our apartment—can I call it ours?—and once we're inside, he releases me. I take two hurried steps away as he drags both hands through his hair.

"You killed him," I say.

He shakes his head and crosses the room toward me. I back up but I'm nowhere near as fast as him. He takes my arms, shakes me. "Where is it? Where is the photo?"

"You can't hide from this, Santos."

He releases me, mutters a string of curses, then digs his phone out of his pocket and types out a furious text.

I look around the room, not sure what I'm looking for but when I see a letter opener on the desk in the corner, I go for it.

"Why did you do it? Why kill my uncle? He was innocent. He never hurt anyone!"

"You didn't know him like you thought."

"I knew him!"

Santos looks at me, then at the letter opener in my hand. It's sharp. Maybe not as sharp as a kitchen knife, but it'll do some damage.

"Give me that, Madelena," he says, eating the space between us, clearly not worried about me with my letter opener.

"Tell me why!"

"Give it to me. Now," he says, words quieter as he's closer, but no less threatening.

I slip behind the couch because I need to put distance between us. He's bigger than me, faster than me, and he knows how to fight.

"What did I tell you just hours ago? What did I tell you about trust?"

I snort. "You wanted me to blindly trust you and you know what?" Tears blur my vision. "I am so fucking stupid, so desperate, that I wanted to."

"You're not stupid," he says, seeming caught on that word. "Give me a minute to explain."

"Desperate then. An easy target. Get back. Get away from me!" I tell him and turn the point of the knife to my own throat because he won't care about getting hurt himself, but he will care if I hurt myself.

No. Care isn't the right word. His plan will be disrupted if I hurt myself. He doesn't care about me. I was a fool and an idiot to ever believe he might.

"Maddy." He holds his hands up, palms to me. "Put it down."

"I'm not Maddy to you. I already told you never to call me that!"

"What did I tell you about hurting what is mine?" he asks, changing tactics.

"I. Am. Not. Yours!" I push the edge of the blade into the tender spot at the center of my collarbones, feeling that familiar sharp pain of skin breaking, the warmth of blood streaking flesh.

"Madelena!" Santos leaps toward me, and he's so fucking fast that I scream when his hand closes around my wrist and his weight forces me backward. I trip on something behind me and we go tumbling down. He mutters a curse, wraps one arm around my middle, and releases my wrist to cup the back of my head just before it bounces off the coffee table. He curses again as he flips us before we hit the floor hard, the sound of the crash of his head against hardwood deafening—all while he keeps a tight arm around my middle, so I bounce off him, his body a firm cushion. Air wooshes from our lungs and warmth pools between us.

I try to push off him, thinking he's going to attack but his arm around me keeps me pinned to him. But there's something else. His expression is off. He's blinking hard like he's trying to process something.

"Tell me why, Goddamn you!" I scream, finally sitting up as his arm slips from my back.

And that's when I realize what I've done. When he doesn't move, and I look down at us, I realize what the warmth is. The wet warmth.

"Oh my God. Oh my God!" I clasp my free hand over my mouth, my gaze locked on the other which is still holding the letter opener. The letter opener that is lodged in his side. "Santos?"

"Madelena... It's not..." It's barely a whisper. "Give me..."

The door opens, startling me. I look up to watch Val enter. He's typing something out on his phone. We're behind the couch so he doesn't see me right away, and he definitely doesn't see Santos. But when he does spot me, he stops, cocks his head to the side. He walks closer and when he sees Santos on the floor, his phone slips from his hand and clatters to the hardwood.

"Santos!" He's on his knees in an instant.

Without thinking, I pull the letter opener out, feeling the strange almost squish as I do, and fall backward before scrambling to my feet. Val reaches for his phone, and I watch him close his hand over Santos's bleeding side. He dials, trying to wake Santos as whoever he calls picks up.

"Get up here," he commands. "We need a doctor!"

I look down at Santos.

Oh, God. Santos. He's perfectly still, though. There's too much blood and his face has lost all color.

"What did you do?" Val screams at me, and before I can think I'm running. I'm running out of that room and out of the apartment. The elevator dings and I charge past it to the stairwell and down the stairs, stumbling all the way, falling down full flights before I catch myself, that bloody letter opener in my hand as I sob because I don't think he's going to make it.

God.

I think I killed him.

When I reach the ground floor, I use the emergency exit to get out of the building. An alarm sounds, but I don't care. I can't.

Rain stings like shards of glass. I hunch over and hurl up dinner. The taste is bitter in my mouth as I run. I run and run, and maybe it's subconscious where my feet are taking me. Maybe it's where I was meant to die all along. Maybe all my mom did all those years ago was condemn me to living a life that wasn't meant to be lived.

I stabbed him. Did I kill him? He asked me to trust

him, asked me to give him a chance to explain, and I stabbed him. I didn't give him a chance.

My feet carry me to the lighthouse entrance, my hair blowing wild in the wind. I'm freezing. Only when I am inside do I realize how cold I am. In here, the wind stops hissing. The waves stop crashing against the killer rocks.

Killer.

Am I a killer?

I clutch my stomach, sick again as I make my way up the winding stairs to that small room. I still remember it like it was yesterday. It was so cold. It's always so cold here, but that day, there was snow on the ground and a new storm was brewing. Mom's hair was a wild halo around her face. She was so beautiful with all those dark waves and her pale face, with her strange eyes that I realize now had that sheen to them in her manic periods... when she was off her meds.

She'd been crying. She'd cried so much her face was pink and puffy. She kept petting my hair so hard it hurt. I remember when she let go of my hand. When she stopped trying to pull me free from the railing I clung to because I didn't want her to take me. I knew what would happen if she did. She stuffed the note into my pocket then, and held my face and asked me to forgive her.

Is that what it is? Is it the words *forgive me*? Is that why I belonged to Santos from the first moment he spoke them to me? Because my mother had said the same two words to me. They were the last thing she said before she killed herself.

I remember crying, reaching out for her, because even at five I knew what she was going to do. I knew. But she didn't look back after that. Once the door closed, it was only seconds before it was over.

I didn't see her fall. I didn't hear her body hit the ground. If she screamed, it was swallowed up by the ocean waves constantly crashing against the rocks. But I knew when she was gone. A stillness settled over the place like nothing I'd ever felt before. The stillness of death. The finality of it.

When I reach the top of the stairs, I drop to a seat, unable to go on. It's dark. The only light is from a lamp that burns at the window. My stomach churns, my head throbs, and I swear I can taste his blood. Setting the letter opener down on the ground beside me, I rub my face. Salty tears burn my eyes, leaving streaks along my cheeks. It takes me a full minute before I look up, look around. I listen for that stillness. That same silence. I press the heels of my hands into my face to stop the tears, but they just keep coming. I press them to the space over my heart to stop the pain but that, too, just keeps hurting.

What happens now? What happens now that Santos is gone?

Just then, lighting breaks overhead, illuminating a shadow that moves along the window. I let out a scream and scramble to my feet, tripping backward against the wall. I don't know what I'm expecting. Who I'm expecting. My mother's ghost? Santos's?

Sirens wail in the distance. I shake my head to clear it. There's no one here. It's just me. My heart thuds against my chest as I look around. What am I doing here? There's only one thing to be done, isn't there?

I shift my gaze to the door that leads to the catwalk. I remember my father talking about the lock they'd installed after my mother's death. Too late, he'd said. She'd have found another way, I think.

Confused, I go to it, turn the handle to push it open. The sound it makes is one I'd forgotten, but now that I hear it again, it reminds me of that night fifteen years ago, the night my mother jumped to her death. It's like fate when I step out onto the wooden planks laid over the damaged catwalk and stand in the fury of the storm.

Are you so unaccustomed to being wanted?

He'd wanted me.

And now he's gone. I made sure of that.

A sob breaks from my chest, and I take a step toward the railing, ignoring the yellow tape warning of danger.

I can almost see my mother as she disappeared that night, her hair a dark river down her back. My hands shake as I reach for the rail. I grip it and make myself look down. Rain slashes my face, my clothes, soaking me through as the sea crashes against the cliffs, the water so high the rocks are almost invisible.

Is this where she went over? I don't know. I close

my eyes, listen to the chaos around me, and wonder what I'm doing here. Am I going to jump, too? Is that why I came?

"Stop!"

I gasp, startled, spinning around, the railing wobbly behind me. The beacon pans over the sea and between that and the lamp at the window, I can make out the face of the man who must have been the shadow I saw. Except that it doesn't belong here. He doesn't belong here. I bring my trembling hands before me holding the letter opener between myself and the hulking man with the scar that circles his neck. The cool, steel eyes trap me as they take in the state of me.

Thiago Avery's eyes.

He holds his hands out, palms up, and looks me over. I look down at myself, too, to see what he sees. The bloody mess of me. I wonder if he hears the low keening coming from inside my chest over the fury of the storm.

"What did you do?" he asks, taking a step toward me.

I walk backwards away from him, away from the door that leads back into the lighthouse.

He follows me, but he's cautious. "Stop. It's not safe."

The wind seems to grow angrier as I look over my shoulder and down at the sea below.

"You can't be here, Madelena," he says.

When I look back at him, he's closer. "Get away

from me!" I yell, brandishing the letter opener between us.

He looks at it, then back at me. I see another shadow through the window, this one inside the lighthouse. I'm sure I'm not imagining it when Thiago glances at it as the shape moves.

"Give me that," Thiago says.

I look up at his open palm and shake my head.

"I am not your enemy," he says, taking another step toward me. I'm almost out of space. The railing is broken, and the catwalk is closed off a few feet from me. I can't go around. That shape inside moves again, and again, Thiago glances at it. When he looks back at me, he seems angry. "Your enemy is much closer to home, and in his veins is the blood of a monster."

The sound of the heavy metal door opening has us both turning, me trying to see around Thiago, him looking over his shoulder. Between the darkness and the rain, I can't see who it is. What I know, though, is that I need to get away. Heavy footsteps approach us, and as I look around me for an escape, the railing I'm holding onto whines.

A moment later, there's a sharp crack, and I scream as it gives way and cling to it as my feet lose purchase on the slippery planks.

Thiago calls out my name, lunging toward me and just as my grip beings to slide from the railing and I'm sure I'm going to go over, a hand wraps around my wrist and I'm jerked to a stop, jerked again when he hauls me up onto the catwalk. The air is knocked out of me for the second time this night as I crash against the wall, my head hitting unyielding stone. My vision falters, going dark, stars dancing. I'm going to be sick again.

Thiago says something, or someone else does. I force my eyes to open. Lightning crashes, illuminating the sky, and I see Thiago. His attention is on the man who is a shadow to me. Just before the night falls dark again, I watch that shadow lunge for Thiago.

I scream, rain pelting me when I look up to see that terrible scar circling Thiago's neck, the cold steel of his eyes, and finally, the terror in those eyes as a hand slams against his chest. Thiago reaches for that hand, managing to catch the wrist momentarily, but it's too late. He's lost his balance.

Something clatters to the catwalk, bouncing and I hear the grunt of air leaving Thiago's lungs and then the scream as his body goes toppling over the edge, that broken railing hanging useless behind him.

Before I can process what's just happened, before I can scream or even breathe, the man who just pushed Thiago over grips my jaw and slams my head so hard against the wall that this time, there are no stars, no blurry vision. No momentary reprieve. There is only darkness.

THANK YOU!

Thanks for reading *Forgive Me My Sins*, book 1 of The Augustine Brothers Duet. I hope you are enjoying Santos and Madelena's story.

Their story ends in Deliver Me From Evil, the final book of the duet.

ALSO BY NATASHA KNIGHT

The Augustine Brothers

Forgive Me My Sins

Deliver Me From Evil

Ruined Kingdom Duet

Ruined Kingdom

Broken Queen

The Devil's Pawn Duet

Devil's Pawn

Devil's Redemption

To Have and To Hold

With This Ring

I Thee Take

Stolen: Dante's Vow

The Society Trilogy

Requiem of the Soul

Reparation of Sin

Resurrection of the Heart

The Rite Trilogy

His Rule

Her Rebellion

Their Reign

Dark Legacy Trilogy

Taken (Dark Legacy, Book 1)

Torn (Dark Legacy, Book 2)

Twisted (Dark Legacy, Book 3)

Unholy Union Duet

Unholy Union

Unholy Intent

Collateral Damage Duet

Collateral: an Arranged Marriage Mafia Romance

Damage: an Arranged Marriage Mafia Romance

Ties that Bind Duet

Mine

His

MacLeod Brothers

Devil's Bargain

Benedetti Mafia World

Salvatore: a Dark Mafia Romance

Dominic: a Dark Mafia Romance

Sergio: a Dark Mafia Romance

The Benedetti Brothers Box Set (Contains Salvatore, Dominic and Sergio)

Killian: a Dark Mafia Romance

Giovanni: a Dark Mafia Romance

The Amado Brothers

Dishonorable

Disgraced

Unhinged

Standalone Dark Romance

Descent

Deviant

Beautiful Liar

Retribution

Theirs To Take

Captive, Mine

Alpha

Given to the Savage

Taken by the Beast

Claimed by the Beast

Captive's Desire

Protective Custody

Amy's Strict Doctor

Taming Emma

Taming Megan

Taming Naia

Reclaiming Sophie

The Firefighter's Girl

Dangerous Defiance

Her Rogue Knight

Taught To Kneel

Tamed: the Roark Brothers Trilogy

ABOUT THE AUTHOR

Natasha Knight is the *USA Today* Bestselling author of Romantic Suspense and Dark Romance Novels. She has sold over a million books and is translated into six languages. She currently lives in The Netherlands with her husband and two daughters and when she's not writing, she's walking in the woods listening to a book, sitting in a corner reading or off exploring the world as often as she can get away.

Contact Natasha here: natasha@natasha-knight.com

www.natasha-knight.com

Made in the USA
Columbia, SC
27 April 2023